I0536364

Unruly Magic

Stella Mayweather Series

USA TODAY Bestselling Author
CAMILLA CHAFER

Copyright: Camilla Chafer, 2011

All rights reserved. The right of Camilla Chafer to be identified as author of this Work has been asserted by her in accordance with sections 77 and 78 of the Copyright, Designs and Patents Act 1988.

First published in 2011
This paperback edition published in 2023

No part of this publication may be reproduced, stored in retrieval system, copied in any form or by any means, electronic, mechanical, photocopying, recording or otherwise transmitted without written permission from the publisher. You must not circulate this book in any format.

This book is licensed for your personal enjoyment only.

ISBN: 978-0-9569086-5-0

Visit the author online at www.camillachafer.com

ALSO BY CAMILLA CHAFER

The Complete Stella Mayweather Series

Illicit Magic
Unruly Magic
Devious Magic
Magic Rising
Arcane Magic
Endless Magic

Deadlines Mystery Trilogy

Deadlines
Dead to the World
Dead Ringers

CHAPTER ONE

For the first time in six months, I woke up without the shaking after-effects of a nightmare. Instead, my first thought as I edged my eyes open, had been *peace*. I stretched out on my bed – in my bedroom, in my home, as I had to remind myself frequently – while I listened to the quiet of the outside world. I spread my hand out hopefully across the covers as I did every morning and felt... nothing. No Evan.

Pushing sleep away, I opened my eyes fully and yawned. I strained to hear sound, any sound but, as per usual, there was nothing. This was as close to bliss as I could possibly get right now, which was good because by this afternoon, my short lived peace would be blown to smithereens. If I'd known that when I woke up, I might have stayed in bed.

I lived on the fringes of a little town called Wilding. Situated just a few miles out of town, my home was completely isolated but for the only other house within screaming distance, which happened to be right across the road. As we were well off the highway, few cars came this way, and, as such, few people either; bar the mailman, whom I'd yet to actually see.

As far as close company went, my neighbours were it, of course, and I was fortunate that they were a friendly pair. They made me feel very welcome right from the day I first pitched up, unannounced, on my doorstep. I had to dissolve the wards that protected the house for two decades before I could enter.

My neighbour, Annalise, who was only a few years older than I, seemed positively overjoyed at some close company and made it her business to be my friend. However, Gage was the first one I'd seen, on the same day I moved in. Though he seemed less enthusiastic about getting a new neighbour, he was pleasant enough, even if he hadn't gone way out on the welcome committee.

Though I had been in Wilding for only six months, it was already one of my longest ever residences. I moved around a lot as a child, thanks to a long stream of foster homes. Even when I got out of the system, I still moved around a lot through a series of icky house shares. All that was thousands of miles away both from my memory, as well as geographically now. I left all that behind with barely a blink of an eye. I hadn't even gotten homesick.

My new home was a much appreciated refuge from the horror and terror of those final days. I was nearly scared witless by what I had seen – and what I'd done – at the safe house where I'd been ensconced for my training. I'd been there only a few weeks and barely escaped with my life... And I was one of the lucky ones! Not that I really considered myself lucky when I thought about what and whom I left behind.

"Get a grip, Stella," I groaned, getting ready to give myself a firm pep talk. So much for finally overcoming my nightmares; I couldn't help but rehash those memories every single time I woke up. It was always the same – what could I have done differently? What if the outcome were different?

What if wasn't getting me anywhere.

I pushed back the covers and slid out of bed, my feet hitting the cold hardwood floor. On auto pilot, I turned around to smooth the covers flat again and padded into the adjacent bathroom where I went about my morning routine. Afterwards, I pulled on jeans and a cotton shirt plus a pair of bright Havaianas suitable for plodding around the house.

In the kitchen, I flipped on the coffee pot, a vice I picked up at the safe house, to make my morning fix. There was always a competition for priority in my veins – coffee, magic or blood. Today the coffee was probably going to win.

Just like every morning, I pulled out my map from where I kept it folded in a drawer, and spread it across the table. I was careful to smooth out the fold creases that made the thin paper buck against the smooth grain of the tabletop.

I held the long ribbon loop of the crystal I'd bought and be-spelled and dangled it over the centre as I did every morning. With a flick of my wrist, I set the crystal in motion to spin clockwise while I willed it to find Evan and give me his location. The crystal was supposed to lurch to a spot on a map but after a few seconds of fading momentum, it petered out and hung limply in the middle, giving me no direction or indication whatsoever that Evan was anywhere to be found, at least not in the States. Perhaps it was time I widened my search, or gave up crystal scrying. One thing was for certain: I had spent months looking for him and I wasn't giving up until I had an answer, one way or another.

I folded the map and placed it back in the drawer, returning the crystal to its pouch and tossing that in on top. With a sigh of annoyance, I cast a glance out the kitchen window. This side of the house overlooked the back of the property. There wasn't a lot to see, just the bushy shrubs that badly needed pruning back for the winter months and a dark tangle of trees that signified the beginnings of the tree line. That ran for another mile or so alongside the road heading north and goodness-knows-how-far back.

All I could hear was the sound of the pot bubbling away next to me, and nothing from outside at all. Just the thought of that was niggling at my subconscious in a way I couldn't quite fathom. Lately, it had begun to strike me as weird. Sure, no traffic was great, but where were the birds? Why did I never see a dog or a stray cat? Or a groundhog? I really wanted to see one of those funny creatures, or at least something native... except skunks. I'd give those a miss.

Occasionally, I heard howling in the woods that bordered the back of my property but I'd never seen any animal close-up in the day time so I had no clue what might be living out there. Come to think of it, I don't recall ever seeing an animal in Wilding, which seemed odd for a town that had several thousand people. Compounding that was the fact that the environs was rural, so there should have been something mewling or stirring up a racket. I shook my head. I was being silly. Of course, I was struggling to adjust: I was a city girl who was used to lights and noise, a constant barrage of unwelcome sounds at all hours.

Anyway, yeah, I was the lucky one, not that it really felt that way, I thought. I stirred two level sugars into my steaming mug. When Evan's face lurched into the front of my mind, I had to grip the counter to hold myself upright, the force of the sudden memory almost making my legs buckle.

Evan. *Oh*, Evan.

His name alone felt like a vice squeezing my heart, leaving me breathless and disorientated. Even the thought of him could still reduce me to tears, after all these months. What was worse was the speculation that I replayed in my head a thousand times. What happened to Evan and where was he? He saved my life, but had he lost his? I just didn't know and it was not knowing that made everything so unbearable. After all this time, waiting for news or some kind of sign, I didn't know if I would ever know the answer but that didn't stop me looking. It was solely that determination that gave me strength.

All I knew was that the last time I saw him, Evan had been badly injured and I poured all of my energy into him in a bid to save his life. He had been alive, barely, when our friends Étoile and Seren took him to safety. All I could do now was cherish my thoughts of him, and keep searching for him when it didn't reduce me to a puddle of sobs.

I glanced towards the front of the house when an engine roared to life outside – finally, a sign of existence – and I recognised it as the sound of my neighbour, Gage's, motorbike. I figured he was heading out to work and wondered if that meant Annalise would come by soon. She worked from home and could pick and choose her own hours, so she often came by for breakfast. I enjoyed her company. I eyeballed the coffee pot; there was plenty more. All I had to do was take deep breaths, put on my happy face and pretend that everything was normal... that I was normal.

A quick rap at the front door jolted me from my maudlin thoughts and I moved through the house, from the kitchen at the back through the living room, pasting a smile on my face as I went to answer it. Annalise waved through the window at me and her sweet, perky smile automatically gave me an energy boost. I privately thought that the phrase "a sight for sore eyes" must have been coined right after meeting her. She was one of the nicest people I'd ever met and I couldn't have picked a better neighbour.

I unlocked the door and let her bound in like a new puppy, blonde curls bouncing all over the place, streaks of pink flicking out like carnival candyfloss.

"Oh good, you're up. Have you had breakfast?" she asked, her eyes bright and shiny.

I shook my head. "Just on my first coffee. Come on through."

"Uh-uh," Annalise said, grabbing me by the hands, her eyes alight with mischief. "I've come to invite you over to us today. Gage has just gone to get pastries and we thought we'd eat on the porch, if you'd like to join us?"

"Sure, thank you," I said, pleased.

"Oh, it's no thanks at all! I practically eat you out of house and home as it is."

"You know I don't mind." I'd happily have

Annalise for lunch and dinner too, her company was so nice. She had helped me settle into town in such a joyful, gracious way. Out of all the potential neighbours in the world, I was glad I struck lucky with her. Plus, she had no idea how grateful I was to her for not letting me live my life in a terminal fug.

"Well, you're sweet but today breakfast is on us. You'll need a sweater," she said looking down at her jeans and padded coat. "We're kissing goodbye to the sun today."

"Just let me put my mug back in the kitchen and I'll come on over."

"Okay, I'll wait on the porch for you." She skipped back outside, leaving the door open. That was the thing out here. No one came this far out of town so it didn't seem totally necessary to close the door all the time. Plus, there had been wards on my house for years – when it was my parents' house. They left it under a stasis protection spell during their absence, a spell which faded as soon as it recognised me. Lately, I'd begun to spin new ones of my own for protection. It had been very much trial and error.

The first spell I created caused my house to throw out a "go away!" vibe. At least, it didn't take me more than a few days of watching Annalise approach only to turn right around and go back to her house again for me to realise my error.

I undid the spell and tried again. I thought I'd finally gotten it right, though I didn't really have anyone to check with. Anyway, what would be the point of protecting myself if I called up the Council and asked them to check out my wards? In angry moments, I rather thought I was protecting myself *from* them.

I went back to the kitchen and put my mug in the sink to deal with later. I grabbed socks from the drawer in my bedroom and kicked off the Havaianas by the front door and sat on the floor to pull on my socks and sneakers. I picked up my jacket and zipped it up. I didn't pick up anything else – I wasn't going anywhere far and hadn't troubled myself about getting a cell phone as no one would ring. Then I shut the door behind me and locked it, my fingers leaving a few boosting sparks of magic as I touched the lock. I wasn't sure why I bothered, but it was habit that was hard to break.

Annalise was standing on the path waiting for me. "You know you should think about painting this place," she said when I caught up to her. I looked back at the house and saw it through Annalise's eyes. The paint was starting to peel in places. The stasis spell had held it suspended in time for more than twenty years, and now that it was gone, I wondered if time was catching up to the house as quickly as it could. Quite a few things seemed to be breaking an awful lot lately and the peeling exterior was one more item to add to the list.

"I don't think I can do it myself," I said, thinking of the sanding and painting and the sheer volume of work. At least there was only one story to deal with.

"I bet one of Gage's friends could probably fix it for you," Annalise said. I thought she was referring to one of the gaggle of guys that seemed to come over to their place a couple of times a week. I was invited over one Friday night and arrived in the middle of a rowdy poker game that looked to be on the verge of breaking into fight. But mostly, they seemed like a nice crowd and shared a common history in the way that residents of small towns did. They knew everyone and everyone knew them. By the same token, they had all heard about the new girl in town so I was new blood to look over and gossip about. "Come over tonight and maybe you can ask one of them to take a look."

"You think they'd have time?"

"One of them would make time for a pretty gal like you," Annalise winked at me and I knocked her playfully on the arm. She pretended to wince.

Knowing there wouldn't be any traffic to look out for, we crossed the road and stepped onto the grass that signified the edge of her property. Her house was a little different from mine, being that it faced out onto the road and had two stories to my single.

The wide wrap-around porch, painted in a creamy white, was my favourite spot of her house. With a big swing and lots of colourful plant pots, it was a welcoming space and I could often hear the tinkle of the wind chimes from across the street. I had never been upstairs in her house, but I knew the downstairs had a similar floor plan to mine.

We both had a big living room straight off the front door, an eat-in kitchen and another smaller room that Annalise used as a work room. Mine differed by having a dining room-sized space – currently empty – off the living room and bedrooms beyond that. I also had a sun room that was really anything but at the moment, given that fall was making way for winter.

Annalise had already laid out a little table on the porch. There was a tray with glasses and a big pitcher of juice. Plates and napkins lay on top, each a mismatch of colour and pattern that spoke to me of

Annalise's eclectic style.

"How long have you lived here?" I asked as we settled next to each other on the swing. I thought that I should get one for my house. It would be nice to sit out and kick up my heels next summer. As it was, I hadn't really done much with the furnishings inside or out yet. There was a lot of tired decor that really needed to be dealt with if I were going to stay here long term. The repairs had more urgency now that it was getting colder. It wasn't easy getting to grips with homeowner complaints after a series of rentals that I could have done nothing about even if I wanted to, but I was trying to relish it. Begrudgingly, anyway.

"Oh, always. This was my parents' house."

"You've always lived here?" Well, duh, she had just said so. For a moment, I imagined living in the same place forever. It sounded lovely. If my parents had lived, I might have had those kinds of roots. They were killed when I was young and I had to bear that cross even though I had, finally, made peace with their passing. At least I had the answers now.

"Well, I moved away for a few years then I just came on back." Annalise shrugged like her years away were nothing more than a blip in her existence.

"It must be nice having Gage around," I said conversationally.

"Sure is. Always good to have a big guy in the house, right?" Annalise was slightly shorter than I, but even so, I knew what she meant.

My heart tried not to sink a little and I leaned forward to pick up my glass, mostly so my eyes wouldn't betray my pain, and took a long drink. In the stillness of the morning, we heard the engine's throttle long before we saw Gage skirt around the corner onto the driveway. His feet dropped onto the blacktop, stabilising the bike as he came to a stop. Annalise stood up to wave and I noticed her glance down at me curiously, like she couldn't quite work me out. Some things were just best left that way.

Gage kicked up the motorbike supports before swinging one powerful leg over the seat. He raised a hand to wave, then eased off his helmet, shaking his crop of hair out with a swing of his head. He tucked the helmet under his arm and came towards us carrying a big rucksack. Taking the side steps up to the porch two at a time, he unzipped the bag to pull out two large brown paper bags. When he bent down to kiss Annalise on the cheek, he caught her in a quick hug and I felt that familiar pang of sadness, deep in the pit of my stomach.

I couldn't remember the last time I had been touched with affection. I shivered and shook out the pity party that was going on in my head. I couldn't grieve forever, and I couldn't be sad at other people's happiness. It just wasn't right.

"Danishes," said Annalise with undisguised glee as she cracked open the bag and spilled the big pastries onto plates. "Help yourself. There's no such thing as formal eating here, as you know."

Gage sat down on the rocker across from us and stretched out his long legs. They seemed to go on forever. He was a lovely looking man, tall and broad with a dark crop of hair, wide brown eyes and perpetual day-old stubble. He was built lean and strong, with a broad chest and neat waist. He kept his jacket on and the well-worn leather creased in supple lines as he reached forwards. "Plate, Stella?" he asked, interrupting my gaze.

I accepted the plate with a quick nod and, at once, dropped my eyes. What was I thinking of in admiring Gage's physique when my friend, his wife, was sitting right next to me? When I coupled that with being wrenched apart from Evan only six months ago, I felt more than a little ashamed of myself. There was no excuse for being a rubbish person.

"Got any plans for today, Stella?" Annalise asked and I gulped. Feeling guilty should take up most of my day now, damn it.

"Uh, no, not really," I mumbled.

After my first month of wallowing here, struggling to even get up every day, I slowly started to explore the area, first tentatively venturing into Wilding and, occasionally, beyond. Annalise introduced herself within a day when she came bearing a steaming casserole to welcome me. That had been the first of our many suppers together. She had also been incredibly useful recommending stores to go and get new bed linens from and crockery to update the ones in the house.

Though I was careful with my money, I had to spend quite a bit of cash on these necessities to make the house liveable, especially as things snapped, tore, and just plain broke.

Strangely, I'd found myself enjoying it in the moments when I could stuff my pain far away from my consciousness. As such, Annalise helped me become the proud new owner of smart sets of bed linen, kitchenware, crockery, new cushions – pillows, as she called them – and other bits and pieces. She introduced me around town as well. At first, she was simply a useful guide for me – though one whose company I enjoyed – and now I was happy to call her my friend.

Gage, who I thought was her husband, although she didn't wear a wedding ring and neither did he, was much more of an enigma to me. I saw him from time to time and he was always polite and nice but a bit more reserved. He seemed to be pretty popular when their friends came over for game nights. It might sound parochial, even hokey, but their game nights seemed like real fun and they always had a lively crowd over. Though I had been a couple of times, I didn't want to just assume I could pitch up whenever I saw the lights were on, so mostly I stayed to myself and didn't try and wedge my way into their lives.

"You could keep me company. I've got a few more things to sew. Then I need to package up my stuff to take to the fair tomorrow." Annalise was a whiz at sewing and crochet and her business was creating pretty home things that she sold at fairs. Right now, I knew she had stockpiled a huge collection of things to sell and I knew she would be successful because she hardly ever came home with anything. Even her pricier stuff was so beautifully made that she never had to worry about not selling it.

I ended up staying for the rest of that morning and well into the afternoon. Annalise tugged her baskets of goods out onto the porch and we sat there, bundled up, drinking coffee. She was much better at hospitality than me, but then she'd had a lifetime of doing it. It was well into the afternoon by the time I left, and I had an invitation to their house for game night, and strict instructions to remember my list of repairs.

"See you," I called, skipping down the steps, waving over my shoulder at Annalise as I cut across the grass. Gage was flat on his back on a tarpaulin on the driveway, tinkering with his motorbike, a deep frown of concentration creased his forehead. I looked over my shoulder as I started to cross the road and he looked up briefly before waving a hand at me. I smiled and waved back then jogged along the path to my door.

If I'd been more alert, I might have made something more of the feeling I got in the air as I took the steps up to my porch. Just as my body was getting soft, and my magic rusty, my senses had also gotten sluggish over these past few months. Even when the idea that someone had entered my space, someone with a signature that I should recognise, trickled into my thoughts, I didn't bother to turn it into fully fleshed curiosity.

I paused at my door, my hand on the knob, and turned around, hesitating for a few seconds. I had the faintest sense that someone had been here and might still be here, but when none of my senses gave me anything to work with, I shrugged and let myself in.

I still locked the door behind me.

~

My afternoon was as idle as idle could be and mostly spent poring over my list, which was growing every day. Painting the exterior of the house came after more than twenty other urgent bullet points that included checking out the kitchen plumbing and finding the source of the clanking pipes. There was also cutting the grass, which had shot up. I wondered who had been doing it over the past twenty years that the house remained empty. Maybe that had been under a spell too. Re-grouting the bathroom and a bunch of problems that seemed to be cropping up all over the house were added. Pulling a face, I wrote, *paint entire inside of house*. After a thought, I added *porch swing* to the bottom of the list.

I sank back on the sofa, tapping my pen against the pad of paper, and wondered if, since magic had kept everything pristine for so long, would it be possible to use it for the house's upkeep too? I had no idea if there were rules on that kind of thing. Surely that would mean every witch could have a perfect house? I had absolutely no idea.

By late afternoon, I was so bored that I was actively looking for things to do. I really needed some kind of purpose in life, I decided. So I started cleaning the kitchen countertops with hot soapy water. The new Stella might be awfully house proud, more through boredom than by design, but it didn't take the place of getting out there and doing something.

I didn't even have my studies to keep me distracted. They ended abruptly with Eleanor Bartholomew's attack and now there wasn't a witch for miles. At least, that's what I thought. I was sure I hadn't come across any and I could recognise the vibrating signature of my own kind's magic now.

Besides, I didn't even know if I wanted to continue in training, especially if that meant getting caught up in witch business again. From what I had learned about the Witches' Council — some sort of quasi-governing body that monitored and assisted our kind — I found them mostly weak and inept. They were certainly to blame for a chunk of my past troubles, even if they had been there in the moment that I really needed them. Or rather, Étoile had been there and I owed her big time.

I huffed and scrubbed harder. It all seemed like so

long ago when I was alone and terrified, then gradually happy, and finally, in the arms of the man I adored. It had all ended too quickly, too abruptly. I channelled my anger into scrubbing the counters furiously.

When I could almost see my reflection in the super clean surfaces, I finally wrung out the sopping cloth and laid it over the sink edge to dry, scowling at my face in the kitchen window.

My top was clinging to me in wet patches. Nights at Annalise and Gage's house were as casual as casual can be, but I still couldn't turn up as a wet mess which meant I would have to tackle my washing. Boring.

Tugging my laundry basket through, I sat on the kitchen floor, separating colours from whites and made untidy piles next to the washing machine. That was also on my "must replace" list, thanks to the ominous rattling sound it made every time it spun a cycle. I suspected corrosion was catching up with it thanks to, like everything else, being part of the stasis spell. I bet homeowner's insurance didn't cover it, I thought with a snort. I shoved the first set of laundry in and turned the sink faucet on so I could wash the few leftover dishes that languished there.

The surge of magic that bloomed into the kitchen through the open doorway nearly knocked me for six. It wasn't the force of it, and I didn't sense any malevolence, but I was so surprised I dropped the glass I'd been washing. It splintered into a bunch of little pieces on the floor. I looked from my feet to the doorway, my body rigid with anticipation.

"Hello?" called a small female voice from my living room. "Is there anyone there?"

Slowly, carefully, I stepped over the shards and edged towards the voice, panicking all the time. I didn't get the feeling I was about to come to harm, but one could never be too careful. So I prepared to shimmer out of there the moment things looked dicey. Teleportation certainly had its advantages.

"Where the hell am I?" demanded the girl standing in the centre of my living room. She was in her late teens with glossy dark blonde hair that hung about her shoulders in a feathery cut. She was dressed in skinny jeans, acid pink heels and a white jacket that sat on her hips with a little pleated flounce. She clutched a thick book in her arms that looked heavy and old against her new and shiny self.

"You're in my living room," I replied, bracing myself for whatever would come next.

"Am I in England?" she asked in disbelief as she looked around in distaste at my furniture. "I did *not* think England would look like this."

"No, you're not."

"Huh?" The girl looked around again, then gave me the once over. "You *are* Stella Mayweather?" she asked.

"Who the hell are you?"

"I asked first!" I thought she might stomp her foot. I certainly felt like it but I settled for glaring at her instead. Obviously, it was the more mature option.

"I'm Chyler," she said at last, and dropped onto my sofa, the book perched across her knees.

"What are you doing in my living room? How did you get here?" If my wards were dogs, they'd be in the doghouse right now. How had she gotten in here when I'd done everything I could to keep everyone out, especially people who could just flash in, like she had, in the blink of an eye.

"I said the spell," Chyler replied, patting the book like she couldn't help it, "and I just ended up here. You are Stella, aren't you?"

"Yes," I said after assessing her for weapons. She looked too scared to be thinking about hurting me and I didn't think the super tight jeans could conceal anything.

"Yes!" Chyler's fist pumped the air. "I just knew it! The book said it was you and now here I am." She beamed at me.

"What book?"

"This book. It's the family spell book," she said, slowly, like she had to spell it out. Groan. One bright blue nail tapped the aged leather exterior of the book. "You don't have one?" she asked, catching my frown.

I shook my head. "But what are you doing here?"

"I need to hide," Chyler said and all the confidence seemed to drain out of her. "I asked the book and it said you would protect me. It gave me the spell to find you."

"The book just... told you?" I tried to not let the disbelief show on my face.

"Usually I have to ask it really nicely; but this time, it practically demanded to help," said Chyler as if chatting to a book was a perfectly normal event. At least, she didn't seem to think it was abnormal, which it totally was. "It even had a picture of you." Chyler thumbed through the thick leaves and finally flipped the book open. She held it up to me, the spine pressed against her middle as she balanced it in both hands. Sure enough, there was a pen and ink drawing of my face looking solemnly back at me. "Cool, right?

I'm on the run," she added helpfully.

"From whom?" I couldn't help but ask, but maybe, given the knowledge I'd received in the past few months, I should have been asking *what* rather than whom.

"The Council, of course," said Chyler, her face returning to glum. "They want to kill me and you're the only one who can stop them."

CHAPTER TWO

I pushed a cup of coffee across the kitchen table to Chyler and watched her scowl at it as she blew the steam away with pursed, glossy pink lips.

"You're going to have to tell me more about this book," I said, at last.

"It's, like, magic and it's been in my family, like, forever!"

"Do you think you could not say 'like' so much?" I asked. Chyler threw a look at me as if to say, *you're so old*, when she couldn't be more than a few years younger than I. But then, anyone was old to a teenager, I reminded myself. I'd probably been just as petulant. Even so, I scowled back at her. It was my house, after all and she had just come in uninvited. I wanted an explanation... Now.

"So, the book has been in my family for years and years and every generation adds their spells to it and we use it for our magic."

I nodded. They were spell casters, a different breed of magic from mine, but a valid strain nevertheless. It explained why the read I was getting from her wasn't quite the same as the smooth vibration I felt when a witch with blood magic was nearby. Spell casters gave off more of a fuzzy feeling.

Chyler continued. "I'm next in line for the book after my mom. My aunts had a lot to say about that! They want the book and they'll do anything to get it. It's got a lot of power." She stroked the book and I watched in amusement as the cover seemed to hiccup and the pages ruffled within. If I didn't know better, I would have said the book was being affectionate.

"How come you've got the book then, if it's your mom's?"

Chyler looked confused. "I... don't know."

I changed tactic. "Why do your aunts want the book if it's yours?"

"Duh, do you not get the magic news? The Council is splitting up and everyone wants as much power as they can get their hands on. My mom's sister wants it because she thinks she deserves it. My dad's sisters want it too, because they want to get away from whatever's left of the Council." Chyler looked dejected, like she had already heard all the arguments against her possessing the book. "And it's not just them. The Council wants it too. It's so old and powerful that they'd do anything for it."

"Including murder? Of a teenager?"

"I knew you'd help me." Chyler grinned, her face brightening.

I held up my hands and her face fell slightly. "Wait. I never said that. I don't know why the book thinks I can defend you against the Council, or why it thinks I would." Though, when I said it, I deduced that it probably would think that. Hadn't the last

Council leader tried to kill me? And wasn't I hiding from them for the past six months? I was definitely *not* in their fan club. Not to mention: thinking about a book *"thinking"* was just plain weird.

"I'll show you what it said." Chyler thumbed the book apart, flipping the edges of the thick paper until it heaved open to the page she had shown me before, the page with my pen and ink portrait. She ran her forefinger below the neat black print underneath, reading aloud, "It says: 'Stella Mayweather is whom you seek. Trouble from you, she will keep. She's a powerful witch whose magic goes without a hitch. Go to her and ask for haven, she will help you from the horrid... coven. Say her name three times, and you'll find yourself in her humble climes.' See? Also, I know, the book likes rhyming but sometimes it isn't very good at it. It's old school like that."

"So I see. When did you find that?"

"This morning. Right after the Council tried to kill me. I raced to my room and the book just appeared, opened at that page."

"And you're sure it was the Council?"

Chyler nodded enthusiastically, but her glazed eyes told me she wasn't telling the whole truth.

"Saying my name isn't much of a spell."

"It is if the book says it is."

"You've got a lot of faith in that book."

"It's all I've got. Please help me, Stella"

I sat back in my chair, my hands warming around my mug as I pondered this new information. I'd been trying to keep out of the magic business. Although it might have saved me, it caused me nothing but heartache and pain, ultimately. It had even turned me into a killer, albeit in self defence.

I might have been done with the Witches' Council but it seemed like they weren't done with me. My heart sank.

I couldn't decide whether it disturbed me or not that the Council was fracturing like Chyler said. I wondered if it was due to the lack of a strong leader, now Robert Bartholomew was dead, or arising from the uneasy division between blood magic witches and spell casters, as well as those who straddled the middle. I knew one thing, however: I couldn't, in good conscience, turn Chyler away and leave her to face her unsolicited enemies alone.

"I'll help you," I said, just as it occurred to me in a jolt of understanding that someone from my past probably wasn't far away. That faint trace of signature that I detected earlier; were they friend or foe? It stood to reason that if the Council really had it in for Chyler, they would be tracking her. No, I realised, I detected it earlier, before Chyler had arrived. Whoever it was was here for me.

"Cool." She seemed remarkably cheerful for someone who was on the run.

"Where are you staying?" I asked.

"I can't go home so I don't know. May I stay here?"

"I don't think it would be wise," I said cautiously.

Chyler barely blinked at my rebuttal. "What should we do? Should we attack first?"

"We won't be doing anything yet and you should lay low until we know exactly what is going on."

"But the book says you're really powerful. Can't you defeat them all and let me get on with my life?" Chyler asked, rather too optimistically, in my opinion.

"Your book's mistaken. I'm not really powerful."

Damn it, I was barely even trained and as far as magic went, it was like asking an amateur to try out for the Olympics. I decided to help Chyler because my conscience told me it was the right thing to do. My mind told me I should get her real help.

"But you're going to look after me, right? How are you going to keep the witches away from me?"

I thought for a moment, trying to resist the urge to drum my fingers on the table as I went through the few options I did have. "We'll have to disguise you," I said, finally.

"There is no way I'm dying my hair. My mom paid two hundred dollars at..." Chyler trailed off and heaved a breath as if something had suddenly punched her in the stomach. She gasped for a moment then steadied herself. I reached over and squeezed her hand and as I did so, I felt a familiar surge of power ricochet through me.

"I've got a better way." I stood and moved round the table until I could put both my hands on her shoulders. I willed her to be hidden and felt the magic flow through me, entirely under my control, seeping around her.

At the same time, I felt something flow back at me and it was like seeing a blurred scene on the backs of my eyes. An attic, Chyler... a knife falling to the floor as someone whimpered. I stepped back quickly, raising my hands from her shoulders to break the connection.

"What did you do?" Chyler whispered. She was shaking slightly, and she held a hand up in front of her as though she were wondering if it were still visible.

"I've masked your magic. I think." Like I said, I

was no master of magic. I just envisioned what I wanted to happen. I wanted to disguise Chyler's magic, not her physical appearance, though I thought I could probably do that too. Right now, the strange vision was at the forefront of my mind. I wasn't sure what I'd seen but I knew what I felt. I felt horribly cold and anxious. Could I have just glimpsed the attack? Even more frighteningly, had I just pulled the vision directly out of Chyler's head?

"How long for?" Chyler was asking me, pulling me back to the present.

"For as long as you need."

"Why didn't you say a spell?"

I shrugged. "I'm not that kind of magic." Though that wasn't strictly true; I could use spells to give my magic a boost and vice versa. I didn't think Chyler needed a lecture from someone who barely understood it herself. Chyler had clearly grown up around magic. It had been in my life, fully, recognisably, for only a year and I was still getting to grips with the basics of what I could do.

"I've got somewhere I can stay. I can go there but I don't know for how long."

"I thought you didn't have anywhere?" I frowned.

"Back-up plan." Chyler shrugged. "Can I come back here?"

"Of course. I said I'd help."

"How are you going to help?" Chyler pressed and, well, she had me there. I hadn't the faintest idea. I couldn't call in reinforcements – not without attracting attention to myself – and I didn't exactly have vast resources.

"Can't your book help you? It brought you here." I eyed the thick old tome and wondered how many secrets and spells it contained. I wondered if my parents had a spell book, and if so, what happened to it.

Chyler stroked the cover. "I don't know. Book, can you help us?" She pushed it to the centre of the table and sat back, arms folded, waiting. Seconds ticked by, then the book slowly began to ruffle its pages, flipping through them until the gaps became wider and the cover rose higher. After a few more seconds, it heaved open to a page. We both leaned forward to get a look.

The book was writing as we watched, the ink looping across the pages. It read: *Hidden in plain sight, something is far from right. Protect yourself witch, beware of the scary bitch.* The ink began to fade until it disappeared altogether, leaving the page blank again.

"Oh, for goodness sake," said Chyler, suddenly sounding twenty years older. She tipped the book shut. "I told you it does stupid rhymes."

"Any chance it gets specific? Like names, times, places?" I raised my eyebrows hopefully but Chyler just shook her head.

"Mumbo jumbo like this mostly. Hey, can I stay here?"

"Um, no. Anyway, you said you had somewhere safe to go. So, you go there now and I'll try and work out what to do."

"But it would be so cool if I stayed here. We could be like, roommates."

"Chyler, you can't stay here."

"Why not?" She looked affronted and there was the tiniest flicker of a sneer rising on her lip; then it was gone.

"I've known you less than an hour so I don't

actually know you," I said gently. "Plus, in getting here, someone might have followed you and we're not prepared to deal with that yet. So please go to your safe place while I work out a plan."

"Fine. Whatever." Chyler scooped up the book and stood up. I saw her mouth move as if she were saying words inside her head, but some of it couldn't help but leak out. In the split second before she winked out of existence, her eyes widened, her pupils dilating. "Stella, help me," she pleaded, her voice nothing more than a whisper.

I sat there for awhile, staring at the space she just occupied wondering what the hell I should do. I was neither arrogant nor stupid enough to think I was a one woman army that could take on who knew how many witches? I knew I wasn't strong enough to take them all; I couldn't rely on even being able to take one! That was if I were only looking after myself, not defending a strange teen witch who merely asked for my protection. Crap. It didn't matter which way I looked at it, things were not looking good.

I made myself a cheese sandwich and a packet of crisps – I still couldn't get my head around calling them chips – and munched them mindlessly while I sat at the table, deep in thought. I couldn't help the feeling that there was something horribly wrong with the whole situation. More wrong than Chyler had even said, thanks to the unnerving feeling I got from the strange vision.

I quickly cleaned up after myself, brushing crumbs into the bin and rinsing my plate before I went into the living room and settled in front of another film about some group of dysfunctional friends searching for love. I must have snoozed for a while because when I woke up, my head was against a blue cushion, the movie had gone off and the digital clock on the DVD player was flashing a quarter after six. I'd have to get a shuffle on to prepare for my night of forced socialisation. At least, it would be better than staring at a wall, willing my brain to come up with a great plan.

I forced myself off the sofa and into my bedroom where I pulled out a clean pair of jeans and a white shirt with a little button-down detail. I finished the look with tooled leather cowboy- style boots with a low chunky heel that I'd picked up in a sale when out shopping with Annalise. They were starting to look appropriately worn in, just like everyone else's did around here. Perhaps footwear was the first step of small town assimilation, I thought with a smile as I sat in front of my dresser. I added the lightest dash of eye shadow and some mascara to make my green eyes pop and ran my hair through my fingers, pleased that it looked sleek and glossy brown.

Earlier, I had put a bottle of wine to chill in the fridge, and I grabbed it by the neck before letting myself out the front door. As my house was side on to the street, I didn't immediately see my neighbour's home. But when I stepped off the porch, I could see they already had a good number of visitors.

Two trucks were parked on the wide driveway next to Annalise's car and Gage's motorbike. Several more cars of varying sizes and ages – nothing ostentatious or showy – were parked along the side of the road, as there were no restrictions here. I could hear music and laughter in the air and I let it wash over me, trying to make it sink in. I could have fun. I would have fun. I chanted that to myself two or three times, hoping it would actually stick.

When I got to the end of my drive, I almost faltered, but just then, two people I recognised as Annalise's friends drove up and parked. They waved to me, so I went in with them as it would have been rude to just turn around and walk away. Plus, I'd have looked like an idiot. As I went in, I couldn't help but look over my shoulder before I shut the door, the same feeling of being watched that I felt earlier was teasing me. I shook off my paranoia, pushed thoughts of Chyler to the back of my mind, and shut the door.

A game was already underway with six players sitting in solid concentration around the circular dining table. For tonight, it had been covered in green baize and there were several stacks of cards as well as a bunch of coloured poker chips. I hadn't the faintest idea what was a good hand or not so I hung back to talk to Annalise as she introduced me to faces I didn't yet know. I nodded politely, said my hellos and had my hand pumped enthusiastically a couple of times.

It seemed people didn't move to Wilding often and, small towns being what they are, everyone knew who I was already and that I'd taken the house across the road. I guessed no amount of wards would have staved off the locals from knowing that! However, I wondered if I should do something about limiting that information and made the decision to think on it some more later. I didn't know if I ever wanted it getting out where I lived especially after spending months trying to live as anonymously as possible. In a small town, where everyone knew everybody, however, my English accent stuck out like a sore thumb.

"Can you play?" asked Annalise and when I shook

my head, she carried on, nodding at the table as she spoke. "Gage learned to play when he was real little and he's pretty damn good. He keeps trying to teach me but it's really never sunk in, in here." She tapped her head and rolled her eyes vacantly.

"You've known each other a long time, huh?"

Annalise looked at me quizzically and nodded. "All our lives, hon'."

"How long have you lived together?" I asked her to be conversational as she took the wine bottle and motioned that I should follow her to the kitchen.

Annalise looked at me like I had gone a little mad as she uncorked the bottle and poured a glass for me, then for her. "Well, except for a few years here and there, all our lives too. Our parents left the house to both of us when they passed."

"I thought you were..." I started, then choked back the words as I followed her back out to the living room. Realisation hit Annalise at the same time and she hooted so loudly with laughter that the players broke concentration to turn and look at us.

"Stella, oh Stella," she howled and tears started to run down her face as she bent almost double, holding her wine glass steady in the air so she wouldn't spill any liquid.

"What's up with you?" asked Gage looking up from his cards, then from her to me, a frown pitting his forehead. Some of his hair had spilled forward and he brushed it back with his free hand, then reached for the beer bottle, touching it to his lips.

"Oh my," Annalise snorted, wiping her eyes with the backs of her hands. "Stella, here, thinks we're ... you know ... hah!"

"You know ... what?" Gage flicked his eyes to his

hand then back to us. I knew he understood when he choked on his beer, earning himself a thump on the back from the player next to him.

I felt myself redden as eyes turned on me when Annalise finally breathed, "Stella seems to be under the impression that we're married, or living together, or something."

His coughing fit over, Gage grimaced. "Gross," he muttered and looked at me like he couldn't fathom why I would think such a thing. Finally he rolled his eyes and busied himself looking at his cards with more attention than they could possibly deserve.

"Why would you think that, honey? Gage is my big brother." Apparently it was the funniest thing Annalise had ever heard.

"Well..." I started. Then, I wondered, why did I think that? I'd gotten their post in my mailbox once or twice and they had the same surname, Garoul, so when I added to the equation they shared a house and didn't look much like each other... Though when I thought about it now, they did have the same shaped eyes – I just jumped to a huge conclusion that they were some kind of – what? Couple? Lovers? It really never occurred to me that they might be siblings. Apparently, I was a ginormous idiot. "I just assumed," I finished lamely, a hot flush burning my cheeks.

"All this time you've been thinking we were... eugh! I don't even want to finish that thought." Annalise laughed as she handed me her glass so she could break open a bag of chips to up-end in two big melamine bowls. She put one on the table for the players and another on the side table by the sofa.

The man next to Gage, the helpful back-thumper,

took one look at the cards he'd been dealt and folded, tossing them on a table with a shake of his head. "You've the luck of the devil," he moaned as Gage put his hands around the small pile of poker chips, pulling them to his side of the table.

"Can't deny it," grinned Gage with a broad smile that would melt an igloo. The good-natured man got up and freed his seat for another player and came over to stand by Annalise. Her whole face glowed as she looked up at him.

"Meet Beau," she said with a smile. Beau looked more like a Butch with his bulging arms, barely restrained by a check shirt with the sleeves rolled up. He had on blue jeans with worn patches over the thighs, and his blond hair was cut close to the scalp. He reached over and pumped my hand. "Beau just got out of the Marines and has moved back to Wilding," added Annalise.

"Welcome home," I said, wincing a bit as he crushed my hand in his energetic grasp.

"It's good to be back," said Beau and I noticed that he had gently looped his arm around Annalise's waist. A-ha! Good job I got my explanation before I'd seen that or I would have thought they were having an affair. That would have been mortifying, not to mention completely confusing.

"We've missed Beau over these past few years," Annalise added, her eyes still fixed on him.

Beau looked at her fondly and I wondered if there had been some history between them. "I was glad to come back and find Annalise still here."

"Couldn't keep away," she murmured.

It seemed that Beau was a popular guy, judging by the reactions he was getting from the room. He was by no means my type, if there were such a thing, but he was broad and tidy looking with an amicable personality that matched his easy smile. For a big man, he seemed gentle around Annalise, who was rather petite, and I liked that. Annalise seemed to bring out a sisterly quality in me and with her easy demeanor. I liked to see people being nice to her.

"Why don't you play a game?" suggested Annalise signalling Beau's vacated chair at the table.

"I don't know the rules," I admitted, feeling like a lame ass. So far, this evening was excruciating for me even though I was trying. I felt like I stood on the edges of fun, not quite able to lean forward and grasp the feeling. I felt like my social ineptitude was rolling off me in waves, but I put my game face on anyway, if only not to disappoint my friend.

"Gage," she called. "Did you know that Stella cannot play poker?"

Gage sat back and looked at me. "Get out. Everyone can play poker."

"I can play Gin Rummy," I confessed weakly.

Gage rolled his eyes. "That's a game for retired folk. Come over and I'll teach you the basics; then we can have a game."

I looked to Annalise and Beau for my escape clause but they were busy making eyes at each other, so I just nodded and took up the spare chair. Seeing that I was a newbie, the other players made their excuses and headed into the kitchen for beers. I looked after them, feeling uncomfortable. "Now I feel like I've ruined the game."

Gage shook his head as he shuffled the deck. "They just couldn't accept that they were all out of chips. They're probably on the first step of drowning their sorrows right now."

"That sucks."

"They'll probably win it all back next week." Gage grinned, dimples popping on each cheek, and I couldn't help smiling back.

Gage showed me the basic plays and we played a couple of easy rounds with our cards face up on the table so he could tell me what to do. I was getting the hang of it but only if I really concentrated on it. At least, it gave me something new to think about, something that wasn't wrapped in sadness or involved in coming up with new and inventive ways to aid my search.

"Ready for a real game?"

"I guess." I pulled a face.

"Are you going to play to win?" Gage cocked an eyebrow at me as he swept the cards up and started to shuffle, letting the cards ripple in his hands in a fancy move.

"I'll do my best."

Annalise sidled up behind me. "How about you put stakes on it? You'll play better if you've got something to lose," she suggested. Her comment didn't strike me as helpful but it did draw a little crowd round us and they murmured their agreement. I wasn't sure if they just wanted to see me lose or, hope against hopes, watch Gage's luck run out. I felt like I was being initiated and, crap, was I about to make an idiot of myself? At least, this evening had a general theme.

Gage looked at me thoughtfully and nodded. "Want to put a stake on it?"

I knew I didn't have a hope in hell of winning so I thought for a moment and came up with the most ridiculous stake that I could, simply because I knew it would never happen. "I win, you paint my house."

The little crowd murmured their approval while Gage considered his request. Annalise winked at me. Heck, it was a good job their house looked freshly painted or I would probably be doing that for the next few weeks. I hope he didn't ask me to do his laundry. There was a line to be drawn, after all.

"I want Stella," he said, at last. He was immediately thumped on the back by Beau who whooped. Gage's cheeks pinked under the stubble. "I mean an evening out. Dinner, maybe."

"Like I cook?" I asked, not sure if he wanted me to feed him. I could do that. Badly. I was pretty sure his sister fed him well, which meant... oh. I started to blush.

"Like a date," he confirmed, "but you can cook if you want. Or we can do something else, like see a movie."

"Oh, lord," muttered Annalise and bent to whisper in my ear. "Take pity on him, sweetie."

"Best of three?" I asked, starting to hope that maybe there was a slim chance he would paint my house because I was not handing over a date and he nodded. It was a good job I was no cheat or I would have considered having a surreptitious magical rummage in that card pile.

"Okay, then." Gage shuffled the cards, clearly showing off a little as he took one hand up high and let the cards rain down into his other hand, then he spun five cards out each with a flick of his thumb. I picked mine up. I had a full house. Unbelievable. And I hadn't even been tempted to me to use magic to get the right cards. I was on a lucky streak all right.

"Deal?"

I shook my head.

"Fold?" Gage asked hopefully.

Again, I shook my head.

"Me neither on both counts. Show me what you've got."

I laid my queens and twos out on the table and waited. The banter had gone out of the room. Apparently our stakes were far more interesting. Gage sighed and tossed his cards down. He had one pair. Win to me! I grinned, feeling a rush of energy crest and flow inside me.

"What colour would you like your house, hon'?" giggled Annalise with a little snort.

"Best of three, remember," said Gage, looking a little surprised at my starter's luck but otherwise not bothered. He eyed me like he was trying to see inside my head and I dropped my gaze to his hands.

"Deal," I said, my confidence taking a little leap of its own. Gage reshuffled the pack and dealt again, his eyes meeting mine in challenge when I raised them for the briefest of moments. Picking up my cards, I held them to my chest and fanned them out. I didn't have a single match. Either Gage's hand had to be just as bad, or he was a clear winner.

I wasn't sure what play to make so I just shook my head. After a tense minute, he laid his out first. We were level one-on-one. My heart thudded. It's just a game, I reminded myself. Besides dinner with Gage would not be horrible, even though this was the longest conversation we'd had as yet. What would we talk about? Perhaps I could just look at him, I thought, which made my heart thump surprisingly fast.

"I like steak rare," Gage teased.

"I'd like my house white," I rebuffed, a small smile playing on my face.

On our third and final set, Gage laid off the fancy moves, shuffling quickly and thoroughly, before dealing our final hands. I waited a moment before picking up my cards and then fanned them in my palm. My opening hand was four tens and an eight. Four of a kind. I was *so* going to get my house painted. I couldn't help the grin that spread across my face as he sighed and shook his hand out on the table. I laid mine down eagerly and heard a whoop go up behind me. My eyes widened just for a moment then I looked down. All clubs, all in the right order. All his. That had to have higher points than mine. Crap. And my heart sank when one of Gage's buddies high-fived him.

Annalise patted my back in commiseration. "If it helps at all, he does chew with his mouth shut and he knows how to use cutlery."

Great.

"Tomorrow night?" said Gage, with a nod of his head, and before I could answer, and tell him that we didn't have to, he scraped back his chair and headed off to the kitchen. And just like that, I had a date.

I couldn't be churlish and cross because I didn't want to be pathetic nor to embarrass him, not in his own house and not in front of his sister and friends. Besides, I accepted the bet, even when I knew I was unlikely to win. So I just plastered on what I hoped was a magnanimous smile, pushed my chair back and left the table to make way for the real players.

For another hour, I hung around and was polite and exchanged conversational tidbits with Annalise's friends. I made polite inquiries to the people I knew vaguely and took their poker jokes on the chin. A couple of the ladies quietly congratulated me and said they'd have played badly for a date with Gage too. I wasn't quite sure what that was all about. Sure, he was good looking and seemed to work hard, but he hadn't said more than thirty words to me in six months, and we were neighbours. Maybe they liked the strong silent types. Personally, I hoped he'd bone up on his conversational skills before we were stuck silently gawping at each other like morons. I hoped our faux date wouldn't be excruciating.

By the time I kissed Annalise on the cheek and stepped outside, the sun had almost set, leaving a faded red tinge on the inky black horizon. I'd just walked down the steps when I heard the door open and shut behind me, a quick burst of noise escaping, and footsteps sounded on the steps as someone followed me out. I must have forgotten something, I thought, as I turned round to face Annalise. Instead, I almost face planted into a man's chest. I looked up and got Gage.

"Have I offended you?" he asked looking down at me, his face completely unreadable.

"Um, no."

"Good." He looked at me, his eyes boring into mine briefly, before saying, "You don't have to go out with me if you don't want to."

I thought about that for a moment, probably a moment too long, and his face seemed to fall a little bit. What else had I planned? A big, fat, nothing, that's what. Who could say we wouldn't have a nice time? And it wasn't like it was a real date. It was just for fun. I needed fun. "No, that's fine. I'm happy to go out with you," I said, keeping my weak justification to myself.

He smiled and, there, under the moonlight, I thought him quite lovely. There was no denying he was handsome. At least, he'd be nice to look at on our pretend date, which I was not going to think of as a date under any circumstances. Not even when my stomach was doing little flips. Not even when I felt the frisson of first date nerves. "So... I'll pick you up tomorrow night at seven?" he said.

"Okay."

"Okay," he repeated. Hmm, we were big conversationalists, all right.

Gage looked at me for another moment, then nodded in that curt way of his and turned to go back inside. I stepped forward, reaching out so that I caught his bare wrist where he'd folded the sleeve back. He was hot, literally hot, and I could feel his vein pumping, strong and vital. There was something about the feel of his skin that suddenly made me feel very alive. I wanted to feel alive. Gage turned back to me expectantly, his face starting to fall again like he really expected me change my mind so quickly.

"Do I need to get dressed up?" I asked, withdrawing my hand, my thumb rubbing against my palm where I could still feel his heat burning against my skin.

Gage thought about it for a moment, then shook his head. "No, casual is fine."

"I'm just relieved I don't have to cook." I tried a coy smile on for size.

Gage laughed and turned back to climb the steps. He paused, one foot on the top plank, the other stretched, long and lean. I admired his physique for probably a moment too long. He smiled down at me, like he knew exactly what I was thinking and welcomed it. "That's for the second date," he grinned and before I could argue that I hadn't agreed to two dates, he bounded inside and shut the door firmly on me.

"Hah," I said to the still night.

I stood there for a moment looking at the closed door, wondering what had just happened. Then I shook myself out of it and went back over to my house, shadowed under the dusky clouds.

It wasn't until I stood on my porch that I saw the parcel propped in front of it. I walked towards it cautiously. It was way past the regular mailman's hours and I hadn't heard a truck pull up, but then, some people left before I had and I barely noticed their engines on the road either. I picked up the parcel, bulky but soft, and took it inside.

Just inside the door, I reached for the light switch and flipped it on, then took the package over to the sofa. My name was printed neatly on the outside, but without an address. Odd.

Leaving it perched on the sofa for no more than a minute, I rummaged for a pair of scissors in a kitchen drawer. Scissors in hand, I sat down next to the parcel and carefully slit open the taped ends which snapped with a gentle pop. I peeled off the paper, letting it slide to the floor as I shook out the coverlet that was inside, allowing it to fall over my knees. It was gently sprigged with hand embroidered pastel flowers and I recognised it at once.

A small white card fluttered down to the floor and I stooped down to retrieve it. *Dear Stella*, said the note, *thought you might be missing this*. No name. Or return address, though I knew where it had come from.

The same coverlet had been on my bed every night at the safe house. I'd slept under it, dreamed on it, cried into it.

But what the hell was it doing here? More importantly, who brought it to Wilding?

CHAPTER THREE

Thanks to Chyler's big intrusion and my surprise gift, both arriving within a few hours of each other, my nerves were on edge all day. Before I went to bed, I was careful to lock the doors and check that every window was closed and locked tight. I didn't take the coverlet with me. Instead, I left it bundled up on the sofa overnight and it had stayed there all day too. Finally, I got a grip and made myself pick it up, shake it out and fold it neatly over the back of my sofa. I even sniffed it just to see if I could pick up the scent of any magic on it. I couldn't. That's when I realised how ridiculous I was being. I couldn't fathom why anyone would want to magic a coverlet.

More pressing, however, was who had been at my house last night and why did they leave it? I couldn't work out if it was supposed to be a gift or a message. It had been almost a year since Steven, one of the Council's elders, gave me the parcel of documents that contained the deed to my house. Unless, he copied everything – and I didn't think he had – I could count him out. Besides, he had never been to the safe house and wouldn't have known the coverlet was ever on my bed.

Plus, now that I thought about it, Steven was extremely careful about giving my parents' things to me personally, so I doubted anyone else had seen the contents. I sighed. This much I knew: things were about as clear as mud.

No, it had to be someone from the safe house. There were only a few survivors to choose from: Étoile, Seren, Kitty or Marc. The sinking feeling inside me told me that without a sign of him after all this time, Evan must not have survived. I was sure he would have come for me, then and here, if he could have. He had extensive wounds the last time I saw him and my hopes of his survival were fading every day.

Whenever I thought of Evan, my heart flipped and sank. I had been falling over the edge of loving him and the pain of losing him was almost too much to bear. During the few weeks that we shared, I felt our connection grow fast and intense like thick cords binding us together. Now, however, that connection felt like gossamer fine thread, waiting to break at any moment. I didn't know enough about my witch heritage, or his daemon ancestry, to know if I were imagining things or if there really were some kind of supernatural connection that we'd initiated, which never petered out.

I hovered near the coverlet looking at it, feeling strangely superstitious about touching it. How was I supposed to narrow it down to a sender? Kitty had been horrendously injured too and I certainly had no guarantee that she survived. Not if there were internal injuries on top of everything else she suffered.

It was also unlikely that Marc would do something as odd as deliver a coverlet under the cover (hah!) of darkness. It had to be Étoile or Seren. I was closer to Étoile. She saved my life once and, though she was bossy and persnickety, I liked her and trusted her.

Still, that didn't explain how anyone knew I was in Wilding. I was fairly sure I hadn't left a trace, human or magic, to follow. I was very careful when I travelled here, criss-crossing back and forth, covering my tracks. I was sure no one knew about the house. It was very puzzling.

I spent the day pottering about the house, growing increasingly frustrated. I tried all my usual pursuits. I read my book, and gave up when I realised I'd not registered a single word in several pages. I watched some more movies from the DVD box set Annalise had leant me; but abandoned that when I realised my mind drifted too much to know what was going on. I even tried having a nap but, after tossing and turning for an hour, I had to accept that sleep just wasn't coming to me.

I tried spending some time thinking about my poker-bargain date tonight and wondered where Gage might be taking me, but I couldn't help feeling guilty. Wasn't it too soon to go on a date? Even a faux date? Especially, when Evan was never far from the edge of my mind and I thought about him so many times a day, I eventually decided I had to steel my heart from the hurt and frustration.

"It's just one date," I told myself firmly as I browsed my wardrobe late in the afternoon. "It's just an evening, with a friend." A hot friend, my brain added, rather unhelpfully, and it was a date, not just a casual evening out.

I finally pulled out three outfits and analysed each of them heavily for any untoward signals they might give off (too short a hemline, too much cleavage... too damn Puritannical) I finally threw my hands in the air and pulled a face in the mirror.

Why was I getting so wound up about it? It wouldn't take more than a few hours out of my life and then things could get back to normal with us waving hello whenever we saw each other and otherwise getting on with our lives. It was nothing to get stressed about and, with that, I pulled out the figure-hugging black jeans and a slouchy silk top in a punchy orange to hang over my closet door until it was time to dress. With heeled boots picked out, I put an end to the clothing dilemma. Considering I didn't know what Gage had planned, it seemed like a good idea to choose an outfit that covered every kind of venue or activity. This would have to suffice.

I wondered what we would talk about. Now that I'd discovered from Annalise that they'd grown up here and were siblings, I had that angle covered. She worked from home, Gage worked in a nearby town.

I wasn't even up to temping at the moment. Well, that meant careers were out, unless he wanted to tell me about his. And we didn't have any shared history of the town or people we knew, because everyone I knew here, already knew him.

The rest of the afternoon I spent cleaning the house and rearranging the furniture. For the first month I left it entirely alone in the way you do when you first move into a place and don't like to touch what isn't yours. Then, I finally accepted that the house was mine and there was no one to stop me doing anything I wanted in it.

So my newest game – and sort of workout routine – was experimenting with the positioning of the furniture. The latest layout wasn't working for me, so now I tugged the sofa into its new place away from the hallway wall, allowing myself a short burst of magic to help ease it into position without straining too much. It was easy to push the coffee table and the rug underneath to their new angles, within cup-reaching distance, but I left the other sofa where it was, in front of the window, as well as the armchair with its back to the shelves. It was far too much seating for one or two people and I wondered if my parents had company often when they lived in the house.

Over the months, I'd been slowly filling the shelves up with books that I'd picked up and the odd ornament that I'd find tucked away. It felt strange, and slightly exhilarating, to be adding my things to so much space. I was even considering painting the room white instead of the slightly dreary off-yellow. Maybe I'd hang new curtains too, something with less of an obnoxious, old-fashioned print. Who knew that I would be so house proud?

Finally I went into the garden to cut some greenery. My neighbour's house was quiet, though I could see the truck and car as well as Gage's motorbike, so I guessed they were both in. Back inside, I tried arranging the green branches in some artful way in a vase to add some fresh colour to the room and, when I was finally happy with the cluster, I set it on the low corner table where a potted plant used to sit.

The first day I arrived at my home, there were

plants dotted all around. I slept on the sofa overnight, not quite comfortable with climbing into one of the beds. When I woke in the morning, the plants had all crumbled to dust.

It took me some time to surmise that while things could exist in stasis indefinitely, once they were brought out of it, after any duration, they would wither and die, their life processes having been sped up.

Unfortunately, my house only proved that my initial guess was correct. Though nothing crumbled quite as actively nor decisively as the plants, plenty of other things were breaking – a chair leg here, a handle there. I guessed if my parents returned frequently, they simply deactivated the spells and time caught up. Unfortunately, it had been twenty years of time that was catching up in just a matter of months. Still, it was nothing I planned to deal with today. At least, the main furniture was holding up for now. Although I could swear another spring popped through my mattress last night...

I looked over the room. Now I was getting used to making changes; I could envisage how it would eventually look. Maybe I would even paint the living room in the next few days if Annalise could direct me to a paint store. It would give me something to do, now the weather was turning cold. Not to mention, the physical action would be beneficial as well.

A glance at my wristwatch made me squeak. I left myself thirty minutes to get ready and was dusty from moving the furniture. I showered quickly and washed my hair, taking my time over blow-drying it before I got dressed in the outfit I previously selected. I kept my jewellery light, just studs for my ears.

I picked up my mother's brooch and turned the pretty coloured bird over in my hand. I hadn't risked wearing it out yet just in case it slipped off and I lost it. It seemed a shame to keep the brooch hidden away in my room so I took it into the living room and propped it next to the photos on the mantle-piece to look at it. Just as I trailed my fingertips over it, smiling, a knock sounded at the door. I looked over my shoulder and could see Gage waiting on the porch so I went to let him in.

"You look lovely," was the first thing he said and I wriggled my toes in my socks self-consciously. "Orange suits you."

"Thanks. Come in." I stepped back to let Gage walk inside. He looked around while I took in his dark blue jeans and open necked shirt in a deep green that set off his dark hair and tan skin.

"Looks exactly the same as when I last saw it. 'Cept where the furniture is," he said, his eyes coming to a stop on me.

"When was that?"

"Around twenty-five years ago."

I whistled. "I wasn't even born then."

"I know. I remember your mom and dad. They were friendly with my parents."

"I didn't know that."

"Annalise never said?"

I shook my head. Then, when I realised we were still just standing there facing each other, I remembered my manners. "Please have a seat. I've just got to get my purse and put my boots on; then I'm ready."

"Take your time."

I tried to be as quick as I could, sitting at my

dresser to brush on a little makeup, just a touch of eye shadow and a sweep of mascara, nothing more. Afterwards, I zipped up my boots and went back into the living room, with my jacket hung over my arm. Gage was standing by the mantle-piece, looking at the photos I had next to my brooch.

"Family?" he asked congenially.

I shook my head. "I don't have any family left. These are friends." There was a picture of Kitty, Étoile, Seren, and me all together and another one of just Evan and me. It had been taken on a beach one night, so long ago now. His arms were wrapped around me, both of us smiling straight at the camera. It made me happy and sad all at once. I planned to get around to framing them.

"They going to visit you out here?"

"I don't know." I turned away before he could say anything else. "Shall we go?"

"Sure. I brought my car, seeing as I didn't know if you were wearing a dress or not. I figured you wouldn't want to be on my bike," Gage remarked as he opened the door. I pulled it behind us and locked it, my fingers retracing the magic the lock retained. If he thought locking my door was odd for this small town, he didn't say so. I stood on the porch for a moment, a faint tingling niggling my skin. I looked around into the dimly lit garden, wondering what it was in the shadows that bothered me so much. I shivered lightly and hurried over to Gage where he was holding his car door open and waiting for me. I kept trying to shake off the feeling I had of being watched.

"I thought a movie then dinner, or drinks?" Gage asked as he folded himself into the driver's seat after closing my door. He was very gentlemanly, which was something I hadn't quite expected from him. "There are a few shows on. I don't know what you've seen recently."

"I haven't been to the cinema in a long time so I haven't seen anything," I confessed. "I didn't even know Wilding had a cinema."

"It doesn't, as such. We're too small to sustain one so we'll go to the next town over. Annalise might have mentioned there's a coffee shop in town that does screenings of old movies, if you like that sort of thing. They do shows every Friday night."

"I'll have to get her to take me."

"You'd better book your time." Gage flashed a smile at me as he turned the car onto the road and pointed it towards town. "She's been spending a lot of time with Beau."

"She seems pretty happy that he's back," I ventured. Annalise hadn't told me much, but I guessed there was some history between the two of them.

"They were high school sweethearts back in the day. Thought they might even get hitched but they split up during their senior year — I was away at college by then — and Beau went off to the army. Annalise, well, she moved on eventually."

"And here they are again."

"Here they are again," echoed Gage.

We fell silent while I wondered if I were supposed to make small talk to fill the gaps. Gage never struck me as overly talkative, but I didn't want him to think I was in some way put out about our date, even if it were the result of me getting a smack down in poker.

When I thought about it, however, I was actually

fairly pleased to be going out and on a date, no less, with Gage. There was no denying that he was an extremely attractive man. And he liked me. That thought made me bristle with pride just a touch, along with a little pang of guilt. I brushed it off. I was going to do my best to enjoy myself. I had to live.

"What're you smiling about?" asked Gage.

"I was just looking forward to this evening."

Gage flashed me that smile again, the one that made me melt inside. "Me too," he nodded and flipped his blinker so that we could switch roads and start the route out of town, instead of toward Wilding.

"So, how come you don't have any family?" Gage asked, as he shook his head. "I'm sorry if you think I'm rude. I just wondered because you came here out of the blue and you said back at your house that you didn't have family."

"I think you were there when I told you that my parents left me the house. I didn't know about it until a few months ago though. I don't think they ever took me there."

"I would have remembered if the Mayweathers ever brought a kid with them and I don't remember you. Did they pass recently?"

I shook my head. "When I was little."

"That's rough."

"You said you knew my parents?" I pressed, changing the subject slightly, suddenly eager to glean any knowledge about them.

"Well, sure. I've lived here my whole life, 'cept for a few years during college and after, so I remember your mom and dad coming out now and again. They used to pay me a couple of dollars for doing the lawn."

"They got a good deal." The lawn was big and took a lot of effort as my aching muscles could testify after this summer.

"A couple of decades ago, that was a great deal."

"Did you continue to cut the lawn when the house was empty?"

Gage nodded but kept his eye on the road. "Every month, money turned up from some law practice in New York in return for keeping the lawn trimmed and doing the odd bit of maintenance. My parents used to keep an eye on the house for your parents; and when they passed, I kept it up. The money stopped coming when you arrived."

"I don't understand how anyone could have known I was here." I wondered if I should ask him if he minded the money no longer arriving.

"Someone knew," pointed out Gage.

I guessed that might explain why I received the mystery gift waiting on the porch. Perhaps it was something to do with Steven's law practice. I hadn't seen him since that fateful evening in New York when I first arrived in the States. That day, he gave me my parents' last effects and the key to the house. Of course, I didn't say any of that to Gage. Instead, I said, "I'm sorry about the money. I didn't know you were expecting it and I'll make it up to you."

"No you won't. That money was not our livelihood and we were always a bit surprised when it kept on coming after our parents passed on. We've been paid, Annalise and I, for keeping an eye on the place and now we don't have to, so for that, I'm grateful. Plus, now I only have to keep on cutting one chunk of grass, so I'm grateful for that too."

"Well, if you're sure."

"I'm sure and don't go offering to pay your movie ticket either." I wasn't totally sure if Gage were offended or not so I let that slide.

"What is it you do anyway?" I asked. He had a nice house, inherited like mine, so I assumed there was no mortgage to pay. He had a nice car, and his motorbike, and I knew he worked out of Wilding, though I wasn't quite sure what he did.

"For work? I'm a graphic designer. I design logos and artwork and stuff like that."

"Wow," I said with admiration. I was lacking in the creative department but I made up for it with an awesome ability to stick out dull jobs. Or, at least, I used to.

"And you?"

"Until I came here, I used to do office work. Typing, filing, things like that... not nearly as exciting as graphic design."

"You wouldn't think it was exciting after the five hundredth cheesy logo you'd drawn. You going to be looking for office work here?"

"Maybe. I don't really feel like it's my calling, but I don't know what is."

"It'll hit you one day," Gage said kindly.

"I hope so. Maybe more of a gentle thud though. Hey, maybe I'll go to college. I never went. Or I could do some correspondence courses." It was something I thought a lot about over the years but never pursued since I always worked long hours. So much had changed this past year, maybe one of them could be positive.

"That would improve your prospects and help you get ready for when you do know what you want."

"Maybe. I'll look into it."

"Ask Annalise. She used to teach at the local college so she'll know how to get you started."

"I didn't know she taught."

"Yep, textile design. That's why she's so good with all those things she makes."

"How come she gave it up?" We were on the outskirts of Deliverance, our neighbouring town, now and heading towards the main street. Annalise had taken me here to buy lamps a few weeks before and we stayed for lunch in the town. It was a bustling place, both day and evening as it sucked in the people from the surrounding smaller towns.

"She had a real bad... accident a few years ago and she didn't go out much after that." Gage was gripping the steering wheel and his knuckles blanched to white. "Gave up her job, moved back home and then she started her craft business. She's almost back to her old self now."

"Oh? She never said." I wondered what he was going to say before he said "accident." I got the impression he was smoothing over the details.

"She doesn't like talking about that time of her life. That's why I'm happy she's happy. Especially with Beau. He's a decent guy and he'll treat her right."

Gage took one hand off the steering wheel to point along the street. "The movie theatre is just over there."

We got tickets for a Johnny Depp film and shared a bucket of hot buttered popcorn. He didn't do anything cheesy like try and put his arm round me; but he did rest his arm against mine on the armrests. Later, when we left, he wrapped his hand around mine and I let him. He was toasty warm and I allowed myself to enjoy the simple pleasure of a handsome man holding my hand.

"Do you want to go for a drink?" he asked as we lingered for a moment outside the doors of the theatre, the cold night air whispering around our faces. The street was shot with artificial light spilling from the doors and overlaid with the soft glow of moonlight. A long line of people snaked down the street. It was date night from the number of couples waiting.

"I'd like that," I said.

He nodded to a bar across the street. "Let's go there."

The sound of the band hit me as soon as we went inside and I let Gage, being the taller and broader of us, break our path to the bar. He was greeted, and clapped on the back by a few guys and I couldn't help but notice more than a few women look casually over him from head to toe and then look coolly at me. I got it. He was in demand and I was in the way. *Tough, sodding luck for them*, said the little defiant voice in my head.

Gage ordered beers for us and pointed to a table for us to perch, all the while holding my hand so that I was swept along in his wake. I shrugged off my coat and hung it over the back of the chair.

"Do you come here often?" I asked.

"Worst line ever. Does it ever work for you?"

I blushed and he squeezed my hand lightly. "I'm kidding, Stella. And no, I don't come here often but I've been a few times. If I want to go for a beer, I go somewhere closer where I don't have to drive."

"Like the bar on our road?" I asked. The Loup Garou, as it was called, was a few miles down the road from our houses. From the times I'd driven past, it seemed to attract a motley sort and I never had any desire to go there. I doubted I was missing much.

Gage took a long sip from his bottle. "From time to time."

"I've never been." Annalise had recommended a bunch of places but never that bar, even if it were the closest one to us.

"I don't think you'd like it much."

"Dirt floor and angry barmaids?" I asked, making light of it and Gage laughed.

"Not quite. It's fairly rough and ready though. I wouldn't take you there."

"I'll take that as a compliment then."

"Gage! Stella! Hey!" I twisted my head and saw Annalise and Beau bearing down on us. Annalise was wearing super tight jeans and a strappy top. Despite the cold, she was only carrying a light jacket. Beau was more dressed for the weather in jeans, boots and a thick check shirt. Still no jacket. I was glad I'd taken my jacket off or I would have felt positively overdressed next to Annalise. She slid over to me, smiling. "Well, hello. Are we crashing your date?"

"Not at all." I would have signalled that she take a chair if there were any to be had but the other bar patrons had gotten them first, so I stood to give her a quick hug instead.

"We're going to see that Johnny Depp film, now. Shame he's not a pirate in it, but a girl can't have everything." She shrugged and Beau slipped his arm around her shoulders so that she could snuggle into him.

"We just saw it," said Gage.

"Then don't say anymore because you'll spoil the

surprise. See you later... maybe." Annalise winked at me as she hugged me again, then Gage. Gage shook hands with Beau in a friendly man-way which involved clapping each other hard on the shoulders and not wincing.

"You're right, she does seem happy," I said, watching them retreat out the doors until they were lost in the crowd.

Gage nodded. "You want to stay for another drink?"

I shook my head. "You're driving and it wouldn't be fair. We should go."

Gage drained the last of his beer and I took another sip. We'd been in there less than half an hour and I hoped he didn't think I was trying to cut our date short. I'd actually surprised myself into having a good time.

"Want to dance before we go?"

I looked over to his line of vision and saw a small space had been cleared for no more than a few couples to dance. The band were playing some thumpy, up tempo numbers and the crowd were getting loud right along with them.

"Sure," I replied and it wasn't until we were on the dance floor and Gage spun me out and pulled me back to him that I realised that the last time I danced was with Evan. Suddenly, my heart seemed to plummet through my body. I swallowed quickly and forced myself to move in time with the music. I would tackle my grief later, privately. I wouldn't let it consume me. For this moment, I just wanted to feel happy.

Gage was a good dancer. Rhythmic, vibrant and with good footwork that told me he had never lacked for a dance partner. As the number drew to a close, he picked me up, his hands on my hips and twirled me around before setting me lightly on the floor, my body sliding against his.

I wasn't a genius at man-woman stuff but I recognised a come-on when one slammed into me. He smiled down at me and, for a moment, I thought he was going to kiss me, but instead, he took my hand and tugged me outside into the cold night air.

"Let's get you home." Gage chatted congenially about the film as we drove back and when we passed the Loup Garou I couldn't help but check out the number of cars and motorbikes in the lot. The lights were on but it seemed quiet inside tonight so we flashed by and, five minutes later, Gage turned onto my drive.

"You're welcome to come in for a drink, if you like." I thought about what I might have in my kitchen. "I have wine, or coffee. No beer though, sorry."

"Wine is fine by me." Gage cut off the engine and walked around my side to open the door for me. I fumbled in my bag for my keys as we took the steps, then unlocked the door and held it open for him.

"Make yourself at home. Put on music if you like. I'll get the wine."

Gage took off his jacket and hung it on the rack by the door as I retreated into the kitchen. It felt strange having someone in my house. So far, there had just been Annalise and me. Gage was officially my second guest; (I decided Chyler didn't count, seeing as she wasn't invited). I picked up two glasses with long stems and the white wine from my fridge. I hoped he wasn't a wine snob because otherwise he was going to suffer disappointment.

When I went back in the living room, he'd turned on my TV and was looking through my stack of dollar bin DVDs. It would have been less mortifying if I'd had some more cerebral movies selected. Unfortunately I hadn't.

"You're just as bad as my sister," Gage laughed.

"I like happy movies," I said, sitting next to him on the sofa, and then started to protest when he took the wine bottle and corkscrew from me, but he just shook his head. I waited until he'd uncorked the bottle, then held out the glasses for him to fill. He set the bottle on the floor and clinked his glass lightly against mine.

"What are we drinking to?"

"Bad poker hands and good dates?"

"I'll drink to that." Gage smiled and I returned the smile before taking a sip. The wine slid down my throat easily.

"Okay, let's see if you have anything watchable."

"I'm going to take offence at that."

"Most people would take offence at your preferences," Gage teased as he shuffled through my less than intelligent offerings.

"I'm definitely offended now."

"Drink your wine. It'll dull the pain." I got the pleasure of him yelping as I bashed his arm with a cushion.

"Fine, fine." Gage paused, holding up a disc box. "You want to watch *A River Runs Through It*? No drooling over Brad Pitt."

I laughed. "Sure." I settled back on the sofa as Gage loaded the DVD before sitting next to me, legs stretched out, wine glass in hand as the credits rolled.

He looked very at home on my sofa. If he were my boyfriend, I would have pulled the coverlet folded over the back of the sofa over us and snuggled up to him; but he wasn't so I didn't. As soon as I thought, if he were Evan, I wiped it from my mind. The rawness had only just begun to heal; but every so often, it would tug at me as if to remind me it was still there.

As it happened, we didn't really end up watching much of the movie; instead we talked about them. A line here would remind Gage of something he'd seen and then we'd talk about that. Or maybe a scene would remind me of another film and that would lead on to another topic, which would make us laugh.

I didn't even realise that I was flirting at first as my body responded naturally to his. By the time I did realise, I was warm with wine. When Gage flirted with a touch of his hand against mine, or our legs would bump together and neither of us would draw back, I didn't mind one bit. Then, finally, his lips brushed mine, his hand soft against my cheek, I didn't hesitate to slip my arms around him and pull him in for more. It wasn't just human contact I craved; it was the warmth of his skin on mine, the feel of *him* on my lips.

CHAPTER FOUR

My head was swimming as I cranked my eyes open, groaning with discomfort. My recall of the night before and falling into bed was muddled and indistinct. Kicking off my clothes and climbing under the covers was a distant, hazy memory. In my half-sleepy, fuzzy state, I smiled at the memory of dancing with Gage. I remembered him coming back to the house with me, where we shared a bottle of wine and I (vaguely) recalled opening another. We watched another movie and talked and laughed for hours. I knew I hadn't drunk that much, but I wasn't a big drinker so the effects of the alcohol didn't really hit me until I knew I was already very merry. By the time I'd cut out the alcohol, it was too late.

I touched a finger to my lips. We kissed. *Oh...* Yes, we definitely kissed.

I rolled, stretched and... Jeez! I froze. There was someone in bed with me. The body shifted and a long arm stretched over me, curling around my body.

"Morning," came a gruff voice and my eyes

widened. I did *not* remember this. I did not remember going to bed with... I tilted my head to one side. No, I did not remember going to bed with Gage.

I shuffled, a small, tentative movement and felt the sheets cool against my skin. I wondered if I could peek under the bedclothes to see what I was wearing. I was fairly certain I was wearing something. I'd better be wearing something.

"Um... hi," I said, flustered. "Um..."

"Um?" Gage mumbled, his hand sliding down my arm to lace his fingers around mine, and his thumb rubbing my palm. I untangled our fingers and carefully pushed his hand back over to him before rolling onto my back. Slowly, I turned my head fully. Yep, there he was. Head on my pillow. I raised my head a fraction, just enough to see his clothes on the floor at the foot of my bed.

"Ah... did we... um..." I trailed off, my head thumping.

"No, we didn't 'um'." Gage paused a beat. "You would have remembered if we 'ummed'."

"I would hope so."

"You definitely would."

"Bit full of yourself."

"Wish you were full of me."

"Gage!"

"Sorry," he mumbled into the pillow and I only just heard him say, "Meant it, though."

"Why are you in my bed?" I asked.

"Home was too far away and we just fell asleep."

"You live right across the street... and you're not wearing anything."

"Anything could have happened in the dark. Late night. Lone man..."

I raised my eyebrows at him. I hoped I wasn't raising a line of day old mascara too.

"I live in hope."

"You do know Annalise is probably looking outside right now, seeing your car parked in my driveway and putting two and two together to make thirty five."

"She might think I just left it here until morning."

I shook my head. "She would have been at your door offering you coffee or something as soon as it was decent."

Gage thought about that for a moment, then grinned. "Don't worry, I'll keep our dirty little secret to myself."

"You do that." Oh, wait... "There is no dirty little secret!" I protested.

"Seeing as I'm keeping quiet, my sister will never know that." Gage looked smug now. He should. Annalise would absolutely surmise the worst... or the best, depending on whose point of view she was working from.

"I should probably be cross with you."

His face fell a bit as he looked at me from the next pillow. "Are you?"

With his morning stubble and the slight curl of his hair, he was a very attractive man to wake up to. If I were a red-blooded female, and if I were in my right mind, I would have been taking advantage of this situation. As it was... "No, but you should go home."

"But I'm warm," he protested sleepily.

"You can be warm in your own house. It has a heating system that works. Go use it," I said, probably a touch too harshly as I tried to peek under the covers to see exactly what I was wearing. Or if I would have to tug the covers off to wrap around me when I got up. What if Gage were naked under there? I felt my face redden. I couldn't look. But I kinda wanted to. There was no "if" about it, I *was* a red-blooded female, judging by the thoughts surging through my brain. I tried to quell them with a mental sledgehammer.

"What are you doing?" he asked me, amused. "If you're you trying to have a look, I'm not shy."

I flushed bright red this time. "I. Am. Not! I'm trying to figure out what I'm wearing."

I probably shouldn't have said that because it wasn't my hand trailing over my shoulder and running the length of my body under the covers. "Bra," murmured Gage, as he slipped a finger under one, barely there, shoulder strap, then his hand moved lower.

He raised his eyebrows. He seemed to be taunting me into telling him to stop. Or goading me into not asking at all as his hand rested against the flat plain of my stomach. Then it drifted lightly, lower, until he was brushing my thigh. I could feel a familiar pit of excitement swirling inside me, spiralling heat from my core, something I hadn't felt in a long while. "Something very silky...," he murmured. I felt his foot rub against mine and he flicked an eyebrow again. "Oh, you took off your socks. Good girl."

Gage didn't move his hand and I didn't push it away and he most certainly took that as a signal as he leaned in to kiss me, his lips softly pressing mine. The taste of him now slightly bitter, swirled with the memory of the kiss we'd shared last night. I liked him, it was clear. I liked him a lot. Some parts of me liked him a great deal. I could feel a very definite part of him announcing he was very pleased to see me, as he manoeuvred himself on top of me. I couldn't help the groan that escaped as I slipped my arms around him and let him press himself against me, running my hands down the thick muscular cords of his back. He smelled of grass and pine, earthy, natural things and I inhaled a deep, intoxicating, lungful.

But it was just too soon.

I broke away with a firm push against his chest.

Gage looked down at me, leaning on his elbows so his chest was barely lifted above mine, not with reproach or hurt, but just calm appraisal. I hoped I didn't have a bad case of bed head. "I can wait," he said, his body telling a different story. "I have time."

"Okay," I replied slowly, because I didn't want him to think I was asking anything of him or giving him the great never, ever rebuttal. Truthfully, I was fighting arousal, fighting what my body was demanding, struggling against the voice of reason.

He smiled before sliding off me and out of bed, leaving a cold pocket of air between the sheets and me. I was trying to ease into a sitting position, pulling the covers with me but they wouldn't give until he got up. When he did, he released them all in a swoosh that nearly knocked me on my back.

With his back turned, I could see he was wearing black shorts that were very form-fitted, which made me bite my lip. After a brief moment of disappointment, (I was human, after all, well, sort of), came relief. He pulled on his jeans and I saw his hands work the buttons on his shirt. I forced myself to be glad. If he turned around or pressed the point, I might have changed my mind and I couldn't decide how I felt about that.

"I'll let myself out," he said, padding out of my room. I heard his footsteps grow further away; then the front door opened and closed gently. A minute or two later, his car engine started up and I guessed he was reversing across the street to his own drive.

I sat, staring at the wall, feeling dizzy. After looking at the clock and seeing how early it was – I just couldn't get out of the habit of waking early – I hunkered down for another hour and slept peacefully alone. It wasn't until later, when I was looking thoughtfully at the indentation Gage's head had left in the pillow next to mine, that I realised I'd had another nightmare-free night.

I ate a very late breakfast in the kitchen – cereal with a big, healthy glass of milk – and the radio turned on to a local station. The annoyingly cheerful host made my head pound. When I heard a shuffling and scraping noise outside, I got up, pulled my cardigan around me, belted it and went to explore. I already knew it was unlikely to be animals rooting through the trash.

"What are you doing?" I asked when I stepped outside the front door, my eyes blinking from the cold glare of the sun, already high in the cloudless sky. Gage was standing on my porch in jeans, stained with old paint, and a tee, a big swatch of sandpaper in one hand. There was a pile of things on the porch; big tins of paint, brushes and roller trays. He'd already laid drop cloths across the porch to catch any spills.

Gage held up the paintbrush. "Painting your house," he said, like I hadn't guessed.

"Why?" I asked, trying not to be awkward because he clearly wasn't, even though we'd spent the night together. I gulped. Not doing anything, I reminded myself.

"You kept your side of the bet."

"But you won!" I protested. "The loser is supposed to... lose."

"I know."

"You need to get a grasp of the rules, you know."

"Maybe."

"You don't have to do this."

"I know that too."

"So... why are you?"

"Because we're neighbours and that's what neighbours do." Gage turned back to the house and crouched on his heels, turning his attention back to the boards under the window where the paint was flaking the worst.

"Ah."

He swivelled on his heels and gazed up at me, a mischievous look in his eyes. "Are you going to watch me all day or are you going to make coffee?"

"Make coffee, I guess."

"How many mugs you got?"

"Um, four, but I'll make a flask, if you're that thirsty."

"It's not for me, it's for them." Gage thumbed a hand over his shoulder and I looked up just as a truck turned into my driveway. Four big men jumped out and I recognised them all from the poker night, even if I could only remember two by name. One was Annalise's Beau, the other, a small swarthy man, named Joe. I waved at them as Gage added, "They're going to get thirsty too."

"I can't believe you'd all do this for me."

"If it makes you feel better, Beau is helping out because he thinks it will help him get into Annalise's pants faster," Gage said in a low tone so Beau, who was pulling paint tins out of the truck bed, couldn't hear him.

"Will it?" I whispered back conspiratorially.

He grinned. "Absolutely. She's loved him since junior high; not that she's going to tell him that and I've never seen her happier than since he came back to Wilding."

I mimed zipping my mouth. Then I unzipped it to say. "Just let me know what I owe you."

"You can always cook for me in return."

I looked at the tins and the brushes Gage's friends were piling on the porch.

"I'd be cooking all month. You might as well move in."

"If you insist." He winked at me so I knew he was joking. At least, I thought he was; but he turned away before I could give him a retort. "Coffee when you're ready," he said to the wall.

"Coming up, but one of you will have to share a mug." I stomped inside the house, wondering when Annalise was about to show up. When I caught sight of the coverlet, I wondered who else would soon be my guest.

I made coffee for the entire painting crew and took out the mugs with bowls of sugar and creamers and a big pack of cookies, leaving them all on a tray on the porch. Inside, I was plotting an exciting afternoon of finishing my laundry – which now included stripping my bed – and brainstorming job options or whether to take a correspondence course. So far, I had drawn a blank on who might employ someone with limited qualifications, a lot of experience and without much of a paper trail.

I was careful with money but it wasn't going to last forever and eventually, I'd have to tap into my funds. That would probably draw attention to me just as if I had a red flashing beacon right over my head. But I couldn't sit around and do nothing. It just wasn't in my nature, not that I was entirely sure what my nature was any more.

I pulled out my map and the crystal, half-heartedly hanging it in the centre and set it in motion with a flick of my hand. It wheeled once, twice, then with a sharp tug it lurched down. I gazed at it for a moment then put my thumb on the spot where it landed. Tulsa. Huh? I stared at the spot marking Oklahoma's second biggest city for a long minute before I picked up the crystal again and flicked it into motion. This time it spun and spun before hanging limply by its ribbon in the centre of the map. No lurch, nothing. I tried again and again.

After a frustrating hour where the crystal didn't give me any indication that its first try had been anything but a fluke, I pulled on my running clothes and went outside. Gage and his friends had sanded a good portion of the flaking paint off and there was some discussion about treatments and paint and the weather that sailed right over my head. He broke off when he saw me and walked over, leaving the debate to continue without him.

"I'm going for a run," I announced in case he couldn't guess. My head had started to clear but I hoped the exercise would give me a boost.

"You run often?"

"Now and again."

"Stick to the road," Gage said, his firmness surprising me.

"I will. Cross country isn't my thing."

Gage just nodded at me and went back to whatever he was doing. I jogged off the porch and didn't look back to see if he were checking out my butt. I could feel his eyes on me.

I ran as far as I could, until my lungs heaved and I felt my legs going weak. I was in poor shape all right, and it was all I could do to stand there in the road, swinging my arms in circles as I paused to catch my breath. I could feel my leg muscles tighten. I hadn't stretched properly before setting off and I was risking an injury, but I needed to be out here in the open where I could stare into the far reaches of the mid-morning sky. I needed to force my body to work, to feel connected to my senses.

I could feel magic ripple through me like it was waking up. I'd dulled it for so long, and fought to hold it at bay; but now, it felt like pure joy to let it surge through me. When I held my hands up, I found them bathed in a soft glow like they had their own inner luminescence but, with a quick shake, it vanished.

Turning back, I pulled a face. I'd run too far, almost to where the tree line ended and broke into fields. Hearing a twig break somewhere off to my left, I froze and looked about me. Then, hearing nothing, I started the slow walk back. After a few minutes, I stopped and crouched by the side of the road, my fingers reaching for the small indentations I could see, puzzling at the clear imprint of a large paw in the mud.

I stayed in my crouch, looking past the shrubs. The print looked fresh, definitely made within the last day or two, but if there were a wild animal out here, it seemed to be long gone. I got up and walked on, moving into the centre of the road.

By the time my house was in sight, I started up a slow jog, not wanting to embarrass myself by appearing a heaving, panting, sweaty mess. Hey, maybe that would put Gage off. I smirked to myself.

Gage was standing on the driveway, almost like he was waiting for me, and fell into step beside me as I slowed to a walk.

"Enjoy your run?"

"I might die," I admitted.

"You run every day?"

"I try to."

"Same time?"

I shrugged. "Not really. Just when I feel like it."

"It's not safe at dark, so don't run at night."

I stopped. "Why?"

"Animals. We're isolated out here, so... What if you twisted your foot, or something?"

I thought about the strange print I'd seen. "Oh, right. I guess. Well, thanks. And thanks again for this." I waved a hand at the house. I opened my mouth to ask him about the footprint but he was already walking away.

"No problem," I heard him say.

I stumbled into my house, my heart still pounding from the run, but at least my head was clear again. I was pushing myself too much for someone so under exercised. I'd have to take it easier in future, or risk pulling a muscle.

I froze a few steps into my living room. Just as I had time to think something wasn't right in my house, I felt the familiar feel of magic drift towards me. Out of the air, Chyler materialised. I will have to do something about the wards, I thought as she took on form. It wouldn't do to just have witches popping up out of nowhere in my house.

"Hi, Stella," she said brightly.

"Chyler, hi. Is everything okay?"

"I wanted to know if you found anything out. From the Council, or from... Are there any other witches around here?" She studied me for a moment. She was wearing the same outfit as the previous day, but her hair was pulled into a low ponytail and didn't look like it had been brushed properly.

"No, there aren't any other witches around here. That I know of anyway."

"Oh. Too bad." Chyler's tone wasn't exactly sincere.

I gestured at her to follow me into the kitchen where I poured myself a big glass of water and glugged it down before offering her a drink. She shook her head, so I knocked back another glass and then leant against the counter, tugging at the zip of my sweat jacket.

"So no one's come looking for me?" Chyler swept a finger across my counters and then checked it, like she was inspecting it to see if cleanliness was a top priority in my house. I hoped she was satisfied at my super clean kitchen, elbow grease powered by boredom.

"No one, yet," I said, adding a little caveat.

"Oh. Good."

"I guess. Why don't you sit down and tell me more about what's happening?"

Chyler wobbled over to a chair like a baby gazelle taking its first steps and I frowned at her.

"Are you okay?"

"Fine, thank you. So, I don't really remember much. I was just practising some spells and bam! Something flies out of nowhere and hits me. I think something backfired."

"And that's why the Council came?" I couldn't see the Witches' Council bothering about something like a spell backfiring. Unless it was something really hideous.

"Yes!" Chyler exclaimed. "They just turned up and they were really mad and they wanted to take me somewhere, and I was scared so I just grabbed the book."

"Did they say where they wanted to take you?" I asked, trying to recall the details of the vision I had when I touched her. Something smelled off.

Chyler shook her head. "They were really scary, Stella, and I was frightened, so I didn't stay and ask." She shivered and clasped her hands in her lap, her head bowed.

"What spells were you practising?"

"Um... I don't remember."

I didn't miss the flicker of Chyler's eyelids. She was lying, I was sure.

"They're really bad, you know. They want power, any power, and they'll do anything to get it," she said, her eyes flicking up to look at me from beneath her lashes.

That didn't exactly strike me as untrue. Chyler had intimated before that there wasn't any successor to Robert Bartholomew and I wondered what it meant to have the Council fractured without leadership.

"And you think they want yours?"

"Sure, and I bet they'll make up a bunch of stuff about me to make sure no one wants to help me.

You're my only hope, Stella. I need to know I can rely on you." Chyler darted another look at me from under her lashes. A tear slipped from her eye and her jaw wobbled. She looked vulnerable as hell but something in me still didn't want to trust her.

"No one is going to hurt you," I said, but I didn't add: *I promise*. Promises could be broken.

"And you'll zap them if anyone..." But Chyler didn't get to finish her sentence because just then, my front door banged open. I hadn't locked it like I normally did.

"Stella?" Gage called to me. I put my finger to my lips and mimed *shh* to Chyler. I scraped my chair back to get up and flapped my hand behind me as I walked out of the room, hoping she got the hint to stay back. I pulled the kitchen door so it was closed except for a sliver as I went through to the living room.

Gage stood in the centre of the room, his chin raised up and he seemed to be sniffing the air. He started when I approached him. "You okay?" he asked.

"Sure. Why wouldn't I be?"

"Thought I heard something," he murmured, his nostrils flaring slightly as he looked about him.

I shrugged. "Just me. How's it going out there?"

"Okay. The guys are fast workers. Your house will be looking new in no time."

I grinned. "You know, this is probably the best loser deal ever?"

"If you keep making out how great a deal you're getting, I'll have to make up something to ensure I really won." Gage laughed and his eyes creased with laughter lines. There was something captivating about him and I felt my breath catch in my throat, as well as my heart race a few beats faster than normal. He stopped looking around like he was searching for something and instead, his eyes narrowed as he focused on me, keeping eye contact.

I breathed shallow breaths and finally, when my heart was under control, I said. "Let me know if you need anything else."

Gage nodded and backed out of the door. "Shout if you need anything."

I pushed the door closed after him and went back into the kitchen. Chyler had moved into my vacated seat where she wouldn't be seen from the other room. "Who's the hottie?" she asked.

I raised my eyebrows. "That is my neighbour, Gage."

"My neighbours are dorks," she sighed. "I wish I had neighbours like him."

"And that's probably the last time you'll see him," I said, feeling strangely proprietary as I explained. "Seeing as you should stay out of sight. If anyone comes asking, people only know that I live here alone and that there aren't any supernatural teens in residence."

"So you won't tell the Council that I'm here?"

I shook my head. It wasn't like I had a direct line to call up and report a missing teen, not that I would anyway, given my past dealings with the Council. They were largely the source of all my troubles.

Their last leader, Eleanor Bartholomew, was the wife of the head of the Witches' Council when she tried her best to kill me. Although she failed in her attempt with me, she succeeded in killing her own husband, Robert. She had also driven my friends' – Étoile and Seren's – sister, Astra, mad with her power-hungry struggles.

Our elderly housekeeper, Meg, took a hit and as she died, fading into ashes, I learned she was a vampire and over a century old. I still puzzled at the irony that the first vampire I ever met had turned out to be a sweet old lady rather than a glamorous, brooding hunk. C'est la vie, I thought, then grimaced when I realised, actually, it was more, c'est la morte.

Meg hadn't been the only casualty, of course. Jared, Christy and Clara, the other young witches who lived with us, had all died, having been caught unawares in the conflict. They never stood a chance. My close friend, Kitty, was also terribly hurt, part of Eleanor's warning to me.

Evan was hit by a powerful pulse of magic aimed at me when he pushed me out of the way and absorbed the whole hit himself. I tried to help him as soon as I could, after Eleanor wasn't a threat anymore. He was still breathing, but his blood was doing strange things and he wasn't able to heal himself thanks to Eleanor's devilish meddling.

I didn't find out until later, when the "cleaners" were sent by what remained of the Council, what Evan was. After they surveyed the scene, they disclosed to me that Evan was a daemon. The man I thought I loved,was concealing a massive secret from me, despite everything. A secret just as shocking as it was revealing.

I tried my best to save him and he was still alive when our friends, Étoile and Seren, came to retrieve him. But they said they weren't powerful enough to teleport all of us and they didn't come back for me. It had taken me some time to realise that I was still in shock when I left the safe house.

It had been months now, and I hadn't heard a word from any of them. Even a random teenage witch had managed to find me, I thought with a sudden shudder, so why couldn't they? I didn't want to accept the possibility that Evan was dead because a part of my heart would die with him.

I killed Eleanor, but it was in self defence. I never thought I'd be able to take another life, but when it came down to seeing her killing and maiming my friends, while aiming for me, it was quite simple. I killed Eleanor Bartholomew and, while I couldn't shake the awful feeling that I had taken life from another being, I never regretted it. She had done so much damage in her life and killed so often in her pursuit for power... And lust, I reminded myself. It was her lust for my father that started all of this when he spurned her because he loved my mother.

Eleanor's deception went back many years. When I was a little girl, Eleanor killed my mother right in front of me. My father hid me with his magic before she could kill me too. He rejected her and she murdered him next in her fury. She spent years trying to find me. As the child of two witches, she knew my powers would mature one day and she was terrified that I would recognise her. She was afraid I would destroy everything she had managed to obtain – her power, her privilege, her status.

I didn't remember her, of course, but she made it her mission to track me down and tried to get rid of me nonetheless. She became just as dangerous as the witch hunters that plagued me before I was rescued. Her husband had gotten in the way of her pursuit of power and she was so afraid of losing her foothold in the hierarchy, that she even spellbound her son, Marc.

She hamstringed his potential, lest he overtake her. Marc got his powers back as soon as she died, however, and, even though we had somewhat of a falling out, I often wondered how he was getting on. He was a late-comer to magic, like me. I tried not to blame him at all, even though it was hard at first, because he was being manipulated by his mother too.

It was imperative after Eleanor died. And when everyone was finally safe, and the injured were treated, I was ignored and abandoned. Being unhurt, I was left behind in the care of another witch, David. I waited and I waited. I thought they would come for me but they didn't. While I waited, I eventually became unsure that I wanted them to come back, especially if Evan were dead. The Council had dragged me into this life, putting me in the middle of their struggles, and no good had come from it. I'd had it. The shock ensured my reasoning was skewed.

That was what pre-empted my decision to come to Wilding, to my parents' house. So here I was, facing another witch who sought my help to protect her from the Council.

"I won't tell the Council, but look, Chyler, you found me so there's no reason why they can't. They'll work out where you are and they'll come looking. You can't stay here."

"I know, but..."

"No buts. It's safer if you keep hiding wherever you are." I tried to stay firm without being unkind. "How can I get in touch with you?"

Chyler shook her head and her shoulders heaved up and down like she was utterly despondent. I would be too, if I were her. "I'll get in touch with you," she said and, before I had chance to protest, she muttered a few silent words and vanished again, leaving me with a massive problem that I had no idea how to deal with.

I changed back into my clothes, giving myself a fresh spritz of deodorant and body spray, and folded my running gear into a pile on top of the dresser, trying to fathom the whole time what I was supposed to do. I badly needed some help.

Maybe things would look a lot better if I were outside in the crisp fresh air, watching my house get a fresh coat of paint. That idea felt really good. I walked out the open door through to the living room, not quite prepared for my heart to leap into my throat when I realised, once again, I wasn't alone.

I was still for a moment as I watched Gage, who stood with his back to me, tilt his head upwards. At first, I thought he was inspecting the ceiling but then he seemed to sniff the air just like he had done earlier.

Slowly, he turned to me, his eyes flickering as though they registered something unseen. His mouth slipped into the easy smile that made my heart flutter, then shudder as he inhaled the air in one deep lungful. It was almost like he were tasting it, tasting something on it.

He looked at me as if he wondered what my secrets were, but I would never tell.

CHAPTER FIVE

The probable answer to the riddle of my coverlet was waiting for me on the porch the next morning. She was just standing there, leaning against the posts that held up the overhanging roof, almost as if she belonged there. Étoile Winterstorm seemed like she had all the time in the world. She looked amazing, as usual, in a short black dress, a blue wool coat open at the top with a white scarf, tossed casually around her neck.

I, however, had gotten a poor night's sleep, as I woke up every other hour wondering how I could help Chyler and whether she was okay. My morning grouchiness was quashed as soon as I saw Étoile, but replaced with wary delight when I opened the door.

"Hello, Stella," she said softly, barely turning her head as I stepped out.

"Hey." I smiled tentatively, hanging back a bit until Étoile crossed the small space between us and hugged me warmly. She held the tops of my arms in her hands as she looked at me, a flash of anger briefly crossing her face. "Do you know how long it took me to find you?" she asked.

"I'm guessing six months," I replied, somewhat facetiously. "Was it you who left me the package?"

Étoile nodded. "I thought a peace offering might pave the way before I came to see you."

"Well, at least I knew someone was here, though you could have signed the card."

"Didn't I? Oh." Étoile shrugged and looked out at the garden, then across the street. I followed the direction of her eyes and saw Gage tackling the job of weather-proofing the furniture on his porch. "Lovely view," she said to me, then, without missing a beat. "Shall we go inside?"

"Please come in." I stepped back and held open the door.

"So you've been here this whole time?" she inquired, looking around, taking in the plain decor and dated furniture. "Why here?"

"It was my parents' house," I answered, keeping it short so I didn't scream at her or shake her, not that it would have done any good. Once my grief faded, I found myself becoming increasingly calm but even that was threatening to dissolve fast. I was furious at her... but equally delighted to see her.

"When I came back for you, you were already gone. David was in a terrible panic." Étoile cut a glance at me like she was checking to see if I were paying attention. Her tone was just short of scathing.

"I waited three days." My voice came out with a slight upturned edge that was in danger of turning into a whine. We were standing in the centre of the living room, facing each other. I crossed my arms across my chest defensively. "Where were you?"

"Eleanor's magic weakened us terribly. Seren and I couldn't shimmer again after we travelled so far while holding on to Evan and we had to recuperate before I could come back. When I did, you weren't there." Étoile enunciated the last words carefully and looked at me pointedly.

I brushed it off. "What happened?" I asked at last, weakly. I wanted to hear and I didn't. I wanted to know the truth and I wanted to hide from it. I stared at my toes and steeled myself to finally hear the truth. To finally lay Evan to rest, if that were what it took.

"It was touch and go for a few days," said Étoile. She took a deep breath like she had a lot to say and didn't want to pause while it poured out. "You saved him, you know. Whatever it was you did back there, it healed the major damage, but Evan was still very, very ill. Witches and daemons don't mix well. Too much negativity in the energy expended, I think."

I looked up at her sharply. "Evan's alive?" I whispered, not quite sure I'd heard her correctly.

Étoile smiled at me, a broad, happy smile that lifted her whole face. "Of course, he is!" she exclaimed, like I just asked the dumbest question ever.

"What happened? I thought... I thought..." I stammered as my mind raced ahead of me, picking through all the scenarios I'd considered and dismissing them just as fast, puzzling what I should do next. Where was he? Could I get to him? I wanted to go to him now.

"He's not dead," said Étoile, simply but not unkindly. "He was completely out of it for a month. Eleanor's magic, and my sister's, affected him very badly and it took another month after that for him to heal. Do you know how bad that is for a daemon? Taking that long to heal?" Étoile paced away from me, looking back over her shoulder to see if I were taking it in. She paused to look out the window, surveying the view, before glancing back at me. "He was lucky you seemed to develop healing powers just at the right moment," she added.

I did understand how badly injured Evan must have been to take that long to heal. Sort of. I'd seen him heal a cut right in front of my eyes when he'd been hurt once. But that was a minor thing compared to what he endured on the last day I'd seen him. When he pushed me out of harm's way he took the brunt of the supernatural blast himself.

"Where is he?" Does he want to see me? I wanted to ask. Does he blame me? Instead, I asked next, "Where has he been?"

"He's been looking for you for four solid months. We thought something happened to you. He was ready to kill Astra to find out for certain." Étoile shuddered. For all the bad her sister had created, Astra suffered a terrible injustice too. Eleanor Bartholomew had used her for her enormous power, draining her magic and treating her like a broken puppet.

Étoile rescued her sister and took her somewhere safe as soon as Eleanor was incapacitated, or, more bluntly, when I killed her. I had to; I didn't have a choice, I reminded myself for the umpteenth time. She was insanely violent and out of control.

"But here you are in Nowheresville. Quite fine too, by the looks of you," continued Étoile. She was wandering around my living room, finally resting her eyes on the two photographs I'd propped up there.

"I really thought he must have died," I said after a long moment. I let the flood of tears course from my tear ducts and over my cheeks until I put my hands over my face and soaked them too. I stood there shuddering and shaking until Étoile guided me to the sofa and made me sit, wrapping her arms around me, until I could get a hold on myself. The relief was immense. I felt euphoric. Evan was alive!

Then, I felt horrible. I kissed Gage! Crap. I didn't know what to feel. I wiped my wet cheeks with the backs of my hands and sniffed in an ungainly way before asking again, "Where is Evan?"

"Three hours away."

"Seriously?" I looked at Étoile with my eyes wide. Three *hours* between Evan and me? After months of nothing but fading hope, there were just three hours separating us. It was both too long and no time at all.

"Yes, we were driving here and I thought I'd *zap*, as you like to say, ahead." Étoile made it sound like she simply switched train lines rather than moved herself through space a few hundred miles.

"Didn't you stay after your last visit?" Now that I was close to her, I could read the signature I'd felt a couple of days earlier as, quite obviously, hers. She had done nothing to disguise it, I realised. She meant for me to know.

"I stayed long enough to drop off my gift. Then I went back to tell everyone that you were fine."

"How did you know I was fine?"

"I saw you heading out with that hunk of yum across the road. Nice outfit, by the way. Was it a date?" Étoile asked casually but I could see her watching me from the corners of her eyes, waiting to see what I would say.

"Sort of. He won a bet." I knew someone had been watching me. I'd felt it.

A flicker of a smile sprung up at the edges of her lips. "Classy. Is that why he's painting your house?" So, she noticed that too.

"That was my winning prize. He's just doing it anyway to be neighbourly."

"I'm sure he is." Étoile choked back a laugh.

"Is that why you came ahead?" I asked, when it dawned on me. "You wanted to make sure Evan wasn't about to interrupt something?"

Étoile didn't bother to look embarrassed; that really wasn't her bag. "Pretty much. It would be a *terrible* reconciliation if you were."

"Well, now you know. Are you going to zap back?" I swallowed the anxiety of guilt I suddenly felt. Nothing happened, I reminded myself. Except a kiss, or two... if you didn't count how long they lasted... or where they had taken place.

"To Evan? No, he's driving and that would be unsafe. I might not even shimmer into his car. I'll just wait until he gets here."

"Is anyone else coming?" Meaning, how was everyone else, of course. Had they all survived? Fortunately Étoile got that.

"Kitty is fine, although her leg is still in a cast. But she'll make a full recovery, you'll be pleased to know. Shall I tell her where you are? Marc is with her. David and Seren are on their way here too."

It would be quite a houseful when they got here. I knew I hadn't enough cups for six, let alone anything else. Where did they expect to stay? I could hardly say no. I just couldn't imagine the imminent reunion.

"I've booked rooms at an inn in Wilding," said

Étoile and it wasn't the first time I wondered if she had a direct dial line straight into my thoughts. "I'm sure you and Evan have some catching up to do. Plus, I just love playing third wheel to Seren and David." She put her finger to her mouth and pretended to gag. Like Evan and I, Seren and David's relationship began at the safe house. It was heartening to know they were still together.

"Is Evan mad at me?" My voice came out like a whisper.

"Oh, Stella, no. Of course not." Étoile took both my hands in hers and looked solidly at me. "He's just been worried sick. He's a tracker, probably the best there is and he couldn't track *you*. He's been desperate to find you, and fairly intolerable about it too."

I couldn't even begin to fathom what Evan must have thought. A ball of anxiety was growing inside me. At least, I thought it was anxiety. There might have been a pinch of fear, and excitement too. I was going to see Evan! Now that I knew it was going to happen, that he was real and alive, that he was on his way to me, the time felt like it slowed to a snail's pace. It couldn't go fast enough for me. I stood up, then sat down, and stood up again like a hyperactive kid who knew Christmas was only a few hours away. I wanted my present, damn it, and I wanted it now.

"So, show me around," said Étoile, "and tell me what you've been doing the past few months and then I'll tell you what's been happening while we wait. Or you could stand up and sit down like you're the only one playing musical chairs and I'll try and look entertained."

I grinned at her usual sarcastic self. "Missed you," I said.

"Missed you, too."

I showed Étoile around my house, which didn't take long and she said nice things about the sizes of the rooms and what I had done with the place, which wasn't much. She was more interested in hearing about the wards that were woven around my home.

"Frankly, it wasn't easy to track you down. The wards are strong and they definitely masked the presence of magic, certainly for those who aren't so inclined."

"So how did you find me?"

I swore I saw a faint trace of red creep onto her cheeks. If I didn't know better, I'd have said Étoile was blushing. "Land records," she said eventually. "Turns out tax records were much more helpful than magic. I came here to check. I was fairly certain once I'd caught your trace, and seeing you clinched it, naturally."

"Thanks again for the coverlet." It was still lying over the back of the sofa and I thought I'd keep it there; it was cosy. "I appreciate it."

"I'm sure Meg would have wanted you to have it."

"You know I never guessed Meg was a vampire." I was surprised how easily that came out. Meg owned the safe house where I was hidden and she was an elderly, fussy housemother type who favoured night time walks. She was always cold to the touch. But I had no idea she was a vampire until I saw her body flake into ashes.

A year ago, I would have giggled at the idea of saying, never mind thinking, such a stupid thing. But then, a year ago, I thought I was a clumsy freak and had no clue that I was suffused with a deep and ancient magic that I could bend to my will. It made me wonder what else I didn't know about.

"She wasn't exactly your archetypal vamp. Definitely not of the black leather and chains variety. Don't be fooled into thinking they're all like Meg though. Vampires are dark beings, mostly, though there's always the exception. Generally, they are not the ilk you or I would want to consort with. Meg was an exception, though a dangerous one. We still took measures, even with her."

I let that sink in and wondered how much danger we had been in every night at the safe house. I wondered what became of the house itself now, whether it stood empty or passed to the descendents that she'd been turned for. Meg had herself turned specifically to provide a home for her grandchildren after she discovered she was sick and dying and had no other options. Her own daughter had died before her, so her grandchildren had no guardian or family left but Meg.

Étoile flicked her wrist so she could glance at her watch. "What shall we do while we wait? Do you want to fill me in on what you've been doing? Or do you want to do your hair before Evan gets here?"

I looked at her sharply. "What's wrong with my hair?"

"Oh, nothing." Étoile quickly shook her head. Her hair was a little longer than the last time I saw her. It was still closely cropped on the sides but now with a longer top that swept forward across her forehead. It softened her angular face slightly.

"We don't all have New York salons to go to, you know."

"I've been in Oklahoma for the past few months."

"Oklahoma?" I remembered that was where Tulsa

was located. Apparently, scrying hadn't been such a waste of time after all!

"You were hoping for somewhere more exotic? LA, perhaps?"

"I don't know what I thought."

"Oklahoma is perfectly lovely, so long as you aren't stuck in a hospital."

"But you weren't hurt..."

"No, I wasn't, but I was still weak and needed to recover and others were hurt. It took Seren and I two weeks before we could shimmer again, and even then, we had to draw strength from each other. David had to drive us back from Meg's house and we stayed to help. He looked all over for you. He said you used your magic."

I thought back. "Yes, I shimmered out of the house and I covered my traces."

Étoile cocked her head and considered me. "We caught a trace of your magic and then nothing. So you see, we did think, for a while, that something must have happened to you. You have no idea what it was like telling Evan. He's formidable when angry."

"I'm so sorry."

"Don't be. It's all right. Now, tell me what you've been doing."

I told her from the beginning. When I found myself alone in Meg's house, I'd remembered the key to my parents' house amidst my panic and decided to go. From then on, I'd done very little except make myself at home.

A light pinged in my head. Now that they knew where I was, I could use my bank account. I could be a little more adventurous in looking for a job or starting college since I didn't have to be so cautious anymore about giving away my location. Things were looking up indeed.

"What about you?" I asked when I finished.

"Not much. Seren and I were ensuring our sister was safe and in a place where she couldn't harm anyone else. Her doctors have high hopes that she might recover. Eleanor meddled with her mind, you know. Hateful woman. And, of course, we stayed with Kitty – though Marc has been staying with her most of the time – and with Evan, too."

"How come I could use my magic, if you couldn't use yours?" I asked, after I thought about it for a moment. Étoile and Seren's power had been weakened by Eleanor but mine hadn't abated then or now. I just stopped using it so much.

"I was wondering the same thing, though it didn't occur to me at the time. Seeing as we thought you'd been captured."

"I said sorry!" I got up and walked over to the window as if looking out would make Evan arrive faster. I turned. "Who did you think had captured me?"

Étoile took a deep breath before explaining. "The Council is broken, splintered into different factions. Some want to be left alone. Some want power and they'll do anything to get it, including snatching witches."

This reminded me: Chyler. She said something quite similar.

"What would they want with witches?"

"To reinforce their own power; wipe out other clans; who knows what nefarious reasons they have? Some think with Eleanor out of the way, it's time for a new order."

"And that's a bad thing?" It didn't sound bad to me.

"Eleanor was not nearly the worst of them, unfortunately. Speaking of the worst, let's snap to the best. I have something for you: Kitty's phone number." Étoile rummaged in her bag and produced her pride and joy, her BlackBerry. After pressing a few buttons, she offered it to me.

"I can call her?" I asked.

Étoile rolled her eyes. "Just press dial. Do you mind if I take a nap? I'm exhausted." Étoile was already kicking off her heels so I suggested she take the sofa, seeing as the guest room wasn't made up. Actually, there just wasn't anything even vaguely guest-like in the guest room, but I'd worry about that later.

"I'll wake you when they get here," I offered, taking the phone.

"Do, though I'll know when Seren is close by." With that, Étoile pulled the coverlet over her, sank back on the pillows and closed her eyes. She seemed to go straight to sleep.

I wasted no time in hitting the dial button and, after what seemed like an eternity, a female voice picked up just as I stepped into my bedroom. "Hello?"

"Hello? Is that Kitty?" I sank down on my bed.

The voice on the other end of the line squealed. "It is, and I know that voice. Stella, I'm so glad you called. Étoile must be there, if you're calling, and Evan, too?"

"Étoile is here. She shimmered ahead but Evan is still driving. I'm waiting."

"And the time can't go fast enough, huh?"

"It seems like it's going slower," I laughed, giddy at talking to Kitty, as well as Étoile being here, while feeling beside myself that Evan was alive.

"Well, that I can relate to, honey. I've been in hospital ever since that day and boy, am I sick of it."

"I'm so sorry, Kitty. I'm so sorry you had to go through all of that. I wish there was something I could do."

"I heard about everything you did, and you've done enough. Besides, you don't have to apologise to me. You did not do this, Stella, you hear me?"

"I hear you." But it was still hard for me to accept that my actions were purely in self defence. I heard Kitty shuffle and tried not to imagine her in casts, in a hospital bed, with injuries bad enough that she had been hospitalised for more than six months.

"Is anyone with you?" I asked. "Who's taking care of you?" I didn't have much to go on, and while I understood that she, and the others, had not been at a regular human hospital, I wasn't sure what an... *irregular* one was like.

"A great team of doctors and nurses. There are supernatural medical professionals who do a rotation through here." Kitty paused, then said, "Brace yourself, honey. Marc stayed here the whole time."

That wasn't huge news to me, Étoile had already said as much; plus, I had an inkling that Marc's feelings for Kitty went far beyond friendship. "You're back together?" I asked.

"Hold up, girl. I haven't finished telling my story yet." Kitty laughed. "He's been great, really great, but just when I was seriously thinking about it, I opened my door and found him playing tongue twister with the nurse and that, my friend, put paid to that."

"I'm sorry."

"Don't be. I'm just glad I realised Marc was still the same Marc. It's almost reassuring, you know, that some things never change," she added.

"I guess. Is he still there?" I had a lot of time to think about Marc but I didn't know whether he blamed me for everything that happened. I hoped not.

Kitty seemed nonchalant when she said, "Yes, for now." Changing the subject quickly, she said, "Evan, however, has pissed off just about everyone in the building. He was furious when he woke up and no one knew where you were."

"I've been explaining that to Étoile. I panicked when everyone left and no one came back. I just hightailed it out of there and came to Wilding."

"What's in Wilding?"

"My parents' house; they left it to me."

"You'd have thought one of them would have figured that out a bit faster," sniffed Kitty. "I sometimes think they should try and use their brains, instead of their magic."

"I guess. Étoile said she found it through land records."

"You can never escape taxes, honey."

"Apparently not. Kitty, I have been looking for you guys. I tried everything, but nothing worked. I didn't give up, I swear."

"Honey, no one said you did and of course, it didn't work. The magically injured come to this hospital for a reason. No amount of spells or magic would let you find us here. It's very well protected." Kitty paused. "I thought Evan's heart was breaking, he was so sad without you."

My heart lurched. I didn't want to dwell on that, not now when he was so close. Instead, I said, "I can't believe he's nearly here."

"Better believe it, baby. Now, I have to go for therapy and you have to keep calling me back to fill me in on what's going on. Where can I call you?"

"On Étoile's phone, I don't have one."

"You need to join the technological age, honey. Call me soon. I've missed you."

"Missed you too, Kitty."

~

Seren and David were the first to arrive. With every sense attuned to waiting for Evan, I had no problem hearing their car long before it turned onto the driveway. I went out to greet them.

Seren was a lot like her older sister. Her high cheekbones gave her face an aristocratic air and the same piercing eyes, but Seren was somewhat softer to look at and her hair swung in layers past her shoulders. She was dressed in a soft powder blue sweater and jeans that hugged her legs. Behind her, David Barton, my former spell teacher, and her lover, followed. He was a tall, slim man with an unexplained scar that curved across a very pleasant face. He had a fine crop of curly brown hair, cut very short. Today, he wore glasses with thin rims. I hugged them both and Seren kissed me on each cheek.

"Étoile's inside. Sleeping," I said, putting my forefinger to my lips as a warning.

"I'm awake," came her voice from behind me and I heard the sofa creak as she got up.

"Evan is right behind us," murmured Seren as she swished past me.

"Shall we make coffee, sister dearest?" came

Étoile's voice again. I left the three of them inside so I could wait anxiously on the porch rather than pace the living room in circles, too wired to sit still any longer.

I stamped my feet and wrapped my arms about myself to keep out the cold air and the ball of anxiety in the pit of my stomach blossomed into desperation. Six months felt like an eternity, and these few minutes felt like a lifetime. It seemed as though time was tormenting me by dragging lethargically by.

When I thought I couldn't bear it anymore, a big black car cruised into view and rolled onto the driveway to park behind Seren and David's car. I waited forever for the engine to cut out and the driver's door to ease open.

When Evan got out and stood, turning to face me, sinewy arms leaning on the door frame, blinking against the light of the cold sun, I gasped. I never thought I would see him again and I inhaled the sight of him like a flavourful aroma, from his short crop of hair to the fine cut of his jaw. Finally, he saw me. Our eyes met and I let out a yelp of delight.

I raced off the porch, my feet barely touching the steps as I sprinted towards him. In the same moment, he slammed the door shut and took a few steps towards me, catching me in his arms and holding me tight against him, before spinning me around. I breathed in the citrus scent of his aftershave as he kissed me. After a moment, he set me down and just looked at me like he couldn't quite believe we were both together again. Then he kissed me. His full lips crushed mine and I thought I could never feel such pure joy again.

CHAPTER SIX

We sat in the living room for the big witch powwow.
Seren, David and Étoile were on one sofa, with Seren
in the middle. The sisters were incredibly close and
almost identical although they were born a year apart.
Étoile's hair, however, was as short as Seren's was
long and Seren had always struck me as a casual,
bohemian dresser while Étoile favoured upscale chic.
They shared the same elegant bone structure and
almond, slightly feline, eyes. They were a study in
contrast to their sister, Astra, who looked extremely
unwell the one and only time I had the misfortune to
meet her.

Evan and I sat opposite them, our hands so firmly
entwined, it was like they were fused together. I
couldn't fathom letting go. I was still struggling to
accept that he was right next to me. Every so often,
he gave my hand a little squeeze like he couldn't
believe it either.

"I can't believe you're all here," I said at last.

"It took us long enough to find you," smiled

Seren, without a hint of admonishment.

David took her hand in his and smiled with a mixture of admiration and tenderness. Finally, he turned to me. "I'm very proud of the way you used your magic. We could all feel it when we got here."

"Is that true?" I asked Evan and he nodded. "We could feel the wards, not so much the traces of your personal magic. Have you been practicing?"

I shook my head, guilt seeping through my pores. Evan had been my teacher and it was partly owing to him that I'd gotten my magic under control. "I've been keeping a low profile. I didn't exactly want to advertise myself."

It wasn't just about hiding from the Council, and what I thought they might do; it was the Brotherhood as well. There had been several reports a few months back about witch murders, but nothing recently. I wasn't stupid enough to think they had just given up and gone home; but without any other witches to talk to, the "witchy grapevine," I was relegated to a decent level of paranoia.

The Brotherhood located me in London a year before now and I barely escaped then, thanks to Étoile. There was nothing to prevent them finding me here if I chose to use magic too frequently. It surprised me to realise that I actually missed using my magic and hoped it had not atrophied like wasted muscle without proper use.

"You should practice. We can work together, now I'm here," Evan said.

"I'd like that." My body warmed with delicious memories of the day I first used telekinesis under Evan's tutelage. Ring the bell for round two: I was going back in.

"How come all of you came at once?" I said, before backtracking in case I sounded rude. "I mean, I'm really, really happy to see you and I'm so glad Evan is okay. And I'm glad to see Seren and David too, but it seems like you've all come a long way just for me." Evan I understood, and Étoile too, but all four of them at once? It seemed like a lot.

Étoile opened her mouth to speak but before she could, Seren shook her head. We played glare at the guests in my house for a moment before I had to ask. "What is it?"

"Stella, Eleanor's death caused a lot of problems," David began and I saw Seren give him a swift little kick with the heel of her foot. He frowned at her and she flashed wide eyes at him.

"Am I in trouble?" I asked, becoming increasingly discouraged when no one answered. My heart sank. Perhaps they had come to run me in, though I couldn't fathom where "in" might be. As far as the world at large knew, Eleanor and Robert Bartholomew died in a car accident, driving back to Manhattan. Although I was responsible, like I said, it was only because she was killing everyone else.

I couldn't see any justice in holding me to account. Perhaps I was a very bad person for thinking that. I still hadn't come quite to terms with what I had done. I wasn't sure I ever would. The nightmares I'd suffered for months partly stemmed from reliving it all.

Seren shook her head. "Let me explain. The Council was already becoming fractured when Eleanor went... mental. Without Robert to lead the Council, they splintered entirely. Instead of a national leadership, we've now got splinter groups operating all over the country. Some want to be left alone, some want more power; and those who want more power seek others' power, to have what isn't theirs."

"Étoile said that too," I interrupted, "but I don't understand."

"We're having major problems," David said. He took Seren's hand and held it in his lap. When I first met him, I noticed he'd been badly injured, leaving an angry fresh scar across his face. It had faded now to just a thick white line rather than the puckered welt he once wore. It made him look older and harsher than he was. He never told me how it happened. My mind suddenly flittered to Evan. David wasn't the only one with unexplained scars.

"Okay." I hoped this wasn't one of those times when they were going to tell me stuff without actually telling me stuff. I wondered if they were refugees. Very well dressed refugees, at any rate. Maybe they needed to stay with me, out of the way. I wasn't sure how I felt about that. I certainly wasn't unhappy even though I'd just about gotten used to solitary living. Still, I'd had a lot of practice at that.

"What's left of the high Council think you might have something of theirs," said Seren in such a soft, gentle way that I wasn't sure if she were asking or accusing. "They've asked us to do some checking, seeing as we know you and were looking for you anyway."

"Like what?" I asked, spreading my hands out. "The only things I have here are the things I brought with me. I haven't taken anything." Did they think I stole something? From whom? I fought indignation.

"They think you have *someone*," Seren rephrased. "A young girl that they're looking for. They think she might have come to you."

Uh-oh. Chyler. I kept my face passive. "Why would they think that?"

"Apparently she left a trace and they seemed to think that she was headed for you." Seren was being very careful what she said. The room went still and the air heavy as my mind raced. I tried to blank my thoughts.

"Why would this girl come to me?"

"They don't know. She might want to hurt you," said Seren.

"Good to see that queue has started up again."

"Is that British humour?" asked David, puzzled.

I smiled at him, partly to give my face a break from being wide-eyed and innocent. We'd soon see if I had a poker face. I wasn't going to mention Chyler until I had to. If at all.

Seren reached into her purse and pulled out a picture. She passed it over to me and I studied it. There was a man and a woman, a girl and a younger boy all standing in front of a big house. They were smiling and happy. I'd recognise the acid pink shoes anywhere. "Do you recognise the girl?" she asked.

I shook my head. "She doesn't look like anyone around here," I said, which wasn't exactly lying. Chyler didn't look like anyone around here. "She looks quite young."

"She's seventeen. Her name is Chyler Anderson and she's from a long line of witches. Her mom is, was, one too. It runs in the female line in her family."

"Apart from that, she might be looking for me? What's up with her?"

"Her mom is dead – she was killed – and their family spell book is missing. The Council, well, like I said, what's left of it, think Chyler killed her and they want her to pay for it. They also want the book returned."

"Why would she kill her own mother?" I asked, seeing as it was an obvious question while I worked to keep the shock from my face. *Why didn't Chyler mention that?* "Why would she be looking for me?"

"We don't know," said Étoile, finally, when I started to wonder if anyone would answer. "They seemed to have a great relationship by all accounts. We think she's looking for you because you're..."

"Because I'm what?" I asked in the long pause.

"Because you're on the outside," Étoile said.

I've been on the outside my whole life but having it spelled out to me was a heart sink of a moment. Evan's thumb was stroking my palm, reminding me I wasn't alone, not anymore.

"Don't look so sad, Stella," Étoile added.

"I'm not sad."

"I didn't mean it like you think. I meant, you're not affiliated to any particular group. And you're strong. You'd be a natural source of magic to seek out and..." Étoile trailed off after another sharp look from Seren.

"And what?" I pressed.

Étoile shook her head. "It's nothing."

"Why can't you find this girl?" I asked. Étoile, Seren and David were all powerful. I shifted on the sofa to look at Evan. "And why can't you?" Evan was a daemon, not that I really understood what that meant, but I did know that he was considered an important tracker, like a supernatural bounty hunter. The elation I first felt at seeing him was being edged out by an unsettling feeling that our reunion was part of something far greater.

"It's not my job to find her," Evan said, but he looked uncomfortable. "I haven't been asked and witch business is not my business. I'm here because of you, not because of Chyler."

"So you haven't tried?"

"I didn't say that." Seren and David both looked sharply at Evan's tacit admission. Only Étoile didn't seem surprised. "What I said was ..."

I interrupted him. "So you could find her?"

Evan shrugged. "Maybe." When I looked at him, I got the feeling that there was something more he wanted to say, but he wasn't going to say it then and there.

"Listen guys." I said as I spread my hands out in the universal gesture of I'm-innocent-and-I-don't-know-a-thing. "If she comes by, I'll let you know."

Seren reached into her purse and extracted a small card and a pen. She flipped the card over and began writing on the back. "My cell number is on the front, and I'm writing Étoile's, and David's too. We're staying in town, but if you see Chyler Anderson, or if she tries to contact you, call one of us right away."

I nodded and took the card, tucking it into my jeans pocket.

Seren stood up and smoothed invisible creases from her jeans. David rose quickly to stand next to her, like he couldn't bear to have their bodies separated by more than a few millimetres.

"Stella, she's dangerous," David's voice implored me. "And if she's looking for you, we don't want you to get hurt. Stay on your guard."

"I appreciate the heads up," I replied.

"She won't be in any danger with me," said Evan,

which made my heart jump. He'd gotten to his feet too and was following Seren and David to the door, leaving Étoile to smile at me as if she felt vaguely awkward with the whole speech.

Étoile hung back a moment before saying goodbye. She leaned in to hug me, every bit as tactile as her sister, and, as she did so, whispered in my ear, "Trust no one." Then she stepped away and followed her sister outside with a casual wave of her hand. Pausing on the threshold, her hand on the doorknob, she said, "Don't forget to lock your door. Strange little town, this."

Then Evan and I were left alone; just him, me and my pounding heart.

CHAPTER SEVEN

"I started to think you were probably dead," I said and my voice came out like a whimper, shallow and full of the ache I'd carried with me for months.

"Stella." In the next instant, Evan's manly arms were around me, holding me as I burst into tears, tightening as I heaved against him. I finally let all the fear and pain empty over my cheeks as I headlined another burst of today's tear fest. He felt solid and real, and with me, and I didn't have to be afraid anymore. When I finally regained control of myself, I still sank against him, the sadness replaced by comfort of the most gentle, welcoming kind.

He scooped me into his arms. "Which way?" he said, his voice gruff and urgent. I nodded towards the hall as I circled my arms around his neck and allowed him to carry me into the bedroom. The door was open, so there was no awkward grappling with handles and he took me straight to the bed, laying me down. I was all thumbs as I helped him slide off my t-shirt and my jeans. I rested on my elbows and watched as he pulled off his own clothes, revealing taut, tan skin over a powerful frame that I knew so well. He stretched out next to me and pulled me into him until we were tightly pressed against each other and my head was resting in the hollow of his neck. He pulled the blankets up over us as he kissed me repeatedly.

"I was terrified for you," he said after we'd lain in silence for a long while, just attuning to each other's bodies again. I could only imagine the anguish he felt when he couldn't find me. "By the time I was well enough to move, your magic was so faint I could barely sense it. I could only feel the slightest whisper, because of our connection. Étoile couldn't find a trace at all. We went looking for you, but whenever I thought I picked up a trace again, something disrupted it. Your magic?"

I nodded, my head rubbing against his chest so he could feel the motion.

"You didn't have to hide from me," he said, sounding wounded.

I blinked at him in surprise as I raised my head quickly. "I wasn't hiding from you. I thought, if you died, I didn't want any part of the Council. I wanted to hide from *them*."

"Even Étoile?" He rolled onto his back and was looking up at me from the pillow.

"Anyone, if you were gone."

"I'm here. I'm here as long as you want me. No expiration date." His hands stroked my arms, from my shoulders to the tips of my fingers and back again, sending shivers through me. He pulled me into him again and I wrapped my arm over his chest, my hand drifting down his side, just feeling him. It was almost as though I still needed to be convinced that our almost unclothed bodies were truly pressed together, that he was really lying next to me.

"What happened after she took me out?" Evan asked.

I drew in a deep breath, filling my lungs and shook my head. I didn't want to relive that night. "I thought Étoile told you?"

"She did, but no one knew what happened to you when you disappeared."

"I woke up one morning and everyone was gone. I waited days for Étoile and Seren to get back and they didn't. Then I couldn't find David... and... and, I just wanted out. I wanted to get the hell away from there so I shimmered out of the house, rented a car and just drove. I got here a few days later."

"You ported out of the house?" Evan murmured thoughtfully.

"Yeah."

"And you didn't have any problem using your magic after that?"

I shook my head again, no, although it surprised and concerned me that Étoile and Seren seemed to have problems afterwards. "If anything, it seemed to come easier. Like something just unlocked inside me. Whatever I wanted to happen, happened."

"Interesting."

"Why's that?"

"Everyone else was weakened by Eleanor's magic, but not you."

I edged out of Evan's arms so that I could face him. He was deep in thought, his hand casually moving across my back in long strokes. "What does that mean?"

"It means you're a lot stronger than we all thought. Étoile and Seren had great difficulty using their magic. By rights, as a novice, you shouldn't have been able to use yours at all. You should have been considerably weakened." He thought for a moment. "Who have you told?"

"Only you guys."

"Don't tell anyone else."

"Why?" Étoile's whisper echoed in my head: *Trust no one.*

"Eleanor was a very powerful witch who could disable just about anyone, but not you. I don't think it would be wise to tell many people. Certainly not other witches."

I let that sink in. "Are they going to come after me? These other witches?"

"Maybe, maybe not. You've kept a low profile these past few months. Perhaps, it's best to stay that way, for now, anyway."

"Except Étoile, Seren and David all think this Chyler is looking for me. And other witches want her, right? How can I keep a low profile?" I really wanted an answer to that and I hoped Evan would have some solution. It wasn't enough to rely on his protection when I needed the answers so I could depend on myself. If something were coming for Chyler, and that something, or someone were after me too, I wanted to know about it.

"I need to think some more about that." Evan was silent for a moment before he fixed his eyes on mine. "Do you like living here?" he asked, surprising me.

"Wilding? Sure. It's a lot different from London. *A lot.* But I like it. It's quiet and the people are nice.

I'll introduce you to my neighbours." Gage. Uh-oh. No. Maybe I won't, I thought as a crease of guilt made me wince inside. I brushed it aside, continuing, "I like being in my parents' house, though there isn't really any personal stuff here. Or, at least, nothing that I've found yet. But it's the strongest connection I've ever had to them."

"Do you have a job?"

I shook my head. "No. I've been thinking about looking, or maybe, going to college. I always wanted to go to university in England, but I wasn't really encouraged, so I kind of gave up on it. I'm not too old."

"You're barely old at all," Evan chided. "If you came back to Texas with me, you could go to college there. The University of Texas in Austin is very well regarded."

"Go to Texas with you?" I repeated like an idiot.

"It's where I live. If you wanted to come, that is."

"It's a long way from Wilding. I wouldn't be able to commute," was my stupidly practical non-answer. My new-to-me car wouldn't be able to take the strain and travel-by-broomstick wasn't actually a physical possibility.

Another thought occurred to me. I could shimmer there. Maybe. It was a long way but it wasn't impossible. I wouldn't have to leave Wilding; I wasn't sure I wanted to. This was the first home I'd ever had and it meant a lot to me to have a space of my own to call home. I hadn't realised how much until now. Nevertheless, it didn't override what I felt for Evan, or my desire to be close to him. I couldn't fathom being apart again.

"You could live with me. We could come out here

on vacations if you wanted to," he added.

"Are you asking me to move in with you?"

"I'm asking you to think about it. You don't have to decide right away." His voice was steady and sure like he felt certain what my answer would be.

"Okay."

"Okay... yes?" Evan's voice betrayed hope.

"Okay, I'll think about it," I clarified through gritted teeth because a part of me wanted to shout yes, yes, yes.

Evan resumed stroking my stomach with the flat of his hand, encouraging another part of my being that wanted to shout yes, yes, yes too, but for very different reasons. I sighed at the recognition of that part of me surging forward pleasurably. I could feel the blood leap in my veins.

"I can feel your magic."

"It seems to be drawn to you."

"Magic calls to magic," he whispered as he tipped my chin up to his and kissed me. It wasn't like the kiss earlier, our brief moment of crushing our lips against each other in the delight and relief of our reunion. It was like the kisses we first shared months ago, passionate and deep, full of desire. It awoke me in a way I had almost forgotten. It made me ache for him. Our tongues touched and tangled and I tasted mint on him. I heard him moan with pleasure and, when he pulled away for a moment, his face questioning, I pulled him back in, allowing his tongue to thrust into my mouth, met by mine.

His hand slipped under my back and he unclipped my bra with a flick of his fingers, pulling it off and tossing it to the floor. He dipped his head to trail kisses down my neck, kissing the crux of my clavicle.

Then he took one nipple, circling it with his tongue and drew it into his mouth while his hands moved lower to tug at my skimpy shorts. His head moved lower again, kissing his way down my stomach, further down, until he was kissing my inner thighs, making them tremble with waiting. Then he started licking me, making me gasp as his tongue delved inside and I exploded into stars that swept me away on a cloud of happiness and lust.

I pushed my fingers through his hair as I arched against him, his firm hands holding me still while he drove me to the brink of excitement, before pulling me back, time and again. When I thought I finally couldn't take it anymore, he lifted his head, cool purple-black eyes assessing me. He riveted my eyes to his gaze as he slid up my body. I felt the soft texture of cotton between us, then that was gone, leaving us skin against skin, panting and trembling in anticipation.

'Stella...' he sighed as I touched the hard swell of his cock. I used my hand to guide him inside me, swiftly moving my hands up his back to grasp him as he pushed his way fully into me. I held him as he slid in and out, increasing his rhythm, pressing against me firmly until I could wrap my legs over his. Then it felt like we were melting into each other and I crested the wave of pure longing.

Oh yes, there was a reason Evan rhymed with heaven.

I came moments before him, and his cries outweighed mine before he crushed my mouth with his, his tongue searching for mine with great shudders rippling through him. Panting, sated, he lay on top of me as I gasped air into my starved lungs.

"You've no idea how much I longed for that," Evan rasped, rolling away from me to collapse by my side, then pulling me into him in a tangle of hot, sticky limbs. "Next time, I'll be gentler, I promise. Next time, I'll..."

I raised myself slightly to lean over and put my finger to his lips. "This time was perfect." I sank back into the pillows to enjoy the aftershocks coursing through me. Evan had been my first, and only, lover and the sex had always been outstanding. I wondered if it were like this for everyone, always, or if I'd pulled a very lucky straw. It wasn't that he was eager to please; it was that he knew exactly which buttons to push and when, like we were made for each other.

It was a silly, romantic notion and it galled me when a thought flitted across my head: he must have had other lovers. I heaved a breath and shoved that thought firmly away into the back of my mind. I didn't even know where such an idea had come from. Except that it was just another reminder that there was a lot I didn't know. Frankly, it was spoiling the moment and I wanted to stay in the best part of that moment, the part that had Evan wanting me and only me. That was the only thing that mattered.

"I said we might join the others for dinner in town, if you want to?" he whispered, his hands cupping my face so he could kiss me long and slow.

I raised my eyebrows. "Not right now, surely?"

"I don't think we're dressed for it right now. Seren said eight. We have the rest of the day to ourselves."

"Will you come home with me afterwards?" I asked with a sly smile that belied how hopeful I was.

"I have my bag in the car. I have someone

covering work. I can stay as long as you want."

"I might want a long time."

Evan grinned at that and kissed me again, a soft groan slipping from his throat.

"If you keep on doing that we might be seeing them for breakfast rather than dinner," I laughed.

"That wouldn't be a great tragedy," he mumbled between kisses and I felt something stir against me, pressing into my solar plexus.

"Again?" I asked, surprised.

"Oh yes." Evan grinned wickedly. "That's something you'll learn about daemons: great stamina." Then he set about proving it.

~

Later, after we dozed and he pressed his healing hands against me and taken away the ache of too much great sex, Evan went out to the car to get his bag. When he came back in, he stripped off his clothes and climbed into the shower while I lay in bed and listened to the water patter. Stepping into my room a few minutes later, one soft towel wrapped around his waist and another in his hand patting his short hair dry, he grinned at me. I drank in his muscular body, the firm pecs that met a hard six-pack and smiled happily.

"You are pleased to see me?" he teased.

"Like you would not believe."

"All the way here, I thought 'what if she doesn't want to see me?'" Evan leant against the door frame and waited, almost cautiously, like he was expecting some kind of knockback. Where had the man been for the last few hours?

I was sitting cross-legged with the covers pulled up over my chest. "Why would you think that?"

"I couldn't think of any reason why you wouldn't come looking for me," he said simply. "But I know now."

"Whom could I have asked? Everyone was gone. I didn't know where anyone was. The Brotherhood were the reason that I was brought here and I saw on the news that they were suspected behind a string of murders across the eastern seaboard. I didn't want to attract attention." After a moment, I added, "And I could barely think straight."

"The Brotherhood have been quiet lately," Evan said, changing tack slightly to address my big problem.

"Do you think they're gone? Back to Europe?" I'd once been told I was the last of the English witches, the ones that were magic to the core anyway. Those who spell cast were more easily hidden. I'd been the last one they were going to pick off. Étoile saved me from a desperate and abbreviated fate and, though I never said it, I felt forever indebted to her.

Evan shook his head, shaking a few droplets that were making their way from his freshly washed hair, which now stood in little peaks. "I think they've drawn too much attention to themselves and they need to lay low. I think they'll be searching for witches quietly and when they come back, they'll be back with a vengeance."

"Will we ever be safe?" I whispered.

"I can keep you safe in Texas."

I swallowed the lump in my throat. "What if I stay here?"

"You'll be safer with me," Evan replied, which didn't really answer my question. I got the feeling Evan thought me leaving with him would be a very natural move. After all, what was he offering? A home, the chance of college, safety... himself. It was hardly a poor trade. I would be foolish not to think about it. I was thinking about it. "Just say you'll think about it," he said, like he just read the thoughts spilling from my mind.

"I will," I promised. Like I said, it wasn't a poor trade – it was Evan with cherries on top.

"I left the water on," he said, switching topics abruptly again. "If you wanted a shower?"

"I do."

"I could help." He flicked his eyebrows in a lascivious way, which certainly added to the general appeal of upping sticks and moving across the country.

"We'll never get to dinner if you 'help'," I giggled. I cast the sheets to one side and strode naked into the bathroom, pushing the door behind me so I could dive under the water in peace while Evan dressed. As I dipped my head under the water, I thought I heard knocking, but I ignored it when I heard the soft strains of music flick on in the living room. Instead, I lathered and rinsed until I squeaked with cleanliness.

When I got out, my bedroom was empty and the bed re-made so I towelled off and blew dry my hair until it was straight. I pulled on a simple sheath dress in light blue and slipped a patent belt around it. Both were new, even though I didn't really know where I was going to wear them when I bought them. I smiled to myself, Étoile would have known, but I wasn't blessed with psychic abilities.

I found a soft black cardigan with little jewel buttons to wear over the top, seeing as it was cool, and finished the look with black opaque hose and flats. Evan would tower over me, even if I were in heels, so I went for the comfort option. This would look fine wherever we were eating. Plus, Étoile and Seren were almost certain to be dressed up, seeing as "casual" wasn't in their lexicon. At least, I wouldn't look like the poor cousin.

Evan gave a low whistle of appreciation when I walked into the living room. "Right back at you," I murmured, taking in his black chinos and mulberry-coloured shirt, shot with thin black stripes. The dark colours made his eyes flash and emphasised the ebony of his hair and olive skin. I felt a flash of pride to have him as my date. It didn't hurt to know he would be coming home with me too.

"You look sensational," he said. Then, after a moment, "your neighbour Annalise came by."

"I thought I heard someone at the door. Did she say what she wanted?"

"To remind you that there was some kind of film show on in town and that she wanted to know if you wanted to go with her and her brother."

Right. Gage had mentioned that Wilding had its own version of a citizen movie theatre.

"I said we were going out for dinner and maybe some other time. I hope that was okay?"

"Yes, thanks." I said. I wondered if Annalise recognised Evan from the two small pictures I had on the mantelpiece. "Did she say anything else?"

"She asked if I was the guy in the photo." Evan signalled to the mantelpiece where the two photos I brought with me sat side by side. Ahh, so she did. He pulled out his wallet and slipped something out, which he held to me. It was the same picture.

"I made it to wallet status?" I asked taking a few

steps towards him, and, standing on my tiptoes, I kissed him softly. He just smiled at me as he circled his arms around my waist.

"We should go before I change my mind," he murmured, while stepping away with a sigh and reaching for my black coat on the rack. I spun round so he could hold it as I slipped it on and then followed him out the door. As we left, I trailed my fingers across the lock, out of habit.

Evan drove us in his car, using his SatNav to guide him. It was bigger, newer and considerably nicer than mine, not that either of us drew attention to that. Seren and Étoile were already seated at the restaurant when we got there – a barbecue place with a warm, countrified sense of style from its gingham-checked curtains to the scrubbed wooden tables.

They both raised their right hands to wave to us and we crossed the crowded room. Evan held my seat and had just taken the place next to me when David rushed in, unwinding his scarf, before dropping into the seat next to Seren. He leaned over to kiss her cheek before signalling to the waitress. The sisters were dressed up, as per usual. Étoile shone in wool pants and a silky shirt in cobalt blue and Seren in a long red dress that was nipped in at the waist. I'd definitely picked the right dress to wear.

"How's the inn?" I asked.

"Better than expected," said Seren, flashing a smile at David. "Much more modern than I imagined."

"She means it wasn't quite as Hicksville as we were expecting," said Étoile bluntly, reaching for her wine glass. "Wilding is a nice town. Very pretty."

"I like it," I said, but not defensively because I

could see their point. Wilding was a quiet town with a few amenities and shops that were kept to a strict planning code. If you wanted something bigger or more exciting like clubs, bars, bowling, and, well, all the fun stuff, you went to one of the neighbouring towns whose reach had yet to swallow up Wilding.

Instead, what you got in Wilding was a neat, brick-built Main Street with shop hoardings matched right down to the fonts, all centred around a community square. There were the usual small town offerings. Being a pretty town, there were several gift shops that catered to the out-of-towners that drifted through. Spanning out around this central hub were a variety of homes, tightly packed together at first with the plots broadening the further away from town you got. It was a congenial sort of place: quiet, crime-free and gently stuck in its ways. It was the absolute opposite in every way from my former home of London. I liked it here.

"And what do you like about it, Stella?" David picked up the wine bottle and filled my glass with chardonnay while Evan ordered a beer from the hovering waitress.

"I like its quiet mostly," I said, after a moment of thinking about it. "In London, people shuffled by and tried to avoid eye contact. Here, people make an effort to say hello or ask how you are. I like that." I'd probably met more people in the months I'd been here than in the several years I lived in London. Even better, they actually remembered my name here.

"Do you know anything about the town's history?" Seren asked.

I shook my head. "Not really."

"I looked it up on the 'net," said Seren. She was

picking at a bread roll on her plate, steadily turning it into crumbs without eating a single bite. "It has a strange past. Apparently, there's some strange municipal law that prevents residents from having pets."

"I noticed that, but I didn't know it was because of a law. I haven't seen a single dog or cat since I've been here and I thought there might have been cows or horses, but I haven't seen any of those either. I hear howling in the woods sometimes." I watched Seren and Étoile exchange a look. I guessed they weren't impressed. I hadn't put them down as animal lovers though. Still, I had to agree it was a strange law.

David said, "You should probably be careful at night. Your house is pretty isolated; not the best place to run into wild animals."

I nodded, Gage's warning suddenly echoing in my ears. "I'll be careful."

I was grateful when they changed topics to more trivial things, before switching to catch me up to date on what happened during the intervening months since I'd last seen them. It made me think of how collected and together they were, when I hadn't even begun to make solid plans. I had Evan's offer to think about now though, but neither of us brought that up.

What they said before about the Witches' Council fracturing was all true, but now they filled me in on the details. The Council was already weakened under the pressure of the Brotherhood picking off witches throughout Europe; and Eleanor's death left the Council in a quandary about what to do. With no clear leadership succession, apparently, trying to assist European witches wasn't a popular option. There had been plenty of dissent, but the Bartholomews always insisted on reaching out a helping hand to their brethren, even if it weren't entirely altruistic when it came to me.

I still didn't understand why Eleanor chose to send Étoile to save me, when she could have left me to die and thus solved her problem without any more blood staining her hands. I would probably never understand that. Still, I could comprehend why, to an extent, even if it galled me, that other members of the Council didn't want a European problem in their country. Too bad though, they got the Brotherhood anyway.

So, with the Bartholomews gone, and no natural leader to step in and take command, the remaining members of the Council found themselves unable to keep any semblance of control and were forced to disband over the past couple of months. With the Council dissolved, it was becoming close to impossible to monitor what was going on across the country, never mind with allies overseas. There were some witches who wanted to go their own way, fly under the radar; (I started to make a broomstick joke at that but shut my mouth at the last moment); and weren't all that interested in a crumbling regime.

Of course, there were some that wanted not just the Council united, but the ruling seat with their own Council members in power, and for all the witches to be under a new regime. Those witches were already canvassing for power, making an uneasy time for those who weren't politically persuaded, and especially for those who didn't want to be pawns in another's power play.

"Georgia Thomas is the biggest threat," said Étoile and I watched them all nod in agreement with her, even Evan. "She's never been able to get on the Council."

"How come?" I asked.

"She's never been interested in the good of the Council." Étoile glared at me while I covered a snort with a sip of wine, before she finished, "She's just in it for the power."

"She's very powerful though," pointed out David. "She's always felt slighted. This is a perfect opportunity for her."

"She's as scary as hell," added Seren with a shudder. "You know that saying 'wouldn't want to meet her in a dark alley'? Someone met Georgia right before they said that."

David said, "I hear she's travelling along the west coast, recruiting."

"The further away from us, the better. Do you mind if we call it an early night? We were driving for hours today." Seren sat her dessert spoon down and licked sugar from her lips, her eyelids heavy. Étoile and David both nodded and I noticed that they were looking drawn too.

"Of course not. You're here for a few days, right?" I tried not to look too hopeful, but I really wanted them to stay. It wasn't just for the catch-up, but so I could learn more. Just because I didn't want to be under Council rule, didn't mean I didn't want to know what was going on.

"Yes." Étoile answered for the three of them and, under the table, Evan squeezed my hand. Seeing as we hadn't really talked about how long he was staying, I assumed that he just was, but now a time stamp was hovering with a big question mark. I'd been naive not to think about it earlier when he put forth his offer.

I reached under the table, my fingers fanned, ready to take his hand and squeeze it happily, but as my palm brushed against the top of his hand, I gasped. The restaurant disappeared and I found myself in the midst of flames, colours so intense and vivid in oranges and reds with licks of yellow as they flickered around me. I felt the air suck out of the pocket I was in and rush past me like a back draft, encouraging the flames to leap and cavort.

I turned, feeling like I was caught in slow motion as I felt fear and awe. I could feel the heat, the intensity calling me and then strong arms wrapped themselves around me and, as I opened my mouth to call out, just as suddenly as it happened, I blinked only to find myself back in the restaurant.

Evan's hand was under one of mine, his fingers lacing their way through my fingers, my other hand gripping the edge of my seat. The cool wood contrasted with the heat of the moment.

"Are you okay?" Evan asked, his face etched in concern as I tugged my fingers sharply from his.

"Will you excuse me for a moment?" I said, pushing back my chair with an ungainly scrape and dropping my napkin on the table. I hurried to the bathroom as fast as I possibly could without breaking into a jog.

Installing myself in a cubicle, I felt my chest tighten in sudden panic as my thought processes caught up with the lurch I just felt. I couldn't even fathom what just happened except that it was terrible and awesome, intense and alive. My breath caught in my throat. And someone else had been there with me, wherever "there" was. I gripped the basin with both hands and stared at my stricken reflection.

"Are you okay?" came Étoile's voice from outside the door.

"Um, yeah, I'm fine." My throat felt parched. I ran the water for a moment, then straightened up and unbolted the door to step out.

"You looked like you'd just seen a ghost." She looked at me carefully. "You do look a bit pale. Are you sure there isn't something wrong?"

I shook my head. "Oh no, it's nothing. Probably just drank a bit too much."

"You hardly touched your wine."

"I'm fine, really." How could I explain what just happened?

Étoile touched my arm with long fingers and her eyelids lowered as I let her draw from me what I had just experienced. Her face stayed expressionless and I wondered if she got an instant replay, or just snapshots.

"You had a vision?" she murmured.

"I don't know what it was." I shivered.

"I think you saw some of the future."

"How? I can't do that. You and Seren do stuff like that, not me." I scanned the restroom. We were the only two in there, but I kept my voice low all the same. "I just zap myself places and move things." But I knew it wasn't true. I had a vision when I touched Chyler too.

"And make magic from your natural energy. You heal, I remember that. And now you have visions too," Étoile said, more to herself than me. She ran her fingers through her hair, fluffing it a bit until she achieved just the right volume.

"I don't understand it though. How can I be seeing the future?"

"Possibly some latent psychic skills, or just a new manifestation of your power. What were you doing right before you had the vision?"

I thought about it for a moment. "I'd just put my wine glass down."

"Then?"

"I touched Evan's hand."

"Hmm. I think Evan was part of that vision. It's something that involves you and him in the future."

"It seemed like we were on fire. I should be worried about that, right?" Like, really, really worried I wanted to ask. What if it were the Brotherhood? What if they had captured us both? I couldn't bear to see Evan hurt, not at their hands.

"I don't think you were in danger. That's not the impression I got."

"Are you sure?"

"It *was* fleeting."

"You need to work on your reassuring manner," I snipped and immediately regretted it.

"You're not the first one to say that. Fortunately, I'll always believe I'm fabulous. Back to you though, are you sure you're all right?"

"Honestly, I'm fine. Let's go back." My hands were shaking slightly and I could feel the cold tingle of fear edging through my bones. I wanted to be near Evan, not far away from him. I wanted to put the vision out of my head, and leave my subconscious to deal with it. I hoped my subconscious had a witchy streak that would work it all out and deliver a satisfying cerebral message that would explain everything. The rest of me wasn't holding out any hope. Damn it, I really needed a manual for this kind of stuff.

"Take your time," Étoile was saying. "David got Evan into a conversation about soccer and, really, no one needs to listen to that."

I grinned, relaxing. "We should probably save Seren then."

The bill was paid by the time we got back to the table and Evan leaned over to slip his arm around my chair, without mentioning my sudden flight. I made sure to only touch him with the parts of me that were covered. I wasn't quite ready to experience the vision, or whatever it was, again. "Ready to go?" he whispered.

I plastered on an agreeable smile. "Absolutely."

Our goodbyes were swift and whatever awkwardness had been there earlier was gone now. Just as the vague thought that I hadn't been worrying about Chyler flitted across my mind, I stuffed it back down. I had never been entirely sure just how much Étoile or Seren could see into my brain, but I did know that when they were together, their power amplified. I had to do some investigating before I could talk to them.

For all the talk that had been about the Witches' Council, and the general mess it had become, I had no idea what the Winterstorms' role was. As soon as I thought that, I instantly felt mean. Part of me wanted to immediately tell them about Chyler and beg for their help. Another part of me wanted to understand what was going on before blurting out my little secret.

"See you tomorrow," said Étoile, dropping a kiss on each cheek and I waved a hand to Seren and David who had cosied up to each other.

"I can't tell you how glad I am you're all here," I said to Evan when we were alone as I buckled in. He turned the heating on and a warm blast of air hit me. "It's been hell wondering about you all."

"No more hell." Evan leant over and kissed me. He lingered his lips on mine and I relaxed against him. No vision, great.

A few minutes later, and we left the restaurant in our dust. When we turned out of the last residential street, he asked me casually, "Have you been practising your magic at all?"

I couldn't help blushing and was glad he probably couldn't see it in the twilight. Evan had once been my teacher, for only a few short weeks, before he became my lover. We hadn't had long together after that. I was only surprised that he didn't ask about my practice earlier. I squared up and confessed. "Not as much as I should have, but I do find things easier. And there haven't been any accidents."

"Have you been around people much?"

"Yes, but not in stressful ways. So maybe it doesn't count for much." Growing up, I had lots of unexplained accidents, so many that people actively avoided me. Every time I got stressed, or angry, or anxious, there would be someone to slip, stumble, or fall, or an accident just begging to happen. It left me tense and skittish, and people afraid of me. Accidents simply didn't happen anymore. And it wasn't just lack of stress, there was always stress, thanks to the Brotherhood. But the day to day anxieties of life seemed to not affect me as much.

"It counts," Evan said after he'd taken a moment to mull it over. "It means you're containing your magic. That was one of the things that made it so hard to find you. Not finding all those little traces, I mean. When I first met you, your magic used to hover all around you; it trailed wherever you went."

"I saw something like that with Marc. When Eleanor died, his magic came back and it was incredible." Eleanor had spellbound Marc, her son, since he was an infant for her own cruel, nefarious reasons. When she died, the spell was undone and the magic rushed back to Marc. It had been bright and powerful and shone all around him like the most incredible aura. I wondered what it looked like now, whether it burned with that same intensity or whether he'd gotten it under control.

"Right. I saw him at the hospital a couple of times. It hadn't quite faded."

"You saw each other? How did that go?"

"Fine. We didn't have any long heart to hearts. He wanted to help look for you, so did Kitty, but she wasn't well enough."

"I spoke to Kitty earlier."

"I bet she was thrilled." He glanced away from the road for just a moment to look at me, his mouth curving into a smile.

"I was too." I thought for a moment, then tentatively asked, "How come I don't see anyone else's magic?"

"It's one of the easiest ways to spot a witch. All that magic untamed shows itself as a bright light. Witches are taught to keep it under control, to not let it leak out. You're doing a good job of keeping yours controlled."

"I'm not trying."

"That's even better. It means it's just your natural state, rather than something you're trying to force on yourself."

"That's a good thing?"

Evan nodded. "Definitely. You shouldn't have to be concentrating on containing your magic. You just need to harness it and make sure it's always there to bend to your will. It should be something that's so automatic, it barely takes any of your reserve energy."

"How did it... how did I get like this?"

"Accepting it and embracing magic are two big steps. Training is another. Realising your power and controlling it is the last step. You just need to practice now."

"Always the teacher."

Evan grinned, shadows from the street lamps passing over his face. "You better believe it."

"How come I've never seen your magic?"

"Mine isn't like witch magic. It doesn't show. You'll be able to recognise me, and my kind, in other ways."

Evan turned the car onto the long road that led up to my house. After a few minutes, the tree line broke and I could see the bar that nestled there. Tonight, it was all lit up inside and I could hear music drifting over the lot. I could see Annalise's car and just as we flashed by, I thought I caught sight of Gage standing on the veranda that circled the building. I frowned.

"You ever been in there?" asked Evan, glancing over at me.

I shook my head. "I think it's some kind of members' club. You have to know someone to get in. Don't you think that's strange? Who would have a members' club out here?" And how come Gage and Annalise were there? But I couldn't ask Evan that.

A few minutes later, and we were on my drive and Evan parked next to my car.

"Yours?" he asked nodding to my little car.

"There's not much in the way of public transport here. It's kind of a necessity." It also explained why I wasn't feeling as fit as I used to but I wasn't going to say that either. I'd have to up my running soon to stop the softness that I imagined was creeping up on me. Pre-emptive exercise was better than too late exercise.

"You don't shimmer?"

"I didn't think that would be okay. You know shimmering down to the market then flashing out of the parking lot." I could imagine a few freaked out Wilding faces at that.

"Doesn't mean you shouldn't do it at all though," pointed out Evan. "You need to keep your magic strong and the more you practice, the easier it will come to you."

I held my hands up in surrender. "Okay, I get it. No more being a magic slob." I laughed when he gathered me up in his hands like I weighed nothing and skipped up the steps. There was a moment of awkwardness as I grappled with the key and the lock. Then we were inside and kissing furiously, all thoughts of visions gone and replaced by very welcome touching. We didn't quite make it to the bed but the sofa welcomed us like old friends as clothes flew in our wake.

Later, lying in bed with a sliver of moonlight streaking over us, Evan told me of daemons and their place in the world and I struggled to absorb the enormity of creatures that shared the world with so many oblivious humans. Later, as I was on the edge of sleep, he whispered how much he loved me before his language switched to an ancient tongue that lulled me as I drifted away.

My dreams were full that night, not of terror and death as I'd been afraid of, but of Evan and me, and I felt free, at least. But when I held him in the dream world I could see, over his shoulder, Gage looking at me, and, when my eyes met his, I trembled. It wasn't the surprise of seeing him there; it was that I didn't dare get close enough to see what his eyes would reflect of mine.

CHAPTER EIGHT

I stood, hands on hips, in the centre of the road and stared far into the distance. For the first time, I ran to where the thick, dense tree line broke and now there was nothing for miles and miles but green fields, split neatly in two by the tarmac that snaked its way towards the cold winter horizon.

There was a threat of rain in the air and a freezing light wind, so I tugged the zipper of my jacket up until it was snug under my chin. The temptation to join a gym that I could drive to, and exercise in cute sweats before hitting the hot showers, was never stronger than now.

"What are you doing?" said a girl's voice behind me and I jumped, my heart leaping into my throat. Turning around, I saw Chyler standing there, her hands thrust into her pockets.

"Running," I replied, breathing in and out to slow down my heart. I'd just about recovered from the run when she gave me an impromptu heart rate test.

"On the spot?" she asked sarcastically.

"Um, no. Taking a breather."

"Don't you go to a gym?" Chyler had a slightly nasal voice that made everything sound like she was completely grossed out in a condescending sort of way. She probably listed it as a skill on her resume. "With a running machine or something?"

"How could that be better than out here?" I looked around me. Okay, she definitely had a point and no amount of protesting would make up for the lack of glossy equipment and a pumping soundtrack, not to mention heating, but personal pride made me obstinate.

"It would be warm," Chyler smirked then shivered in her thick padded coat, which reminded me I was only wearing thin layers of jersey. I relied on running to keep out the cold and now I was standing still, and cooling rapidly. I tried to envision warmth, but failed.

"How did you know I was here?"

"The book," she said.

"Where is it?"

"I told it to hide." She shrugged but didn't elaborate any further and, for a moment, I thought she was a frightened little girl, not a snarky kid. Then she said, "It's not safe."

"Where are you staying?"

Chyler hesitated. "A hotel."

"Where are you really staying?" I gave her my special "no nonsense" look that I usually reserved for temp employers who thought their business deserved special rates; and waited for her to wither.

Chyler rolled her eyes. "In an abandoned house, somewhere over there, I think." She flapped a hand in an abstract easterly direction. I noticed her manicure was chipping at the edges.

"How did you get here?"

"Same way as yesterday. I said the same spell from the book. Look, can you do me a favour? That's why I came."

I raised my eyebrows at her bluntness. Now we were getting somewhere. "What kind of favour?"

"Can you get a message to my mom? Tell her I'm okay. I don't want her to worry."

"Chyler, I..." I did not know how to tell her. I never had to break news of a death before. Plus, I was worried about what I'd been told yesterday. My friends thought Chyler killed her mother, yet Chyler was asking me to get a message to her! My vision fuzzed everything; something was really, really wrong with this picture. I looked at her, my heart thumping, and drew a breath that I exhaled with a sigh.

"What's wrong?"

"Some friends came to see me yesterday." I gestured to a fallen tree by the side of the road and, even though Chyler looked askance at it, like sitting on a fallen tree trunk was something only hobos did, she sat down next to me anyway. Her knees bumped together as she shivered. "Chyler, they told me that your mother was dead."

"What? Why would they come all the way out here to tell you that? My mom? She's dead?" She sat looking at her feet for a long, tortuous few minutes in which I wondered whether I should hug her or try to do something comforting. I started to reach over to pat her shoulder but she pulled away, her lip quivering.

"I'm so sorry, Chyler." I waited for a moment just to see if she were listening, then told her, "They're looking for you. They guessed you might want a witch who was on the outside to help you."

"Were they worried about me? Are these friends of yours going to help me?"

There was no easy way of putting it, so I blurted. "They think you killed your mom."

"I, like, totally didn't!" Chyler's jaw dropped open in disgust. She jumped to her feet and paced backwards and forwards. After a minute, she stopped next to the tree trunk and stared me down. "You believe me, right?"

I barely moved my shoulders when I shrugged. "I want to, but someone killed your mother. Did anyone have a motive?"

"Only everyone who wanted the book." Chyler sniffed. "How did my mom die?"

"She was stabbed," I said, watching carefully for her reaction.

Chyler made a noise that was uncomfortably wedged somewhere between a squeal and a sob. "Oh God!"

"I'm sorry." It didn't get any simpler than that. What else could I say? "Well, how many people want that book of yours?"

"My aunts, the Council... I don't know who else, Stella."

"I guess that doesn't narrow it down much."

"Not at all," Chyler wailed as she threw herself back down on the log and picked at the bark. "Can we go to your place? Maybe you can do some kind of spell on me? I don't... I... I feel..." Chyler's whole body shuddered and she lurched forward. I hovered my hand over her back, wondering if she just passed out or was about to throw up, on her shoes, (and should I hold her hair?). When all of a sudden, she sat up, back totally straight and beamed at me. She rolled her shoulders around and laced her fingers together, stretching her arms like she'd just gotten up after a long, lazy lie-down.

"Stella," she grinned, as if our uncomfortable conversation had never occurred. She looked at the bark in her hand and flicked it to the ground, then shook her head so her hair fell down in shimmering waves across her back. There were little twigs caught in it and bits of dust that gave her a slightly unkempt, hippie look. I wondered how rough the abandoned house was that she was hiding in.

I peered at her. "Are you okay?"

"Fine! So, what were we talking about?"

"Your mom."

"Oh, right. Whatever!"

"Whatever?" I repeated, my brows knitting together in concern.

"Yeah. You know what we should do? We should lay a trap for anyone who comes looking for me." Chyler jumped up. "Yes, that's what we should do. I bet you could lay down some pretty cool magic. Like a booby trap?"

I ignored the sudden about-face in Chyler's temperament and asked the obvious. "Why would I do that?"

"Well..." Chyler wrinkled up her face like a pug trying to fathom if it could get a treat simply by raising a paw. "Because they're going to come looking for me and we should get rid of them straight away. They're going to hurt me and you're not going to let that happen. Are you?" She tossed her head and stared straight at me.

"Well, no." I was peering curiously at her, slightly incredulous that there was no sign of the grief that had consumed her just moments before. It was like she couldn't remember having the conversation we just had.

I had Chyler down as a typical teenager but not one that was so scatterbrained she could be heartbroken over her mom's passing one moment, and then completely unperturbed the next. Maybe she had some kind of brain injury? I couldn't imagine why else she would have lost interest so fast.

"Fantastic! Maybe we should go back to your house right now and we can start laying traps. I bet you could take out a whole bunch of them by laying charms around the house."

I gaped at her. "Are you serious? For a start, I don't know anything about charms. Secondly, I'm not about to booby trap my house. What if someone got hurt?"

"Well, that's the whole point." Chyler blinked furiously and a tear trickled down her cheek but she didn't make any move to brush it away. Instead, her chest heaved a bit and she looked like she was going to break out crying. As if to make her point, she sniffled, "I thought you were on my side."

"I want to help you and find out what's going on." I got off the log, brushing off microscopic pieces of not quite dry bark, and started stretching to warm my muscles back up. I kept my eyes on Chyler the whole time. "But I'm not going to try and attack a bunch of strangers, even if they do come to my house."

"Maybe you're just not that good a witch." Chyler stopped sniffing and smirked at me instead, a nasty look passing over her eyes.

"Why don't you go back to where you're staying and I'll keep investigating what's going on." I kept my voice even and firm, but what I really wanted to do was shake some sense into her. Chyler's impudence was starting to worry me.

"I think we should go to your house. And I think you should help me. Right now!" Chyler all but stamped her foot on the grassy verge.

"I don't think it's safe to take you to my house yet. I'm just asking you to be patient." Besides, with Evan there, and Étoile, Seren and David due, (thanks to my open invitation), I didn't want to risk some kind of showdown before I had some of the answers. Or, at the very least, some of the questions.

I didn't want Chyler being taken into custody since I didn't know what that even meant. And I didn't want her going in, all magical hackles raised, before I knew how to help her. However, by helping her, I certainly wasn't going to hurt my friends, or put them in danger. There had to be another way.

"I don't think you get it, Stella, I'm not asking you, I'm telling you..." Chyler raised her hand and her mouth started to move in a strange tongue, something that sounded vaguely Latinate, but otherwise alien to me.

With a circular motion of my hand, I shielded myself in a soft glow that hovered around me. The shield would stop any magic hurting me and was an easy, if not energy sapping, mechanism that Evan had taught me months ago. I hadn't used it until now. It would have been pointless against a witch of Eleanor Bartholomew's strength, but Chyler was just a kid. I braced myself as I dropped my voice an octave to warn her. "Chyler, I don't know what you think you're doing, but this is not the way to get me to help you."

Chyler paused for a moment, then stopped, dropping her hand limply by her side. "I'm so sorry. I'm just, like, really anxious right now."

"I'll find you when I know something. Don't just pop up behind me again."

"Why not?" Chyler had the bad grace to look offended.

"Because it's scary and I don't want you to do that." And you've pissed me off, I thought, but I didn't say it out loud.

Chyler wrinkled her nose. "Fine."

"I'll be in touch. Don't do anything stupid." I didn't wait for an answer. Instead I started to jog back towards my house, keeping the shield even and steady the whole time.

"I'm really sorry," Chyler shouted behind me. "I didn't mean to freak you out."

Without looking back, I waved a hand and powered on a bit faster. I didn't check to see if she looked sincere. I was pretty certain she wasn't.

Evan was dressed and had set himself up on the kitchen table with his laptop and cell phone by the time I returned. He mentioned something about checking on his staff.

"Hi," he said, getting up straight away to kiss me. When he drew back, his face puzzled, he asked, "Are you okay?"

"Sure," I smiled weakly. "I'm just going to change."

"You run every day?"

I nodded then laughed. "I try to, at least. Mostly I

just huff and puff."

"Maybe I can come with you tomorrow?"

"I'd like that." I squeezed his hand and kissed him again because I still couldn't quite believe he was still here. Then I stepped back so I could turn on my heel and head through to my bedroom, peeling off my running clothes as I went and tossing them into the laundry hamper on the way.

Chyler's behaviour puzzled me while I redressed in jeans and a soft sweater in a sugary lilac that would make my green eyes pop. One minute, she was a scared teenager on the run, the next, she wanted to lay down traps and attack anyone who wanted to come near her. I kind of got it. I knew what it was like to be scared, but I also had another side of the argument to consider.

She was a stranger to me and my friends thought she was dangerous. I didn't know what I could do without betraying the trust of someone. I could turn Chyler over straight away and let someone else deal with her and whatever problems she brought, or I could try and help her and lie, not so much to my friends' faces, but certainly by omission. The weight of the decision sat heavily on my shoulders. Chyler's behaviour puzzled me: one moment she seemed terrified and desperate, the next she was action and couldn't care less. Something was wrong, that much I knew.

"What are you doing?" I asked Evan as I stood in the kitchen after getting changed. I was running a brush through my hair, enjoying the feeling. I liked the idea of having long hair again. A series of shoddy room lets with appalling bathrooms had convinced me to trim it severely a couple of years ago. But now I had my own place and could take the time to look after it, I could grow it out. That certainly put a smile on my face.

Evan barely glanced up. "Looking for more information about Chyler Anderson."

"Online?"

"You'd be surprised at what you can find." He turned the laptop around and I bent down to look at the screen. A virtual yearbook was open and I could see a snapshot of Chyler. "She was a popular girl. Clever, too. Cheerleader, debate team captain, volunteered at local hospices." He tapped the mouse pad and changed screens so I could see a newspaper clipping with a picture of the family. Chyler was wearing a strapless blue dress with low-heeled blue pumps. She sat perfectly upright, knees together and hands in her lap, the picture of poise. Actually, she seemed to have that down to a tee. All her pictures, even the casual ones, were frame-worthy, like she always knew she had to sit properly and be ready to plaster on a smile.

"Her family were all active in supporting their community, made good money, sat on charity committees and were well thought of. Some witches like to be very active like this; they think it makes them less of a target if they have a solid community around them."

"Are the whole family witches?"

"Yes to the mother, no to the father and brother, though it seems like they knew and were okay with it."

"Any chance they could have been jealous? Maybe they wanted to hurt Chyler's mom?"

Evan shook his head. "They seemed to be a very

happy family."

"You can never tell though, right?" I was thinking about Eleanor and Robert Bartholomew. They seemed like the perfect power couple with a long marriage and a big bank account, but they had been far from happy.

"I guess not."

"I don't get why everyone thinks Chyler killed her mother."

"Chyler's mom – Andrea, was her name – had talked to their local coven about Chyler dabbling in stuff she wasn't supposed to. She was worried about her and said she was going to talk to her and try to make her understand that what she was doing could have serious consequences. Before they could come up with a way of helping her, Andrea was dead and Chyler was the only one in the house at the time. By the time Andrea's husband found her, Chyler was gone."

I raised my eyebrows. "And that's why she's suspect number one?" Also: Andrea *Anderson*? I wondered if anyone had ever called her Andy, but that was a moot point.

Evan nodded.

"Seems to me like everyone is jumping the gun." I switched streams of thought. "I just don't get why you're looking for her though. I thought you weren't keen on working with witches." Evan had explained, when we first met, that he was only teaching me as a favour to Robert Bartholomew, who had quietly tried to help me as much as he could, despite his own insurmountable problems.

"I'm not here looking for Chyler so much as I am to protect you. You do not want a bunch of covens landing on your doorstep. Étoile and Seren were the ones who were asked to do some investigating into Chyler. Being here is like killing two birds with one stone for them."

"Charming," I muttered. "So you're not going to help them at all?"

Evan leant back in his chair and stretched his long legs, folding his hands behind his head in such a way that I got an eyeful of muscular biceps. "Not if it gets in the way of helping you." There was a piece of me that was really pleased knowing that; Evan was here for me, absolutely for me and his being here was not just a by product of some witchy shenanigans. But I couldn't help the niggling feeling that something wasn't right with Chyler. Now I worried that I might get in the way of anyone helping her by not 'fessing up.

"If you were Chyler, what would you do?" I asked.

"We know that she was looking for you because they found a trace of a spell she cast when she disappeared, so if I were she, I'd wait until you were on your own before I'd try and talk to you. I'd be near the house, waiting somewhere for the opportunity."

"And why me? Why not some other outsider?"

"Just about all witches are connected in some way. You're not because you weren't raised with witchcraft. There's a good chance Chyler would have heard about you and risk trying to get in touch.

"Okay. What if she got the chance to talk to me?"

Evan thought for a minute. "I'd ask for protection. I'd tell you I was innocent. I'd ask you to help me."

So far, so true. I asked, "What if I helped her?

141

What could I do?"

"You could use your magic to mask her presence. You could fight on her behalf. If anyone attacked, you could stop them." Evan seemed a lot surer of me than I was. Another plus point in his favour.

"Who would attack?" I asked, because Chyler had intimated that a lot of witches would.

"Andrea's coven, either to avenge or capture. I don't think they want to hurt her, but it really depends on how accountable they find her for Andrea Anderson's death. Other covens are a risk. Remember, Chyler almost certainly has that book and that makes her even more interesting, especially given the troubles witches are having now."

"You all talk about that like something really bad is going down." Evan just looked at me as I pulled up the chair next to him. "Okay, fine, something bad is happening. What's so important about the book? What if she just gave it away?"

"She can't. The book is bound to her. So long as she is alive, and there's magic there, that book will stay with her. As for the book itself, it's very old and it's drawn power from every witch who has ever held it. The spells it contains would be very strong, and amplified, if someone were to use them. If Chyler were gone, the book would transfer to someone else in her line and that would make them a very powerful witch indeed."

"Can only the spell craft witches use it?"

Evan shook his head. "Any witch but they would have to be blood relatives, unless there's some clause. No other supernaturals though. I couldn't touch it, for example, never mind use it."

"Is it likely that the witches might be more

interested in the book than in Chyler?"

"It's a possibility. We'll have to ask David when he gets here. He knows more about spell craft than any of us."

"Hmm. When are you going to tell me more about this daemon stuff?" I asked, latching on to his claim that he couldn't touch the book as an excuse to find out more.

Evan leaned forward and smiled at me. "What do you want to know?"

I leant forward too, like we were conspiring, and resisted the urge to rest my elbows on the surface. "Anything. Everything. I don't even know the questions to ask. I know you're not evil, like, you're not like a demon or the devil."

Evan clicked on the mouse pad a couple of times then closed the lid of the laptop. "Daemons, like me, look like humans, act like them. We eat, drink, have sex, like any normal human would. But we're not human. We can use magic, like you can, so I wouldn't call you exactly human either. Daemons come in all shapes and sizes and as many of us are good as bad. It probably tips the scales towards the bad, unfortunately, and good is just a loose way of saying not completely malicious."

I shivered. "And what about magic? I've seen some things you can do but that's not all?"

Evan shook his head and, as he did so, drawers opened and closed, then the cabinet doors did the same. Overhead, the light bulb flickered on and off. "I can move things and control things." I felt my chair slide back and then I rose off it, into the air and spun slowly around. I felt weightless and I had no control of my limbs as I was suspended there. I gazed down at Evan in surprise. "I can move you. I could move you to Asia if I wanted," he said.

"Please don't," I laughed and he set me down and pulled me, and the chair, with invisible fingers back to where we'd been. I stretched my arms and flexed my toes just to be sure I was in control again.

"I can disappear." Before I could look up, he'd gone and a moment later he whispered in my ear, his breath cool against my skin. "And reappear." An instant later and he was back in his chair. "You've seen me heal. Human injuries mean little too me. Broken bones, cuts, sprains, I'll heal in minutes."

"Handy," I murmured.

"Magical injuries take more time," he pointed out. "But what could kill you, would probably only disable me. It's very, very hard to kill a daemon."

"Lucky you. What else?"

"I can summon fire." Evan held his hand out to me and uncurled it so his palm faced up. Flames erupted. Not a little candle flame, but great billows of red-hot fire that heated the air around us and, in the centre of it all, his hand remained untouched. He snapped his hand into a fist and the fire was gone, leaving me agape in wonder. "And I can get rid of it. But I don't think you'd appreciate a demonstration in your house.

"However, my real skill is tracking people. All I need is their scent and I can find them, wherever they are. And because I'm virtually indestructible, I'm in demand to a lot of supernaturals when they need confidential things done."

"What kind of confidential things?" I asked, intrigued.

"Taking prisoners. Transporting goods, contracts.

Anything that needs discretion."

"Why don't they just hide from you? You stand out, in a good way." I grinned. "And you're magic, I can feel you're different, so others must also."

"Ahh. That's because I can look like anyone I want." Evan melted into the air in front of me and I forced my eyes not to blink when David appeared in front of me. It wasn't just that, the way my body registered him changed too. It was just subtly enough that I didn't feel that I had a daemon in front of me, but when I concentrated really hard, it wasn't quite David either.

"No way," I grinned.

"Anyone, any time," said David and, when I blinked, Evan was there again. "I have other handy tricks too."

"Like what?"

"Look down."

I glanced down. "Oh, very funny." My clothes were gone and I was sitting in my underwear. Thank goodness, I'd picked a pretty set. At least I wasn't completely naked. Perhaps Evan hadn't been concentrating?

"I prefer you in dresses. What do you think?" He nodded at me and a blue dress, short on the leg and tight on the bodice skimmed over me. I felt a zip tug at the back.

"Very nice. But it is winter and my legs are cold."

"How about leggings? And boots?" Black leggings skimmed over my legs and a pair of heeled leather boots melted on top.

"I like. Hey, can I do that?" That would be useful, not to mention, impossibly cool.

"Probably. I'll show you how."

"Can you turn into anyone?" I waited for Evan to nod before I asked, "How about a woman?"

Evan's eyebrows rose and he smirked. "Don't push it. Didn't I mention I'm very, very dangerous?"

"Excellent taste though." I pointed at the dress, then beckoned him. He was around the table in a flash, spinning my chair to face him and nudging my legs so he could kneel between them, hands on my hips, pulling me into him.

"You're not afraid of me?" he murmured, leaning towards me to press my lips against his.

"Not at all," I mumbled, wondering if he really thought there were a different answer.

"You probably should be." He lifted me, physically this time and sat me on the table, gentle pressure from his hands laying me down across the cool wood. I felt the pressure of his laptop on my back before it disappeared. Then I saw his laptop bag on the floor bulge around its sudden arrival.

I wrapped my legs around Evan and tugged him into me, registering that our contact was now very much skin on skin as our clothes magically disappeared. If it weren't for the banging at the door, I would have been more than happy to let very good things happen on that table.

"Ignore it," murmured Evan, his head bent to my neck, while his fingers traced circles on my inner thighs. "I know you want to."

"I do want to," I gasped. "But we're expecting visitors and they know we're here." Both our cars were parked out front.

Evan pulled me up so I was sitting on the edge, his hands caressing me until I was on the brink of forgetting all about the visitors. Then there was another sharp succession of knocks. I gave him a shove that was about as forceful as poking a T-Rex, so it wasn't nearly enough to make him take the step back that he did.

"Could you, um..." I slid off the table, the floor cold under my feet, and gestured to my lack of clothing. In a blink, the blue dress, leggings and boots reappeared as fast as Evan's own black jeans and t-shirt.

"You are insatiable," I muttered as I slid past him, the skirt swinging from my hips.

"Did I mention daemons have a voracious libido?" I heard him say, behind my back.

I couldn't resist glancing over my shoulder to wink at him. "Yes, I noticed that." Then I went to answer the door, a smile plastered all over my face.

Instead of finding Étoile, Seren and David as I expected, Gage was standing at the door.

"Got visitors?" he asked, which was a fairly poor greeting in my book.

"Good morning to you, and yes, I do. Friends from out of town."

"Annalise mentioned it. She came by to see you last night." He leant against the doorframe, still filling it, but made no move to step inside.

"Oh, right. I was on my way out. Did you go see the film?"

"We did, but it would have been better if you were there too."

"Well, thank you. I'll come next time. Did you do anything after?" I'd seen him outside the Loup Garou bar on the way home, but he didn't know that. Besides, I was being conversational. Neighbourly.

He shook his head. "Just came home with

Annalise."

I looked at him for a minute then shook my head. So he didn't mention he'd been at the bar, so what? It was no business of mine. I stepped back. The awkwardness that hadn't been there a couple of days ago now filled the air between us. "So, what can I do for you? Do you want to come in?"

Gage nodded and stepped inside. I shut the door behind him. "Winter is definitely setting in," he said, nodding at the grey sky that still threatened rain beyond the door.

"Then I'm glad you finished painting the front of my house. You didn't tell me how much I owe you."

Gage delved in his jacket pocket and came up with some crumpled receipts. "Just for paint," he said, handing them over and I smoothed the pieces of paper out without looking at them. "The rest of the house looked okay. It can wait for spring before we paint the rest."

'You know you don't have to do that," I protested, since he'd already done so much for me. "I'll get you the money tomorrow, if that's okay? And I really appreciate it; you didn't have to."

"My pleasure and no hurry." Gage was looking me over, skimming me from head to toe, approval in his eyes. "Nice dress."

"Thanks." I waited for a moment and he shook himself, seeming to remember why he came over.

"So... I came by to say there's a garden store on the other side of Wilding that's having a sale. I drove past it yesterday. You said you wanted a swing for the porch? I figured if you got it now, I could build it for you, store it in our garage and you'd have it ready for next summer. You've already got the joints in the

148

porch roof, so it's no problem to hang it when the weather's better."

I beamed. Something else to cross off my list. "I'd like that, thank you."

"You want to go now?"

I could hear Evan rustling around in the kitchen and then steps came towards us. My face fell a bit. "I would, but I'm expecting visitors again."

"Twice in two days. Someone got popular all of a sudden."

I stuck my tongue out at him and turned to greet Evan who was making his way through the living room. He stopped beside me and slid an arm around my waist, his hand perched on my hip which had been bare only a few minutes earlier. He held out his other hand to Gage. "Evan Hunter."

Gage looked at his hand for a moment before taking it. "Gage Garoul. I live across the street." When I looked down, I could see some crushing fingers going on, though neither of them winced. This didn't seem to be a bonding moment.

"I met your sister last night." Crush.

"So I heard." Crush, crush.

"Do you two need a room?" I asked to lighten the moment and Gage broke off first. He pushed his hand into his pocket and I looked from him to Evan, thinking the displeasure on my face should be evident enough... if either of them were looking. I was starting to think this was less about porch swings and more about Gage finding out if he had any competition. I swallowed back guilt.

"I hear you've been looking out for my girlfriend." Oh. I got it. Territorial pissing.

"I heard nothing about you at all," came Gage's

reply. Ouch.

"Well, thanks for coming by, Gage." I took his elbow and steered him back to the front door. "I do want to come to the store with you, but maybe tomorrow? If that's okay?"

"I'll be at work. We can go next weekend?"

"Great. And if I don't see you tomorrow, I'll leave the money with Annalise."

"Anytime. No hurry. See you, Stella." And he surprised me by leaning down and kissing my cheek casually before pulling the door closed behind him.

"He's got the hots for you," said Evan when I turned back to him with my eyebrows raised.

"Yes, he does," I admitted, though I wasn't going to tell him we'd kissed. Or that he'd fallen asleep in my bed, or that there had been some temptation there. Okay, fine, a lot of temptation. That wouldn't do much to improve the situation. "But that was no reason for you to be rude."

"I wasn't rude."

"I'm surprised you let his fingers go intact."

Evan looked affronted. "That was just a friendly handshake."

"You don't need to mark your territory. I'm here, with you, aren't I?" I put my hands on his chest, sending a small burst of energy to wrap around us like a caress. It glittered briefly before fading and he smiled broadly at my silly little expression.

"So long as you are." Evan pulled me into him, both arms around me. He was trying to look sincere, at least. "I'm sorry. I won't act like a jerk again."

I moved my lips up to meet his. "You see to that," I murmured against his mouth. "Gage and his sister are my friends and I want you to be nice to them."

Which was another reminder to me that I had yet to meet Evan's friends. I had no idea what they were like; it was another jog of how little I really knew about him and how much more there was to learn.

Evan shifted his hips so he was pressed a little closer. "Down boy," I whispered. "We're still expecting visitors, remember?"

He pushed me away like the physical space in between us might help and shook his head like he wasn't quite agreeing with himself. "I'll get my laptop. I was researching when you distracted me, *remember?*" he teased.

"I think you were quite pleased with that distraction," I called to him and was rewarded with a laugh as he strode down the hallway. Minutes later, he was back with his laptop bag as he set up the computer on the sofa.

"Hey, what you did before, when you turned into David... How will I ever know if someone is who they really are ever again?"

"I'll show you but it'll only help you recognise me. If someone else is shapeshifting or creating an illusion of someone else, you might not recognise what they are doing. Of course, sometimes they won't even disguise what they really are when they create an illusion. Amateurs make it easy."

"So, show me."

First, Evan asked me to focus on him. The two of us just stood there facing each other. I took in the scent of him, slightly citrus and fresh, and he helped me practise shifting my focus slightly. He explained if he were a witch, I might see the faint shimmer of magic emanating around him, but with daemons, it was all about the sixth sense. How I registered him was different to what I sensed in witches. Focusing on it just compounded that the periphery of my consciousness picked up naturally what other beings were as I recognised the different notes to register. When I focused on him truly, my skin broke into goose bumps.

"Do you feel me?" he murmured.

I nodded. "You're different from witches. I feel their magic in a different way." It was like there was a vibration in the air when witches were around and it made my skin tingle. The feeling I got from Evan was much different. Not frightening, but slightly unsettling like the feeling you get when you're trying to lie to someone who already knew the truth and you both knew that they knew. If the feel of Evan's magic left me slightly on edge, I wondered what it would be like if I met another daemon. Evan once told me that I'd be glad to never meet any others.

"Magic is like a fingerprint and now that you can tune into mine, you'll know when it's me. I'll look different, but you'll get my essence."

"So how come no one else does the same thing? Surely all the bad dudes will be taking a sniff of you." I shifted my focus back. Evan was smiling in a very self-assured way.

"You can register me because I'm letting you," he said.

"You can disguise it?"

"Yes, just in the same way that you can hide your magic." He didn't say it with reproach, though there was a hint in his voice that he was neither proud nor displeased that I had been able to disguise mine so well. I hadn't made much of an effort over these past few months; I simply hadn't used any magic of a strength worth disguising and the traces left behind faded quickly as a result.

Evan inhaled deeply and his eyes took on a slightly glazed look.

"Are you registering me?" I asked.

"Oh yes," he sighed. "But then, I did that a long time ago, and again, more deeply when I first saw you again. I have no intention of ever losing you again." Coming from anyone else that might have been creepy, but to me, it was a reassuring note. When I looked at him next, his eyes were back to bitter chocolate and he was looking at me with his teacher face. "You need to take your magic seriously. You need to guard yourself. You don't know what you'll come across and when."

"Even in Wilding?" I scoffed. "Where nothing happens?"

"Especially in Wilding," Evan said softly. Before I could ask what he meant by that, he stepped past me and pulled the door open, raising an arm to wave. Past him, I could see that another car had pulled up next to his and our visitors had arrived so my questions would have to wait.

CHAPTER NINE

I sat at the junction, letting the engine of my car idle while I decided which way to go. I should have been going straight home with the few bags of groceries on the seat next to me; but I'd caught the telltale whiff of magic that was luring me in another direction and I wasn't sure whether I should follow it. I could, of course, ignore it completely. I could take the handbrake off, step on the gas and motor home to wait for Étoile, Seren and David to bring their supplies of an entirely different nature. But this tug was strong and unrelenting.

Yesterday's roundtable (minus the round table) discussion hadn't pulled any punches. Even though Evan had pitched in his research on Chyler – it was amazing what you could find out about a person on the web if you just punched in the right keywords, apparently – and Étoile and Seren had been in touch with their contacts, we were firmly stuck on square one. What the Winterstorm sisters found out was hardly helpful.

They reported that Chyler had been dabbling in a darker magic, something her mom had been deeply concerned about. Eventually, it was reported that Chyler had simply said she was over the phase and wouldn't be messing about anymore. But evidence suggested Chyler had just gotten a little sneakier in what she was doing and continued to dabble.

On the day Chyler disappeared, Andrea was found sprawled inside a chalk circle with strange symbols painted around its edge, in the Anderson's attic room, a space that doubled as a living room slash study for magic. It was also where Chyler was being taught the basics of spell craft. With a knife planted through her heart, there had never been any chance of Andrea surviving. Instead, her death had been as fast as she bled out. Since there were no signs of defensive wounds, they surmised that she had been surprised by the attacker and unable to protect herself.

Andrea's coven sisters had suggested that if it were Chyler, and they claimed there was evidence to suggest that she had been the perpetrator rather than a victim. Andrea simply wouldn't have thought to protect herself from her daughter.

One thing working in Chyler's favour was that, even with the mounting evidence, the Andersons' coven sisters weren't completely convinced that Chyler was absolutely at fault. After a lot of arguing amongst themselves, the coven agreed that Chyler could be in trouble too and might be hurt or held captive somewhere. It wasn't much help in Chyler's favour but it was something. Using their connections to the Council, Andrea's family and the coven had requested help. But that still didn't explain to me why the Council seemed so keen to expend resources on a kid, not when they apparently faced enormous problems of their own.

The surviving family hadn't been able to shed any light on things either. Étoile or Seren had not managed to talk directly to them because the coven was shielding them to allow them to grieve privately.

It didn't escape my realisation that I might have been able to provide answers to some of those questions. Chyler was alive and well, even if her erratic behaviour was disconcerting. More to the point, she didn't seem to be anyone's captive, which suggested she was either innocent and afraid, or as guilty as hell.

A sharp honk behind me made me snap to attention. I flipped the blinker lights and, against my better judgement, turned the car away from the direction of home. Light rain had started to patter on the windscreen so I switched the wipers on to deal with it. After a moment, the lights went on too, seeing as the air was turning as dull and grey as the sky. I wanted a romantic winter image, not a reminder of the weather that trademarked London.

After everything was said, I knew I had to go and talk to Chyler. I let myself drive without thinking, just following that vague wisp of magic I'd caught a hint of back on the main road. I might have disguised her to others but there was no mistaking what I knew. When she showed up out of nowhere yesterday morning, Chyler had gestured that her living space was vaguely east of my house and my limited geographic knowledge of the area seemed to support that I were heading in the right direction.

I wasn't sure what I expected when I drew up in front of a modest bungalow with a neat yard on a spacious plot, but it definitely wasn't the poster home for clean neighbourhood living. Chyler said she was staying in an abandoned house so I got it into my head that it was probably some ramshackle old building. I couldn't have been more wrong. I parked by the white picket fence and got out, pulling my hood up over my head to keep my hair out of the drizzle.

A foreclosure sign swung on a post off to the left of the path. I walked through the open gate and went up to the front door. I knocked hesitantly, thinking of a back-up story for why I was on this doorstep in case I'd gotten it all wrong but, after a moment, Chyler opened the door.

"Oh," she said. "How'd you find me?" Chyler had changed into clean jeans and a red sweater that made me think of Christmas. She'd tackled the twigs in her hair and it shone blonde and glossy again.

"A good guess," I lied. "Can we talk for a moment?"

"Sure. Come in." She stepped aside so I could step past her into a broad hallway, then I followed her into the living room. The big pieces of furniture remained but anything personal was absent. I wondered where the people had gone and why the bank had taken the house back. I didn't have to wonder what it was like to lose a home; the pain of that was clear to me. "What's up?" asked Chyler, twirling a loose lock of hair through her fingers.

I decided to jump straight in with it. "You remember I said some friends of mine came all the way out here to see if you had tried to contact me."

"Uh huh. What did you tell them?" Chyler was doing her best not to look worried but I could see the telltale sign of her lower lip quivering and her jaw vibrate with the effort of keeping her mouth shut. She might have a roof over her head, but I didn't get the impression she was dealing with "life on the lam" so well.

"I didn't tell them anything, but I am worried about you. I don't think this is just about the book." The book had barely been mentioned, except in passing when Seren remarked that it was missing. Mostly, they discussed the dark magic Chyler had been suspected of practising; that, and her mother's death.

"What else could they possibly want from me? I know the other witches want it." Chyler sat on the big flowered couch, her knees together and ankles splayed in an ungainly way.

"I think they just want to find you, to know that you're okay. They want to know what happened."

"I'm okay. I just want them all to leave me alone."

I sat opposite her on a velvet-covered stool so that I wasn't looming over her. "Why don't you come back to my house? My friends might be able to help you."

"No way." Chyler shook her head emphatically. "Everyone is totally mad at me. And you know that when people are mad at witches, they do horrible things."

"Like what?" I pressed, which was silly because really, I, of all people, did not need to ask that. I'd been ostracized, teased and picked on and that was just by people who didn't have an ounce of magic in their bones.

"They'll set me on fire!" Chyler wailed, throwing her hands in the air, her face stricken. "And, like, that totally cannot happen. Do you know how much hairspray I have to use to make my hair look like this?

I am totally flammable!"

"Chyler, I don't think they'd do that."

"They might. Fire is the best way to kill a witch, everyone knows that. That's why those crazy Brotherhood dudes do it. I'm not risking it." Chyler leapt to her feet and paced the small room. She was shivering but it wasn't particularly cold inside. "How can I trust your friends? They might be tricking you. They might be just using you to get to me."

"They're not like that. And they won't kill you." At least, I was ninety percent certain they wouldn't.

Chyler harrumphed. "I'm not letting them take me prisoner. I'm free and I'm staying that way."

"I'm just asking you to talk to them so they can help you."

Chyler came to a stop in front of me and stared down, one hand on a hip. "I think you should go. I don't know if they followed you here."

"I swear they didn't."

Chyler just looked at me for a moment then sank down to the ground where she sat, rocking on her heels. "Why don't you stay with me?" she said in a little girl voice. I swear, she even fluttered her eyelashes at me. "We could go on adventures and travel anywhere we liked. There's no one to stop us."

"Except an entire nation of witches who are on the lookout for you," I pointed out tartly. I stood up abruptly, fed up with her near schizophrenic attitude to all the trouble she was in. Chyler nearly toppled over in my wake as I walked to the hall. "Look, don't do anything rash. I only came by to see if you'd come with me, but I'm not going to force you. Stay here until I figure things out."

I heard Chyler huff crossly but when I opened the

front door, she tottered after me, throwing herself at me. Right before I could throw up a shield, she surprised me with a tight hug before stepping back. "Thank you, Stella. I know you're trying to help me." She sounded so lost that I had half a mind to grab her hand and tug her back to my house and order her to get some help; but I had no right to do that, so I didn't.

I tried to smile reassuringly at her but Chyler just looked at me, then around her, blankly. She sauntered back to the open archway leading to the living room, turning around with a confused expression like she couldn't quite work out how she'd gotten from there to me. She paced the few steps back again and shuddered.

"So, you're not going to tell anyone where I am?" she asked, her eyes boring into me.

I shook my head, puzzled by her odd behaviour. "No, but stay put. Okay?"

"'Kay." And Chyler shut the door in my face.

~

Instead of heading straight inside when I got home, I stopped my car as soon as it was fully on the driveway and hopped out and went across the street.

"Hello stranger!" Annalise threw the door open with a wide smile and pulled me inside. I followed her into the kitchen past baskets full of materials and yarns of all colours and patterns. "I'm just making coffee and you are just in time to dish the dirt."

"There's no dirt." I laughed when she raised her eyebrows at me. "Okay, there might be some dirt. But I actually came by to see Gage and give him this." I held up the slim envelope of cash I'd gotten from the bank earlier. "I said I'd pay him back. Can I leave it with you?"

"You can leave it with him." Annalise pointed behind me and turned away just as I looked over my shoulder to see Gage padding towards us.

"Hey," he said and leaned down to kiss me on the cheek before ambling past. I blinked back surprise. I hadn't expected to see him, nor get a friendly kiss. Perhaps the finger-crushing incident hadn't bothered him at all. That said, I had to remind myself I was cross at him about that too, just not enough to say anything.

"Hi. I brought the money. For the paint," I reminded him.

"Just put it on the shelf there." Gage waved his hand at the shelf of pans over the range so I slotted the envelope in between pans so it stuck out a little. "Make me a cup, sis'," he said to Annalise.

"Coming up." Annalise was already pulling mugs out of the cabinet by her head and testing the pot with the back of her hand. "Still hot," she announced as she poured, then invited us to finish it how we liked. There was no standing on ceremony here.

"I almost forgot, I have something to show you, Stella." Gage set his mug down and loped out. I heard him take the stairs.

Annalise slipped into a seat and motioned for me to park myself. "And while he's out of the way, *who* is your house guest?"

"That would be Evan. You've seen a picture of him."

"Ahh, the boyfriend. You never did say where he'd been."

"I thought he was dead." I said, then backtracked a little. "At least, I assumed he might have been, but he wasn't and he's been looking for me." I sighed when Annalise looked at me with her eyebrows raised. Yeah, I wasn't making any sense. "Long story," I said.

"You don't say. And here he is?"

"Here he is."

"To stay?" pressed Annalise.

I shrugged. "I don't know. I don't think he's into small town living. He wants to go back to Texas."

"And you?"

I leant back in my chair. And me? That was a good question and one I'd tried to not focus on. "I was just starting to feel at home here."

"Then don't let a man take you away from that."

"Easier said than done."

"Always," agreed Annalise, "but take it from one who knows. If you try and change yourself for a man, or just give in to what he wants without thinking about what you want, nothing good will come of it."

"Sounds like you know what you're talking about."

"Better believe it, baby."

There was a thump upstairs like something heavy had just fallen on the floor and we both looked up.

"I was married once," Annalise said, surprising me. "And that did not work out well at all. I was miserable."

"I'm sorry."

"Oh, it was a long time ago, but what I'm trying to tell you is, that I'm glad I had a home to come to. Don't think I'm being all noble and poetic though. I like having a neighbour and I like you." She flashed a smile at me and, as if she caught my thought train, she added, "And whatever might or might not have gone on with you and my brother is nothing but your business to sort out. But I can't say I don't have the smallest hope that you might like him back, regardless of hot stuff over there."

Gage clattered down the stairs before I could answer. He held a thick red book in his hand and thumped it on the table between us triumphantly. "This is one of the family photo albums. You remember when Dad was keen on photography, Annalise? He'd bug us all the time taking pictures. Anyway, I remember him being keen on summer pictures and it occurred to me he might have taken some snaps of your parents."

"Seriously?" I had a few pictures, but not many. My eyes widened in hope.

Gage was thumbing through the book, then he came to a stop. "Here we are." He spun the book around and pushed it towards me, then leaned in to point. "That's me and Annalise. I'm clearly the cute one. Our mom and dad... and these two are your parents."

I drew the book towards me and gazed at them. It was a faded colour shot, slightly sepia with age. It had been snapped in front of Gage and Annalise's house and there was a little splash pool, which the children were in while the adults looked on. My parents were holding hands.

"This is amazing. Our parents knew each other."

Annalise nodded. "I remember bits but not much about your parents, more of an impression of them. That was a hot summer though. I got my new pink tricycle."

"There's more." Gage flipped over the page and I trailed my fingers down the sides of the cream card, careful to not touch the snaps as I drank them in. All in all, there were several pages with photos that featured my parents. One was a big party shot where my parents stood slightly to the centre. They were waving red, white and blue paper streamers. "Independence Day, probably," said Gage.

"Thank you." I smiled at him in absolute appreciation.

"I'll make copies of them, if you like?"

"I'd like that." I turned the pages again and started from the beginning.

"They came here a lot. I think our family sold them the house. It's not as old as ours, but I don't remember them building it so it must have been here before we were born, or when we were really little," Annalise said and Gage nodded.

"Did they, my dad's family that is, ever come out here?" I was pretty certain my mother's people wouldn't because they were in England somewhere, if any survived her, and Wilding wasn't exactly on the tourist map.

"I don't know. They might be in some of the old pictures but I don't know what they looked like, so I couldn't say for sure," answered Gage.

"Dad didn't keep the best notes," added Annalise.

I'd nearly forgotten about my coffee so I swallowed it and stood up. I had only meant to drop by for a few minutes, instead I clocked up thirty. "I'd be really grateful if you could make me some copies. I don't have many pictures and as I don't really remember them, anything that comes my way is a boon."

"I'll ask around, in case anyone else's family were friendly with them. They would have stood out so people should remember them, if they were known."

I saw Annalise throw Gage a sharp look. "What do you mean?' I asked.

"Oh, just that they were out-of-towners," Gage replied, almost too casually. He left the book open on the table and followed me towards the door. "I'll stop by with them in the next few days."

"Thanks."

"Maybe we could go out again soon?"

"Sure." I said, not entirely sure what he was asking me but he seemed to brighten a bit. Uh-oh. Maybe he meant a date.

"Are your friends staying long?" he asked, almost hesitantly, and quietly so Annalise couldn't hear him.

"I don't know. They have an open invitation."

"And Evan?"

"I don't know that either." I opened the door and, for a moment, I stood there in the threshold of the light against the grey. I knew Gage was fishing for more information and I wanted to turn and jog away, escaping so I wouldn't have to hurt his feelings. But I couldn't avoid him forever, and he didn't deserve to be ignored.

"He doesn't like Wilding much, huh?" Gage continued and I wasn't sure if he meant it as a statement or a question.

I frowned. "Why would you think that?"

"Seems like a city guy," Gage replied after a pause. I wasn't sure if that were an insult.

"Oh, well, I don't know. We'll have to see," I blustered.

"See you later, Stella." Gage bent down to kiss my cheek again and I stumbled back, waving a hand like an idiot. It was only when I got across the street and passed my car, which I parked, seeing as it seemed silly to roll it only a few feet forwards, that I noticed Evan standing on the porch. He was bent slightly at the waist so he could rest his hands on the freshly painted railings, watching me as I walked towards him. From there, he'd have had a great view across to Gage and Annalise's porch. I stopped by my car for a moment to scoop up the bags, steeling myself against any comments.

"Hey."

"Hey." I smiled. Seren's car was back which probably meant all three were waiting inside. Evan came down the steps and kissed me long and slow, resting both hands on my hips. Drawing back, I could see the purple flash of his eyes that made my spine tingle. With one hand, he took the bags, the other he slipped around me and steered me towards the house. "What took you so long?" he asked.

I didn't look back but I was fairly certain the gesture was as proprietary as it was affectionate, and a warning to Gage who I couldn't be sure wasn't watching. I held back from rolling my eyes. I'd never had two men stake a claim over me before, and I wasn't quite sure that I liked it.

"Errands to run. Took longer than I thought. Then I had to drop something off across the road and I stayed to have coffee." Which was largely true even if a little bit of me was uncomfortable about missing out a large chunk. A Chyler shaped chunk. Speaking of Chyler, something had been puzzling me.

"While you were gone, we came up with a plan," Evan began and I gave my attention to him.

"I'm all ears," I said as I shut the door behind us. "But can I use your laptop while you tell me?"

"Sure. It's in the kitchen."

"Thanks." I waved to the others who were hunched over a sheaf of printouts and they paused briefly to greet me before turning back to whatever they were looking at. Étoile blew me a kiss. "Part of the plan?" I asked Evan and he nodded.

The laptop was open and I sat down in front of it. "What's up?" Evan asked, leaning over me to watch what I was doing.

"I wanted to check something out about Chyler," I said, bringing up Google so I could do a search. Then it occurred to me there was a better way. "You know those sites you showed me, with lots of pictures of her as a cheerleader and stuff like that? Can you bring them up?"

"Sure." Evan put both arms around me to use the keyboard and I had to resist the urge to lay my head against his chest and snuggle into him. A few taps later and he'd brought up Chyler's high school website and opened another tab for a family page. I scrolled through the photos and just as I was about to brush off the niggling feeling, I worked out what was worrying me.

Chyler had such poise, an almost uncharacteristic elegance for a teenager. There was no way she was the type to sit, with her legs splayed, her back slightly hunched. It was upright, knees together, heels to slightly one side, and that was it. I sat back and frowned at the screen.

"What is it?" Evan asked.

I shook my head. "I don't know exactly." The more I thought about it, the more fantastic it seemed but the idea was fully formed now. I wasn't totally sure the Chyler I had been talking to was Chyler

Anderson at all, but the very thought of that was completely preposterous. Wasn't it?

"Do you have any candles?" David stepped into the room just as I saw the reflection on the screen of Evan's mouth as he started to ask me another question.

"Oh sure. Under the sink." I waved in its general direction. I'd picked up a cheap bunch of candles a few months ago on Annalise's advice as she said the power sometimes went out this far out of town.

David opened the doors and rummaged around for a moment and finally came up with a little bag of tea lights. "Hmm. I think I might need something more substantial. Can I use these anyway?"

"Sure." I clicked the red box in the corner of the browser to close the web pages and then I shut Evan's laptop, letting my fingers rest lightly on top of it for a moment. I swivelled in my chair to look up at him curiously. "What are they doing?" I asked.

"Something witchy." Evan sighed. "It's all part of the big plan."

"Why does David need candles?" I scraped back my chair and got up and Evan followed me into the living room, muttering something about how I really hadn't been taught anything. Yeah, like that was news.

"How's that my fault?" I hissed, coming to a stop in the doorway so that he almost bumped into me. "It's not my fault."

Evan held his hands up, then slowly brushed them down my sleeves until he could take my hands in his. He leaned into me, and murmured against my ear. "I'm sorry. I forget how little time you've had in our world."

"Again, not my fault," I whispered back, stepping

forwards, breaking our connection.

Evan put an arm across the doorframe to stop me from flouncing off so I stood still and waited, the heat of him at my back. "I know, but if you came back to Texas with me, you'd have better access to people who could teach you."

"I said I'd think about it, but not right now."

"No hurry," Evan said, withdrawing his arm barrier, but I got the impression that if he thought there actually might have been, or if I said the word, we'd be in his house the next time I opened my eyes. I let it slide, for now.

"What are you doing?" I asked, looking at Étoile and Seren when I entered the living room, with Evan only a pace behind me. The sisters were both sitting cross-legged on my floor, watching David who was marking out a large circle with white grains that looked like salt. I hoped he planned on vacuuming.

"We're going to call Chyler Anderson," said Étoile, looking up from her pieces of paper.

"On the phone?" I asked. Moron.

"With magic," Étoile confirmed.

"Ah. Are you sure no one's thought of that already?"

"I did a divination spell while you were out," said David, shaking the last grains to complete the circle. "She's in the area. You can only do this spell in short range."

"Oh." Hadn't my magic covered hers? I was starting to wonder if I would regret having done that.

"When she gets here, we can find out what's going on," added Seren, like I hadn't guessed that part.

"Are you sure this is the right thing to do?" All

three nodded back at me. I turned to Evan. "What about you?"

"It's the best plan we've got." Evan breathed out and his next words weren't exactly reassuring. "It's the only plan we've got."

"Why haven't you tracked her if she's close by?" I put a big emphasis on the 'if'.

"I can't. I don't have anything of hers to go on. I've never met her and I can't sense her magic. I think something's masking her."

Ah. Oops. I gulped. I was the one masking her, but I'd done it to protect her from everyone else.

"How come David could do the divination spell then?" I asked, wishing there were a textbook I could reach for rather than having to ask what everyone else clearly thought were dumb questions.

David took it upon himself to answer me. "It's more general. It doesn't give an exact location, just a rough area of where the person you're looking for is. It works within a twenty-mile radius. The good news is we were right in thinking she would look for you. I'm glad we found her first."

"So it's not specific... which is why you haven't shimmered in to get her? Like you did with me?" I asked Étoile and she nodded.

David was on his hands and knees shaking more grains into the shapes of strange symbols around the outside of the circle. Seren was following him, stooping down every so often to put a small tea light in the centre of each symbol. When they completed the circle, they stared down at what they had done; then David nodded, apparently satisfied.

"So, what's going to happen now?" I asked, looking at the thick white lines and the swirls and shapes.

"We'll do the spell to call Chyler and bring her to this circle. These symbols are protective." David pointed to the ones that looked like spirals; then to the others which looked like sand art to my untrained eye. "These other ones represent the elements – earth, wind, air and fire – and they're part of the calling."

"Oh." I really, really needed a textbook, and a crib sheet.

"The candles magnify the spell. Seren, I'm not sure these tea lights will be strong enough. Maybe we should get some bigger ones?" David checked his watch. "We won't do the spell until dusk, so there's plenty of time."

I wanted to ask why but I thought I'd already shown myself up as an absolute neophyte quite enough today; so I swallowed the question. Instead, I said, "There's a gift shop on Main Street that has lots of candles and things, or you could try Walmart."

"Seren and I will go together." Étoile moved so fast that I hadn't seen her come to a stop next to me. "Then David can finish looking through his spell book. See you later." She swished out the door, leaving Seren to gingerly close it behind her so that no draught would disturb their efforts.

After we heard the car start up, David settled himself on the sofa with a small leatherbound book. It had symbols etched deeply into the creased and cracked cover.

"What's that?" I asked.

David stopped flicking through the pages and looked up. "My family's spell book. I'm checking to see if there is anything else I should do."

"Can't you just ask it?" I asked, thinking about Chyler's book and how she seemed to communicate with it.

"It's not voice activated, Stella." David had taken on his teacher voice and sounded a little weary.

"Maybe Apple will make one," I teased before I skirted around the circle and went into my room, leaving him to his reading. After kicking off my shoes, I lay on my bed, looking up when Evan paused on the threshold.

"Are you okay?" he asked.

I nodded. "Just tired." I folded my hands behind my head and stared up at the ceiling, making an effort to get my thoughts back to where they had been. I couldn't help but feel something was horribly wrong, not just with Chyler but with the whole situation. However, just when the thought seemed close to developing into a fully formed one, it would disappear, leaving me a new trail to chase. I just couldn't add it up fast enough. Was Chyler really Chyler? Or was something much more dangerous at play?

I should have known to trust my intuition. My bad.

~

"Stella. Stella, wake up." A hand shook me lightly for the second time.

I cranked open my eyes and stifled a yawn. Being woken up was only slightly more annoying than realising I'd fallen asleep and wasted who knew how much time. Evan was hovering over me, a mug in his hand.

"I made you coffee, sleepyhead," he murmured and I felt the bed press down where he sat. "Though given the amount you drink, I'm surprised you can sleep at all."

I made a noise that was half yawn, half groan and deeply unappealing. "How long have I been asleep?"

"A couple of hours. It's nearly dusk, so I had to wake you." He was looking at the other side of the bed with fondness, like he regretted not climbing in and curling up instead. "Perhaps I shouldn't keep you up so late. How about an early night tonight?"

I smirked and shuffled onto my elbows so I was sitting up. I smoothed my hair, then rubbed consciousness into my eyes. "Easy, tiger. I don't usually sleep in the afternoon. I must have been really tired."

"We should take a vacation when this over. I'm partial to hot places."

"Anything to get away from Wilding, huh?" I couldn't help saying it.

Evan shook his head. "I'd be with you anywhere and I know we don't have to talk about it now, but just tell me you're still considering coming back with me. I'll make sure you have a good life. I'll protect you."

It was a warming idea and I leaned over to kiss him, because I really couldn't get enough of him. "I haven't said no, have I?" I grinned.

"No, you haven't." Evan stood up and stretched and I could see the muscles under his shirt work to keep up. As far as sights went, I'd add it to my list of things to see every day of the week. Too bad he had his clothes on. Oh, scrap that thought. I still needed to get up. "They're ready and waiting for us in your living room," he said, the corners of his mouth twitching upwards and I knew he knew I was blatantly admiring his physique.

"They're planning on cleaning up, right?" I asked as I followed him out and he just laughed.

My furniture was pushed back against the walls and the circle exactly as it was when I'd taken my impromptu nap, except the tea lights were gone. In their place were thick stubby candles, their blood-red hue in stark contrast to the white lines.

Étoile, Seren and David were standing in a way that picked out three corners and David motioned for me to take the last corner.

"What about Evan?" I asked. I looked behind me. Evan hadn't come any further into the room and was, instead, leaning against the wall with his arms folded like he was waiting for the show to begin. He was drinking my coffee.

"Not a witch, remember?" murmured Étoile.

"Oh, right."

"You don't need to do anything," said Seren. "David will say the spell and he'll draw power from us to fuel it."

"Stand here and look pretty. Got it."

Étoile smirked.

"Are you sure we should be doing this?" I asked, just as David opened his mouth. "I mean, won't she be pissed off that we're just summoning her? It's not like we're giving her a choice."

Seren shrugged. "If she's innocent, she needs help and we can help her."

"And what if she's not?"

"All the more reason to find her," Seren replied.

I felt my stomach drop a little further. When Étoile mouthed, "What is it?" I just shook my head. I didn't have a good feeling about any of this, but I couldn't protest. There was a piece of me that agreed with them. Whatever Chyler was going through, she did need help.

When Étoile, Seren and David raised their hands to waist height and stretched them out until we were almost touching fingertips, Étoile on my left and David on my right, I followed them. Then David started speaking and I stared at the flickering candle closest to me, trying to ignore the looming apprehension I felt. It didn't matter that I masked Chyler's magic if they found a way to locate her. I tried to quell the anxiety and tell myself that maybe they were doing the right thing. I couldn't help Chyler indefinitely. She needed much, much more than anything I had to offer.

I could feel the air rush past us to centre in the circle and it built up like a mini tornado, absolutely fixed to one spot. Not a single grain of salt moved from its place and, just when I felt like I might get sucked in too, the tornado parted so I could first see long, blonde hair; then a body; then, finally, acid pink heels.

"What's going on?" came Chyler's plaintive shriek. "Where am I?" She wheeled around, rooted to the spot until she fixed on me. "You! You did this? What have you done?"

Chyler took a step towards me, then stopped as she came to the edge of the circle, her eyes flickering to the symbols and their lit candle centrepieces. She held her hands up, touching it like she wasn't sure if she could move past it.

"You *summoned* me?" she snarled, her voice furious. "I told you to back off. I told you not to tell them about me!"

I glanced quickly in either direction. David had his eyes open but they were slightly glazed with concentration. I could feel power moving between the four of us like an open electricity circuit, fizzling and hissing. Étoile and Seren were still but watching Chyler as she jabbed a finger at me accusingly.

"I told you nothing good would come of the witches. They aren't here to help me..." Chyler broke off and her entire body shuddered so fast, it was like she was giving off a tremendous vibration. Her voice stuck in her throat and she went rigid for a second before the vibrating started again, like she was having a fit standing up. I could see the whites of her eyes as her irises rolled back.

Slipping my eyes slightly out of focus, I gasped. I could make out the shape of something not quite corporeal, seeming to edge from her body. This thing took on a translucent shape and I got the impression of dark, wavy hair and a face that appeared to be closer to thirty-something than Chyler's teens. The eyes fixed on me and it made a hideous screeching noise through its drainhole of a mouth. Through my fear, I got the impression of two distinct auras. Two witches.

"Stella," Chyler gasped, her hands clawing at her throat like she was being choked. "Stella, help me. She's in me. I can't stop her... I can't... Stella, *please*!"

The ghost woman whipped her way around the circle, Chyler in the middle, as if it were trying to find a way out. Then, without warning, we were blown back by some unseen force. The salt circle scattered and broke up, the candles skittering across the floor to snuff out. Étoile and Seren hit opposite walls and were scrambling to their feet. I was on my ass, looking up and David was flat on his back as Evan darted forward. His chest was heaving like he was taking a great gasp of air in readiness to pummel Chyler. I wondered if he could also see the dark presence that was coiling about her body, in wisps of smoke and shadows.

"Oh, Stella, help me," was Chyler's last wail as the thing wrapped around her, invaded her, and they both winked out of existence.

Evan was by my side in an instance.

"What the hell was that?" I gasped. Étoile and Seren seemed to have shaken themselves back to their senses and David had gotten to his feet. He was walking a little awkwardly over to Seren, straightening his glasses then rubbing a hand through his hair, his face guarded.

"That was an imposter spirit," said Evan, pulling me up so I could dust myself off. I was covered in salt sprinkles.

"Say again," I whispered.

"An imposter spirit. I'd guess a witch. She doesn't have her own body so she took someone else's."

I gaped at him. "You have got to be kidding me."

Étoile was shaking her head. "I've seen it before and it all ties in. Damn it, I should have seen this! We knew that Chyler was dabbling in dark magic. She must have called something up, or let something through, and it got into her. I bet it attacked her mother too."

That made my stomach turn over and I leant against Evan. Étoile had voiced exactly what my mind was trying to process. The schizophrenic nature of Chyler had been puzzling me. She behaved like a frightened, desperate young girl one minute; defiant

177

and devious, the next. I wondered if I were speaking to both of them at times, but which one had sought me out? I could understand if Chyler needed help, but what would an unincorporated spirit want from me?

"I can't believe I let her get away." David slapped his hand against the door in an unexpected fit of pique that made me jump. "I didn't make the protection symbols strong enough. I was just expecting a weak kid. She shouldn't have been able to blow her way through that or even disappear." He turned to the sisters. "Whatever we're dealing with, she's incredibly strong."

Seren nodded but when she turned to me, her face was hard. "Stella, I think you've got some explaining to do."

Étoile nodded. "She obviously knew you. Did you know she was here? Have you been helping her?"

I took a deep breath and nodded, preparing to be bawled out. "She came about a week ago, just before you all got here."

"Did you know what she was, what was inside Chyler?" asked Evan.

I shook my head. "God, no. No!" I put my head in my hands. What had I been thinking by not telling them? Only about how glad I was to see Evan and the relief that he was alive. How happy I was not feeling afraid every day. How I liked magic not dominating everything I did. No wonder I pitied Chyler, I was trying to protect her from the damage I'd been dealt. But I'd been saved from it and should have trusted the people who were there for me. I felt hot tears prick at my eyes and the shame of feeling so stupid.

It was Étoile who stood in front of me, pulling my hands away from my face. Softly, she said, "Stella, we

need to talk."
Uh-oh.

CHAPTER TEN

The kitchen table was rapidly becoming my least favourite place in the house. At least it was right now. Everyone was seated around it, all of them staring silently, questioningly, at me.

I breathed deeply. I could feel the cabinet doors begin to rattle in solidarity with my anxiety, but it wasn't until the glasses flew out of the cupboard and dashed towards the floor that Étoile took my hand in hers.

"You can control this," she said. Out of the corner of my eye, the glasses hovered a foot from the floor, seemingly unsure of whether to smash or not. I saw Evan nod at them and they floated back to the cabinet from where my magic had flung them.

I forced myself to pull my magic inside where it belonged, and around me the doors began to settle down. It didn't escape my notice that this was the first time in a long time that I'd been anxious enough for something like this to happen, but as far as accidents caused by me went, this was small fry.

"Tell us what happened," Étoile urged and I didn't need her to add, "so we can fix this mess."

I forced myself to meet her eyes. "Like I said, Chyler came to see me a week ago and she was afraid. I told her I would look into things and try and help her." I pulled back from Étoile to spread my hands across the table and leaned forward. "I had no idea you were looking for her then and she was terrified."

"But you knew when we came to visit," Seren protested. "We told you we thought she would try and get in touch with you."

"And I bet you didn't tell me the whole truth either." I threw the words at her like an icy slap.

Seren had the good grace to look guilty.

"I didn't think so." I shook my head, tired. *Witches.* "I've only seen Chyler a couple of times since you came."

"Did you put the masking spell on her?" David asked and I nodded. "How did you do it? I never taught you to do that."

"I just kind of felt it and pushed the magic at her. It was... automatic."

David's eyes widened in surprise, and what I thought was a glimmer of admiration. "You didn't say a spell at all? Interesting." Whatever I thought I saw, however, soon faded into a wary expression as he rubbed his thumb against his jaw, lost in thought.

"When did you see her again?" Seren asked.

"When I was out running. Some mornings, I run and she just appeared when I was taking a breather. That was the day after you came. And I found out where she lived so I went to check on her today."

Seren latched on to the first bit of my confession. "So she could find you?"

I nodded. "She has some sort of book that helps her do stuff. She said it was the family spell book and that's how she found me. And I can find her; her magic isn't masked to me."

Étoile and Seren exchanged a look and I asked, "What is it?"

Étoile pursed her lips and I could feel her thinking before she added. "A family spell book is tied to the family. An imposter shouldn't be able to access it, unless..."

"Unless, Chyler is still here," Seren finished, her eyes far away in thought.

"I don't understand."

"You can't use a spell book unless there's express permission from the keeper of the book, and, even then, it wouldn't necessarily work. The keeper would have been Andrea, Chyler's mom, and she wouldn't have offered it up to something as dark as that imposter. But with Chyler as the keeper, that's a different story," explained Seren, Étoile nodding in agreement at her side. "But what I really mean is, there must be some part of Chyler still there or the book would be of no use at all."

"I'm sure I spoke to Chyler sometimes, but other times, she acted so strangely. That must have been the imposter," I surmised, trying to think this through logically. "So this witch wants... the book? Why? Doesn't she have her own?"

David took up the story. "Not all witches have spell books; plus, when a witch dies, it passes on to her descendents and her power goes with it. Old books like the Andersons' are stuffed with power that the next generation can tap into. It would be quite attractive to someone dangerous, someone who wanted to come back even more powerful than they ever had been."

"She said that other witches wanted it too; her aunts, for example."

David nodded. "That's also quite likely. They would be able to use the book; but they can't be the keeper because they aren't direct descendents of the keeper and that's where the biggest draw is. Do we know if any of the aunts died recently?"

Everyone shook their heads.

"What has someone dying got to do with anything?" I asked.

"This spirit that's got Chyler is almost certainly dead. It needs a body and this particular body can access that book," replied Étoile. "Chyler is the keeper. She's got the potential for enormous power now. The spirit hit the supernatural jackpot."

"At the risk of sounding freaky, Chyler said the book helped her out, told her what to do. Why would it do that if she were possessed?"

David didn't seem that surprised by my question. "It's probably that the book *is* helping Chyler. I've often thought that books take on a kind of persona of their own when they get old enough and suck in enough power. It's all to do with the power they've absorbed – perhaps something of the ancestors coming through to help their descendents."

I raised my eyebrows sceptically. "So there is a chance we can still help Chyler?"

"Possibly. If you're certain you've spoken to her, and not this spirit each time, and the book is helping her, then Chyler is fighting back. We might be able to separate them and banish this thing," said David.

"I'm sure I spoke to Chyler. She didn't even know

her mother was dead."

"That's possible," agreed David. "She was probably possessed when it happened."

I had to ask, "And what if we can't separate them?"

"It's simple: Chyler dies, at least, the Chyler everyone knows does and she'll be taken over completely. Her body will live, but her soul will be gone."

I, for one, did not like the sound of that.

"How do we find her?" Étoile asked our little assembly. "She'll be prepared for a summoning spell again. It won't work."

David nodded. "She won't come back here willingly. As soon as she, this spirit, is in control of Chyler again, she'll be getting the hell away from here..."

"I know how to find her though," I interrupted brightly. "I might have masked her magic, but I can still trace her. I went to see her at an abandoned house about three miles from here. She's been staying there."

"That doesn't mean we'll get anywhere near her. She'll be on the alert for us," pointed out Seren and my shoulders dropped as she continued, "Plus, the chances of Chyler trusting us are slim, that is, if we even speak to her and not the imposter." So much for my great plan.

"I can get her," said Evan. He avoided looking at me so far and instead watched us parry, his arms folded, his face blank. "She wasn't here long enough to take much notice of me and she's only expecting witches, so I might slip through. Now I know where she is, I can get her and bring her here."

"Can we help her?" I didn't know what it would take to get Chyler back to normal, if it could even happen, but I wanted to help. It was my mess and I wanted to fix it before anything bad happened... anything worse, if that were possible.

"We can, but not on our own." Étoile looked sad and I had a sinking feeling about what she was going to say next. "We just don't know how strong this spirit is, or who it is. We need to call the Council."

"I don't want any members of the Council here," I said, but my voice was just a whisper.

"I don't think we have a choice. Not if we want to help Chyler." Étoile didn't seem particularly enthusiastic either. "They asked us to investigate. They will help."

"Why would they? I don't see why they're so interested in Chyler?" I asked, looking between them, trying to read something from their faces.

"Andrea's mother is a Council member. She was the one who called us. We can trust them," Étoile replied.

"Can we?" I muttered.

"This time," said Seren, which wasn't exactly reassuring.

"We need to go." David pushed his chair back from the table and stood up. "Chyler's not going to come back here and we need to get in touch with the Council members and see who we can call in. We need a stronger magic and we need to find out exactly who this spirit is before it's too late."

"Does it really matter who it is?" I asked.

David nodded. "Yes. A name will help us target the spells better. It will make them more effective."

"Do you need me to come too?" It was a half-hearted offer but I felt I should make it. Any fear or apprehension I felt, I'd just have to swallow. A part of me was arguing that it was more important to help Chyler than to keep hiding away. What was the point of my power if I didn't use it for good?

"No, you stay here," said David with a surprising firmness as he pushed his glasses back onto his nose. I got the distinct impression that he and I were on the outs, though he didn't seem as furious as Evan was. Out of the corner of my eye, I could see Evan's posture tense, his fists flexing.

"Just hang tight," said Étoile, rising to join him and her sister. "We'll come back soon. We'll need you."

"Okay." I waited until they left the kitchen, their footsteps echoing through the hallway into the living room, before I turned to Evan who sat still and silent next to me. I had some apologising to do. Apologising stunk.

"Evan, I..."

"You lied to me, Stella. You knew they were looking for Chyler and you hid her." Anger rolled off Evan in waves that crashed into me. "Why would you do that? Why didn't you trust me?"

"Why can't you trust me now?" I pleaded. "Chyler came to me for help and I said I would help her. She was all alone."

"You could have turned to any one of us, anytime, but you didn't. Even if you didn't trust them... I get that, I do. I get what you feel about the Council, but you didn't trust me?"

"I know. I'm sorry, I should have come to you. It was stupid not to."

"How were you planning on helping her anyway?

And what if you got trapped by your heart, instead of thinking with your head, Stella? The longer this thing is in Chyler, the stronger it will get and the less there will be of Chyler. What if you were there when that happened and you couldn't defend yourself?" Evan threw the chair and paced to the back door before looking back at me, fury contorting his face. "Have you any idea the amount of danger you put yourself in?"

"I know now." I swivelled to follow him with my eyes as he paced.

"You put all of us in danger today," Evan continued like he hadn't heard me. "You heard David. His protection circle wasn't strong enough to cope with something like that. They thought they were summoning a frightened kid and look what they got instead! If Chyler weren't still fighting, we might not be here right now."

"I said I was sorry." My voice etched upwards, towards a whiny pitch.

"I can't deal with this." Evan's jaw shook like he wanted to yell, or thump something, and there was something disturbing in his eyes that bothered me. "I'm going to follow the others into town."

"Wait! You're leaving?" I stood up like I could possibly stop him when in my bare feet, I barely reached his shoulders. More than that, his power was phenomenal compared to mine. He even showed that through the control he exercised in keeping his anger checked, though barely.

"I can't stay here right now. I'm so... mad at you." His voice was low and laced with disappointment.

Before I could ask him if he were coming back, he was gone. He didn't walk out, he didn't slam the doors or knock anything over in a fit of pique. Instead, he simply vanished, taking a rush of air with him. A moment later, I heard the engine of a car starting up and I rushed through the house in time to see his car peel out of my driveway. I stood and just watched him leave, knowing there was nothing I could do.

After the red flash of his taillights were gone, I finally turned around. The salt was still there, strewn across the room like a breeze had whipped through a sand dune but Evan's things – his jacket and the ever-present book he was currently reading were both gone. I went back through to the kitchen. Yes, his laptop, too. Everything was gone. I stomped back to the living room and rested against the wall, looking at the mess.

With a flick of my head, I made it all disappear, using my magic to set the candles in a row on the mantelpiece. I channelled my anger into physically pushing the furniture back to where it should be. The resentment inside me threatened to bubble over into acute pain as I shoved the sofa into place. I didn't want Evan to leave and there he was, walking away without listening to me. He hadn't even said if he were coming back.

I couldn't help feeling like something had shifted and things would never be quite right again, never as uncomplicated as the days when our relationship had begun. I couldn't help scoffing at myself. It was funny to think of those days as uncomplicated, when they were really anything but. Now, however, well, it felt like the whole game had changed and I wasn't sure if Evan was still on my team, which flew right in the face of finally feeling at peace with myself.

I put my head in my hands and cried, alone again.

~

There was an unpleasant sense of déjà vu in the waiting but wait I did. I sat and waited, and pottered around the house, but they didn't come back. After a while, I felt the fury creep up on me. I could either be the girl who sat at home and cried, feeling sorry for herself, or, even though my heart felt like it was breaking, I could pull my proverbial socks up and get on with things. Because the world wasn't going to wait for me. Sitting at home, wailing, wasn't going to bring Evan back.

I did the next best thing I could do. I went across the street, dragging my feet like they were concrete weights, to see if Annalise was home.

"Well don't you have a face like a wet weekend," said Annalise, taking in my red-rimmed eyes, beckoning me to come inside and take a seat amidst a pile of yarn. I introduced her to the idiom "wet weekend" a few weeks ago and she thought it was hilarious.

"What are you doing with all this?" I held up a clutch of brightly coloured balls and resisted the urge to sniffle.

"Making knitting kits for the Christmas fair and you can help me. You look like you need to stay occupied." Annalise passed me a heap of plastic bags, which were already stickered with her logo and showed me how to pull a pattern leaflet from the heap on the coffee table, then add needles and a selection of yarn. I packed a few kits quietly and held them up for her approval before Annalise asked me, "So, what's going on with you? I've been watching you guys coming and going all week."

"Well, they're staying in town so they're in and out, and right now they're out," I said sullenly.

"I saw Evan leave in a hurry," Annalise said slowly. I looked up in alarm. I wondered if she'd seen him appear out of nowhere on the drive or if he'd just appeared in the driver's seat. But if she saw anything out of the ordinary, she didn't say.

"That he did." I agreed, looking around. "Is Gage here?"

Annalise shook her head, no. "Just us two, so if you need some girl talk... Well, he won't be butting in."

"I feel like I'm messing up," I confessed after a moment of silence while I gathered my thoughts. "I never thought I'd see Evan again and then he was back and now he's mad at me and he just walked out."

"Did he say he was coming back?"

I shook my head. "But he didn't say he wasn't either."

"Why'd he go?"

"He's mad that I kept something from him."

"Like kissing my brother?" Annalise asked, with a wink.

I blushed the same shade of raspberry pink yarn I was about to package. "No, and for the record, nothing else happened between us."

"Hmm."

"Hmm, *nothing*," I said emphatically. "Gage fell asleep at my house, that was all. Honestly, Annalise. I feel really bad about it because I know he likes me, but there's Evan and... I just feel bad about it, okay?" I choked back a tear and took a few deep breaths to calm myself.

Annalise opened her mouth like she was about to say something, then closed it again and stuffed a few more yarn balls into packets. Finally, she said. "He really likes you, you know."

"I know but I can't worry about that right now." I tried to put a wall between the guilt I felt at liking Gage a little too much, and the other me that had other problems to contend with as I said, "Please understand."

"Bigger problems, huh?"

"Something like that."

"So tell me more about Evan and your friends. Where did you meet them?"

I gave her the short, condensed, palatable-for-humans version. I first met Étoile in London and went with her to New York to meet friends of my parents. There, I'd been given the documents for my house. I stayed with Étoile at a house where I then met Evan. But through all that, I was hazy about details, intimating there had been an accident and we'd gotten separated and unable to find each other temporarily.

I left out the bits about the Brotherhood, the magic, the destruction… The deaths. When I finished my vague account, Annalise looked at me as if she knew there were some other back story I hadn't mentioned, but she didn't pry.

"I really didn't think I'd ever see them again. I feel like I've put roots down here." I finished, wiggling my toes in my boots like they might shoot tendrils into the ground.

"And your friends arriving put a kink in all of that?"

I sighed. "I'm so thrilled to have them here, but

what I want isn't quite what they want."

"What do they want?" Annalise sealed another bag and tossed it in the box with a pile of others, before reaching for the next one to start all over again.

"Evan wants me to go to Texas with him, where he lives," I answered, even though it wasn't quite the question she asked.

Annalise looked up sharply. "That's a long way, honey."

"That's what I said."

"Are you going?"

"I said I'd think about it, but right now, he's not talking to me."

"Men," scoffed Annalise. "And they think we're complicated."

"Right." I nodded in agreement.

"Here's what I think, and take it or leave it, or whatever. I think you should do what's best for you. Don't go because Evan wants you to and don't stay because Gage wants you to either. If you like it here, stay, but that doesn't mean you can't ever leave. You've got a car. There are planes and trains. You can go back to London, or to Texas or wherever you want. You've got friends here now and you've got friends elsewhere too. True friends will work around what you want. They won't just ditch you because you aren't doing what they want. Ya got me?" She sucked in a breath and gave me a lopsided grin, pink highlights dropping around her face.

"I got you."

"Feeling better?"

"A bit."

"Good because we have twenty more kits to put

together. I'll make you dinner if you're a good girl and don't complain."

"Deal."

When I finally threw my last kit bag of yarn in the box, Annalise happily high fived me and picked up the box to stow in a corner of the room.

"You know, you could sell this stuff online," I pointed out, looking at the heap of boxes with Annalise's latest creations. I didn't know how she managed it all. It wasn't just the selling of it, but the motivation to create such volume of skilled craftwork repetitively that awed me.

"Don't you start, too. Gage has been bugging me to do that ever since I started this business, but I like getting out and meeting people and seeing them pick up my stuff and loving it." Annalise turned to me, waving a finger. "It stops me staying at home, at any rate. I may be a homebody but I don't want to be a hermit. Speaking of which, you need to get out more."

"Oh, thanks." I could pretend to be chagrined all I liked, but she was right. I was restless. I wasn't working. I wasn't in education. Yeah, I had money but I didn't want to blow through it, especially with a house – not to mention taxes – and a never ending list of things to fix in it.

I thought again about Evan's offer of living with him and getting enrolled in the university there. It was tempting. I thought about enrolling in a local college here. Temptation struck again. I had options and that was a good thing, if only the magic business would butt out.

I ate dinner with Annalise that night and I was helping her clear the dishes as Gage rushed in like a whirlwind, slamming the door behind him. I saw his jacket fly off and hit the couch in a heap then the thud thud of his boots kicked off by the door.

"Annalise, we've been called to the Loup. We have to go now. I'll drive," he shouted from the front door.

Gage had half unbuttoned his shirt while walking through the living room and was just in the process of pulling it over his head, revealing a tanned swathe of muscle, when he caught sight of me. That didn't stop him. He just pulled his shirt off and grinned at me while I couldn't do anything but get an eyeful of his torso. I didn't know if the universe were telling me that life could be easy; or, when I thought about Evan, very hard.

"Evening." He grinned at me while I bit my lower lip.

"Hi, Gage." I nodded at him, turning away to dry my hands on a dishtowel. I took my time folding it onto the counter, keeping my eyes to myself.

"We have to go now?" Annalise asked, with a slight hint of dismay in her voice as her eyes flashed towards me.

Gage shrugged, sending his muscles up and down in a rather eye-catching way. "They'll wait ten minutes."

"What's going on?" I asked, wrenching my gaze away from his abs which I most definitely shouldn't have been looking at, never mind feeling anything close to lust. It was anger I told myself, anger at Evan. Not Gage. Not *much*.

"Oh, just this thing we have to go to," Annalise replied dismissively.

"At the Loup?" I asked. "The Loup Garou?

That's the bar down the road?"

Gage nodded. "I'd invite you, but it's not my call." He didn't look like he was about to invite me, or that he was even that sorry that he couldn't.

"Oh, I wasn't asking myself along," I backtracked. "Besides, I need to be heading home."

"It's not a very nice place anyway, Stella. You won't be missing anything," Annalise added, then to Gage. "Stop posturing and get changed already."

When Gage laughed, his muscles heaved, lifting firm pecs that were right in my line of vision. Sigh.

"I saw you outside there, when I was driving back a few nights ago," I said.

Gage looked surprised, then shrugged. "I go there sometimes."

I didn't tell him I saw Annalise's car. It was a given; if I'd seen him and her car, then she was there too.

"So, I'll see you tomorrow?" said Annalise, steering me towards the door. I wondered what was so important that they had been called there, something so important that they didn't even seem to want to tell me.

"Sure. Let me know if you want a hand with any more stuff." I said to Annalise as I picked up my jacket and zipped it up. "Have a lovely evening."

"Oh, we will," said Annalise but her cheery smile didn't quite reach her eyes and I thought I heard the hushed start of an argument form just as I closed the door.

As it turned out, I didn't see anyone for two entire days. Gage's motorbike was long gone by the time I got up in the morning – and it wasn't like I was a late riser – and I didn't hear him return in the evenings.

When I called by on the second day, Annalise didn't answer the door but her car was where she always parked it when she was at home. So I didn't know if she were out with someone else, or just avoiding me. I hoped for the former.

I didn't see Étoile, Seren or David and I wondered what they were doing and whether it involved Chyler and if she were okay.

Evan didn't come back.

The anger I'd felt when Evan walked out simmered into frustration before bubbling over to rage the longer I thought about it. Evan knew how terrified I'd been when they left me alone in those days after Eleanor Bartholomew's attack. I couldn't imagine why he would leave me alone now unless... The thought was an unpleasant one. Maybe he wasn't coming back at all.

I could have driven into town to confront Evan, but I wasn't big on confrontations and, as I'd never had relationship niggles, I didn't know if this kind of behaviour were normal or not. I was veering towards *not* okay. Besides, it wasn't like I knew where he was and even if I scryed, it wouldn't be specific enough to give me an address, just the general area.

Instead, I stomped around the house like a stroppy teenager, wondering if I felt sick with sadness, anxiety, or grief over the potential end of a relationship that really hadn't been given a decent chance to thrive. On top of that, I was mad that Evan didn't try to understand where I was coming from at all. Most of all, I just wanted him to come back.

Above all that, I worried about Chyler and how she was faring. She had come to me for help and, so far, all I'd done was keep secrets from my friends, hurt my boyfriend and irritate the spirit that was jostling for space inside her. At least I'd discovered one thing: there was a good chance Chyler was innocent of killing her mother. Unfortunately, that probably meant she was sharing body space with the real killer.

I wished I had a computer so I could do my own research and eventually, I decided that that was what I would do. So I grabbed my bag and coat, added scarf and gloves, and drove away from Wilding to do some shopping.

First, I parked in a small strip mall that held a chain electronic goods shop. After an hour, I purchased a small laptop and a little device that I could plug in to connect me to the internet. Then I bought a cell phone because I was tired of having no way to contact anyone. After depositing my bundles in the trunk, I went into the gift shop a few shops down and bought Christmas presents. This was such a rare treat for me to do, that I spent over an hour browsing candles and photo frames and other knick-knacks.

Eventually, I bought some earrings for Annalise and a little trinket box with roses painted on the lid because she liked flowers, and a photo frame for Gage for one of his father's pictures. I hesitated, wondering if I should get gifts for anyone else, then decided I'd done enough for one day. I paid and went home to play with my new toys.

With the rest of the day to my lonely self, I assembled my shiny new phone and set it to charge. Then I set up my laptop, fumbled with installing the software and checked out the lengthy instructions for the internet gadget. I wondered if I could have used magic to create a wireless connection, or if utilities were out of my capabilities.

I also wondered if I would ever be able to answer my own questions or if I'd always be a novice witch who stumbled her way through magic, hopeful, but never one hundred percent sure. Eventually, I packed everything in and curled up alone in my bed, too tired to think anymore.

~

I awoke at midnight by a howl, high and long. I just cursed under my breath, shoved a pillow over my head and went back to sleep. In the morning, I put my lethargy down to skipping a few days of running. I alternated between being cross, trying to think of ways to help Chyler, and, frankly, just sulking. Back in London, I used to walk all over the city, not just to save money, but for the health benefits. I was out of my dingy flat almost every single day.

By contrast, since I'd been in Wilding, I'd been very sedentary. I lounged around the house and, when I needed to go into town, I drove since it was too far to walk. The effects were going to very evident on my hips if I didn't break the pattern soon.

So, when I stretched on the front porch just as the first light was breaking, I felt good, positive even, that I was pursuing my resolve to get some exercise and keep myself fit. It was good for my soul, not to mention my thighs. Dressed in comfy sweatpants and a zip-up top that fit like a second skin, I was already itching to get outside for my run. I wanted to burn off the nervous energy building up inside me.

Standing in front of the bathroom mirror, I twisted my hair into a ponytail high on my crown and fastened it with a band. I was feeling pumped. My anticipation of a run was setting my adrenaline flowing and I felt like I could run for hours. Realistically, however, I just hoped I could make it a few miles without passing out or straining a muscle.

I stepped off the porch, swinging my arms in circles to limber up my shoulders, then stretched my legs. Across the road, my neighbours' house was dark and I guessed they weren't awake yet. Judging from the quiet stillness, I was the only thing awake in the whole area. The silence sometimes struck me as eerie but I brushed the feeling to one side and jogged out onto the road, turning away from town.

As per usual, I had the whole road to myself. This way led out to back roads that eventually connected to the interstate and wasn't well travelled. There was a more direct route that led out of town, which the locals preferred for the obvious time and gas-saving reasons. I could only assume that my parents had bought this house for the solitude because it certainly wasn't for the swinging social life.

Starting off slowly, I eased my body into a rhythm so I could jog along the road at an even pace. Eventually, I started putting distance, and speed, between my house and me, the cold morning air fighting with the heat I was generating. My muscles felt warm and willing; though I wasn't sure I wouldn't feel the after effects for the rest of the day.

It was pretty out here, now that fall was turning to winter as fast as the leaves could slip from the trees. The quiet was so breathtakingly different from my city life that, though it had taken some time, I was learning to love it, to find it refreshing.

A mile in, I'd only just started to regret not bringing my music player when I heard a noise off in the woods to my left. I glanced over, saw nothing, and pounded on. The rustling stayed with me, even when I increased my pace. Stray dog, said my brain. When have you ever seen a dog around Wilding? said the rational part of my brain. Maybe it was a bear? Oh, God. Bears attacked people. Did bears even live out here?

I felt my chest constrict in panic as the rustling seemed to fan out. I was sure Annalise or Gage would have warned me about big, scary animals. I remembered when, months ago, I was walking home and the world seemed to freeze around me, making me listen intently for whoever followed me. As it turned out, that was the night the Brotherhood caught up to me, but I'd been saved just in time.

The rational part of my mind told me they couldn't have found me here. Even so, I started edging into the middle of the road just as I could see the tree line start to thin out slightly. I wanted to put more space between the dense undergrowth and me and whatever it concealed. Further ahead, but not much, were the broad, wide-open grassy plains that stretched on and on, without a house in sight for miles. What was I doing? I should be turning back to my house, not carrying on into the nothingness. But I was too freaked to stop entirely, so I paused and jogged on the spot for a moment, then bent forward, hands on knees to catch my breath, tensing, ready to sprint.

Behind me I heard a growl, a plaintive rumbling noise that sent a shiver of fear down my spine, seeping through me. Slowly, I turned around and stared in surprise at my audience, my jaw threatening to drop open as I sucked back the fear.

A pack of wolves were staring at me. Half a dozen or so milled about in the road and I could see more, edging from the woods, sniffing at the grass verges and the asphalt, watching me all the time. The biggest in the pack stepped forward. Thick black fur covered its head and its ears flicked forwards and backwards. A mantle of grey fur framed its chest and spread down its front legs. It seemed unfeasibly large for a wild animal. It raised its nose to sniff the air, then focused its eyes firmly on me, a low growl erupting in its throat. Then its lips rolled back over gleaming teeth. I didn't know whether to step back or stand my ground.

One of the wolves prowling by the tree line stepped tentatively onto the road and thrust its head to the sky, emitting a long, loud howl. That stirred up the others, rumbling growls sounding from chests to throats. The big wolf in front of me, the alpha male I guessed, took another step forwards and barked once. Silence settled over the wolves as they shuffled into a pack aimlessly across the road, cutting off my route home. There was simply no way I could get past them and I couldn't keep running in the opposite direction. There was nowhere to go. Running wasn't even an option – no way could I outrun any member of the pack.

The big wolf moved another step closer to me and I braced myself. Rooted to the spot, I couldn't move backwards, I couldn't move forwards, so I dropped my eyes submissively. I didn't want them to think I was challenging them, especially when there was a good chance that they would... eat me. It wasn't the cold that made me shiver this time; it was out and out fear. The wolf thrust its head forwards and sniffed again, its nose quivering as it locked onto my scent.

Another wolf, a smaller one, stepped up alongside the black and grey wolf's flank, its movements elegant and fluid. It took a long look at me before sitting back on its haunches on the cold road in a manner that made me feel slightly less terrified. Its coat was a lustrous grey and... Were there flecks of pink edging its coat? Odd.

Forgetting that I didn't want to give off any threatening signals, I glanced surreptitiously at the smaller wolf and its strange fur. It simply looked back at me, its tongue lolling over its lower jaw, panting. I couldn't help the feeling that there was something awfully familiar about it. I felt my heart thud with anxiety and my muscles tighten as a familiar feeling started teasing my veins and I summoned my magic.

The big wolf sniffed the air again and took a step towards me. It growled and the smaller wolf nipped at its flank with a glint of large, white, super-sharp teeth. With another step forward, the black and grey wolf closed in, leaving only a few steps between us. If I had knelt down and stretched I could probably have touched the tip of its nose. I didn't, of course, because I wasn't stupid.

The pack made no moves to leave; instead, more were coming forth and the road was teeming with them. Some were black and grey like the alpha, but some had solid coats and some were much paler with glittering black eyes that calmly assessed me. I was so close to the alpha that I could see my reflection in his eyes.

There was no telling what they might do. If they attacked now, I'd never survive. I'd be shredded and my death would be slow and painful.

Around me, it felt like the air was losing oxygen, leaving me dizzy as I tried not to hyperventilate with fear. Without thinking, I stepped backwards and the wolf moved forwards again. His movements were so graceful, like he knew he owned the road. It strained its head towards me and curled back its mouth to reveal a set of teeth that looked brutal.

I felt my magic tickle my skin as it reached the surface, then flow readily throughout me and finally dance all over my body. The wolf growled a low sound that rumbled through him and squared its shoulders. Its legs were also tense, like it was poised to launch itself at me.

I took a deep, dizzying breath and got the hell out of there with a great surge of willpower and an even bigger surge of magic that cracked like a whip in the space I left behind.

As soon as I materialised in my living room, I lurched to the front door and tested the handle. Still locked, and the keys were in my pocket. I leant against the door, rasping breath back into my lungs. What the hell did I see out there? No one ever mentioned a pack of wolves roaming in the woods outside my house. It struck me that the pack weren't afraid of humans. Instead, they seemed to make it very clear that they were claiming control of their territory and I was the invader.

I guessed it explained why there weren't any animals out here; they'd just be dinner. At least I wasn't dinner, or breakfast as the case may be. Relief swept through me at my ability to use my magic to get out of there. Even though it was something I avoided using on such a scale over the past few months, it had come to me swiftly and easy. At least, I hadn't lost the knack of it. Perhaps it was time to fully embrace what I could do.

I breathed slowly – in and out, in even breaths – while I tried to organise my thoughts. I'd had the strangest sensation while I was facing them. I thought, no, I felt, that I *knew* the wolves and that couldn't be possible at all. It was uncanny that my senses seemed to register them on some level.

I shrugged off my pants and top and folded them onto the chair in my bedroom, clinging to my relief at being home safe and unhurt. The thoughts were still percolating in my brain when several knocks, quick and in sharp succession, sounded at the front door. It was rather too early for visitors. I pulled on my jeans and a check shirt, buttoning it quickly. Then I padded barefoot to the door as I came to a very strange conclusion. There was no way I could describe what I felt, nor what I was sure was true. It was so far out of my frame of reference that I almost laughed at myself.

When I looked through the peephole, my thoughts on the edge of surrealism, I wasn't all that surprised by who my early morning visitor was. I flipped the lock and opened the door.

Gage stood in front of me, his hair dishevelled, with his usual few days of stubble covering his jaw. He had apparently dressed in a hurry wearing jeans, an untucked tee, work boots and a padded vest, unzipped. He looked wild and unpredictable. I eyed him for a long moment while he coolly glanced over me from head to foot, like he was making a new, and not altogether pleasant, assessment of me.

"What are you?" I asked at last, suspending all that I knew for all that I didn't.

I hadn't expected him to answer my question with a question, but I should have seen it coming.

"What exactly are *you*?" he growled.

CHAPTER ELEVEN

We stood there on the doorstep staring at each other coolly for a moment, longer than what was really comfortable, before I stepped back and let Gage walk over the threshold and into my domain. My mind argued with my heart loudly over this one but my heart prevailed. I'd been living opposite Gage for months and he and Annalise were my friends – I thought they were my friends, at least – and we'd lived without incident for all that time, so there was no reason to be afraid of him. My mind, however, was protesting vehemently – I didn't know what he was and now, I suspected, I wasn't sure I should trust him. Even so, having him in my living room now, I felt I owed it to him to listen to an explanation. The events of the past few days had taught me that much.

As Gage stepped forward, I retreated one step, taking care not to turn my back on him. What if I turned around and he was something else? What if I didn't even have time to turn around?

"What are you?" he said again.

I was tempted to repeat the question back at him but really, it was about time we got past that and down and dirty with some answers. "Don't you think you should be giving me some answers? Or do I have to go to the woods and wait for you to lift your leg against a tree?"

Gage looked at me, unblinking, and I saw his pupils contract into oval-shaped slits. His jaw shifted, longer, lower, his bones seeming to slide under his skin. I caught the flash of his teeth elongating, filling his jaw. Then, in the blink of an eye, he was normal again. If I were less sure of myself, and didn't know that supernatural beings lived amongst regular people, I would have considered questioning my sanity.

"Werewolf," he said at last, "but then, you knew that."

"Knew" was a loose definition of suspecting something that should be impossible; but then, I was the lesson in impossible. There was no reason on earth that I should be able to do all the things that I could and yet, I could. But a werewolf? I should have seen that coming.

Gage skirted around me, circling, like he was herding his prey and I sidestepped to keep a wide expanse of room around me, allowing me space to manoeuvre. I didn't want to get cornered. I shouldn't be afraid, I told myself as my heart picked up a beat. Not in my own home. Not of Gage.

"What are you?" he asked for the third time while sweeping a look that took me in from head to toe, and made my heart race.

"Witch."

I didn't expect him to smile; it was just a flicker of his lips turning upwards at the edges. "Thought so," he said.

"You knew?" I asked, surprised.

He shrugged. "Could smell your magic."

I knew magic could leak, for want of a better word, and others could see it if it were left unchecked... But now it had a scent too? Ewww. I took more steps backwards than I thought I had and my back bumped into the wall. I meant to slide the few inches along the wall to the hallway, but Gage was in front of me in a flash, blocking my route.

"Don't be afraid."

"I'm not afraid." But I didn't sound very convincing and my heart was clamouring.

"I can hear your heart race." Gage's face was inches from mine and I could smell the woods on him, the scent of dew-soaked grass, leaves and earth mingled with something... *otherly*. I held my breath as he dipped his head toward me and whispered in my ear. "I can hear your lungs shudder. I know you're afraid. Don't be."

"Is this where I'm supposed to say 'my, what big teeth you have'?" I asked, rolling my head to look him in the eye. There was barely any space between us and I felt my fear abate into something more... lusty. The danger I'd been in while running, combined with the adrenaline of my magic, the proximity of Gage and excitement swam unabated through me.

Gage huffed a low laugh and the space between us decreased millimetre by millimetre until his mouth was brushing on mine, teasing my lips until the blood rushed in. Then he gently parted them and I allowed his tongue to slide into my mouth and tangle with mine. I could taste him, salty and sweet and, delicious. His arms circled me, pulling me to him until I was pressed against his body and I wrapped my arms around him, suddenly desperate to have him ever closer, his heat flooding me.

He slipped his hand down my spine, to rest in the hollow of my back, pulling me ever closer, before travelling back up my body. His other hand caressed my hair, coiling it through his fingers, before migrating down, brushing my collarbone and lingering at the first closed button of my shirt. Through his urgent kisses, I felt one button pop off and then the next. In the distant recesses of my mind, in the parts that weren't governed by desire, I registered the sound of buttons clattering to the floor.

He wasted no time unbuttoning my shirt. He was *slicing* the buttons off and then pushing the shirt off my shoulders. He barely broke away to shrug his vest onto the floor, before ripping off his own t-shirt and landing kisses on me again. My mouth, my cheeks, my jaw, Gage didn't miss anything with his lips as he leaned in to trail down my neck to my breasts. Now only the skimpiest of material was left between him and me.

I swear, he growled, a guttural, animal sound, and I pulled him into me again, my hands running through his hair and he hoisted me up. I wrapped my legs around him for purchase as he held me against the wall. I could feel him push against me, hard and urgent, and I couldn't help arching my back and driving against him. When he tore my bra, we were nothing but skin against skin.

I felt the wall slide from behind me as Gage tightened his arms about me and tipped us to the floor. With his body pressed against me, and his hand behind my back to protect my body from thumping against the wood, he lowered himself until he was sprawled between my legs. He held me to him, the intensity of his kisses making me faint and desperate as one hand fumbled with the button and zipper of my jeans. I heard him curse as he tugged them open. I arched, my body aching for him. It would have been so easy to shuck off my jeans and take him into me right now, to bask in his urgency and desire, to feel his heat surround me, to take comfort in how much he wanted me.

I barely heard the loud banging at the door over the hunger racing through me.

"Stella!" yelled a female voice. "Stella, it's me." I gasped and my head fell back from Gage as I lay there on the floor under him. We both panted air into our gasping lungs.

"Stella, I just came to check you're okay. Please don't be mad at me." I could imagine Annalise peering through the window, trying to see if I were at home because where else would I be this early in the morning? Where else should I have been? Not out running through the woods certainly, not facing a wolf with... pink highlights! I was glad I moved the sofa so that it blocked us from view.

Gage's hand slipped upwards, trailing slowly up my body until he lay still, fully resting against me. While my breathing became more even, he most definitely did not calm down, if the bulge prodding at my thigh was anything to judge by. I looked into his strange, animal eyes and saw my reflection, hair pooling behind my head, and wild, flushed skin.

I was almost naked, on my floor, with my wolf-man neighbour.

I didn't quite know what to make of that.

"Okay, Stella, maybe you're not there, but just in case you are, I'm really sorry. I should have said something but ... So should you!" said Annalise, indignation etched into her parting words.

She was quiet for a moment like she was waiting for an answer, then I heard her stomp off the porch. I guessed she would walk up the driveway and be in her house within a minute, but it didn't matter. The moment was broken and she probably just saved me from doing something I'd regret. But only after I'd really enjoyed it... Then regret.

Gage kissed me, long and slow without the fever he expressed earlier and, before I could change my mind – while part of me wanted to finish what we'd begun – I had my hands on his shoulders and was pushing him gently, but firmly, off me. He was startled at first, confused even.

"We could continue this in the bedroom," he whispered, his voice singing to the inner part of me that really, really wanted to. "Take our time."

I hardly trusted myself to talk. "We can't," I said, my voice barely a whisper.

"We can." He dipped his head to nuzzle the hollow of my neck, his stubble brushing against my cheek as he lifted his head to nibble my ear lobe.

"We really can't."

"We were about to," Gage pointed out. Oh, as if I didn't know that all too well.

I pushed him slightly further up but was a little too late. As Gage gazed down at me, a smile broadening across his face, I readily remembered that I was still completely naked from the waist up. He bent his head and, before I could wonder what he was doing, he licked me, starting at my naval and running upwards, through my cleavage. My eyes widened in surprise. His tongue was rougher against my skin than a human's should be, not that I had ever let a human *lick* me; but it was deeply, oddly, intimate. He kissed the recess between my collarbones and looked at me almost dreamily.

"You taste lovely," he murmured, his words vibrating on my skin. Then he merely brushed his lips against mine and rolled off me to lie on his back on the cool floor. We lay there side by side, staring at the ceiling. Finally he turned his head to me, eyes flickering down and I groped the floor for my shirt, finally finding it under my fingertips. I eased it to me a fraction at a time until I could clutch a chunk of cotton. There was barely any point pulling it on now that it was missing its buttons. Instead, I just held the shirt across me as I swung upright and rested my back against the wall, my knees self-consciously drawn to my chest.

"So a witch, huh?" Gage stretched out on the floor and crossed his legs.

I raised my eyebrows. "A wolf?"

Gage nodded.

"It's you I hear howling in the woods?"

Another nod. "Or one of the pack."

"Do I know the pack?"

"Annalise, for one." Of course, the smaller wolf with the pink flecks. A dead giveaway. "You know others but it's really not my place to say. They'll reveal themselves if they want to."

"And you knew what I was?"

"Yup."

"Why didn't you say anything?" I asked, confusion etched across my face.

"Wasn't sure if you knew." I frowned at him, so he continued. "I only get a hint of it now and then, not often but it's stronger when you use it, like today."

"Does everyone know?" What I really meant was: how many wolves in Wilding knew what I was?

"Some probably realised, like I did. That show this morning would have confirmed it." Gage shrugged and I tried not to admire his strong chest, finely sprinkled with hair – fur? "I told you, you don't have to be afraid of me. I won't hurt you."

"I'm not afraid of you," I said at last and I really wasn't. Not now, anyway. Early this morning, however, was debatable. "I've never seen a werewolf before. I didn't think they existed!"

"Just like witches are only in fairytales?"

"Touché." Daemons and vampires are real, too. Why wouldn't there be werewolves, as well? Goodness knows what else was out there; I just hadn't expected to meet anything supernatural in Wilding, which just goes to show how little time I had spent thinking about my new world properly.

"I still want to take you to bed." He rolled so that he sat facing me, looking like he couldn't decide whether to reach out for me or keep his hands to himself.

I shook my head, slowly. "It's not going to happen."

"Today," Gage finished, a hint of a smirk on his face as he looked over his shoulder, over the sofa. "Coast is clear," he said, easing to his feet and holding out his hand so I could take it. He pulled me to my feet like I was made of nothing but feather-light cotton candy. I had to quickly adjust my shirt so it wouldn't slide off and give him a full frontal. Again. "I prefer you without that."

When I said nothing, he just shook his head, almost sadly. "I'll make coffee," he said and loped out of the room and down the hallway, leaving me standing there, barely clothed and bemused. I wondered if I should throw him out rather than let him pad around my house like he lived here.

I stooped to the floor, and scrambled for the buttons he'd plucked, and my ripped bra; and, with them in one hand, my shirt covering me with the other, I jogged into my bedroom. I balled up the shirt and dumped it in a drawer, placing the buttons on top of my dresser. I pulled out a new bra and a t-shirt. No buttons, thankfully. The bra I dropped in the bin. I remembered to zipper my jeans. There wasn't much I could do about my flushed skin... or the memory, or the lust that was rapidly becoming replaced by guilt when Evan flashed into my mind. Evan, who had just gone off and still hadn't sent word, I thought angrily, not like that really justified anything at all.

When I finally regained enough control to go into the kitchen, I found Gage lounging against the counter. He'd evidently retrieved his t-shirt from the floor while I'd been in my bedroom because he had it on. He set out two mugs and found the creamer, which I'd started stocking, and the sugar bowl. The pot was perking nicely, filling the kitchen with the aroma of fresh coffee grounds. I sat and waited as I thought about all the things I suddenly wanted to ask him. All the things that would get my mind off sex, anyway.

"What were you doing out in the woods?" I asked at last after Gage picked up the pot and poured steaming liquid into my cup.

"Running," he said, pouring one for himself. "We prefer the night and the early morning, when it's less obvious. Though most people round here are familiar with wolves, it's not something we go out of the way to advertise."

"Why did you all surround me?"

Gage's forehead creased. "We didn't surround you. Approached you, I guess, because our otherness was attracted to your otherness. I did warn you not to go out at night." He waved the spoon at me like I was getting a ticking off.

"Because of my magic?"

"Because we're wolves and it isn't always safe."

"It wasn't night, anyway," I protested. "Just early morning."

"Same difference."

"I can't stay indoors. I like running."

"I'm not expecting you to. I've always made sure the pack respected your boundaries and that won't change now. If any other packs join us, I'll warn you, okay?"

"You can ask them to do that?"

Gage nodded. "I can for our pack, and others have to ask permission to hunt our territory." He thought for a moment. "Besides, you can clearly look after yourself. I've never seen anyone just disappear. How did you do that?"

It was my turn to look nonchalant. "I can just do it. I don't know how."

"There's a lot we don't know about each other," he mused.

"You want to start a witch-wolf outreach programme?" I stirred sugar into my coffee and sipped it while it was still scalding hot. It intrigued me that we had gone from being lustily entwined on my floor to conversing like nothing unusual happened, in a few easy steps. I expected to feel uncomfortable and awkward, but I just felt relaxed with him. Uncomplicated.

"I think we've said our hellos."

"Is Annalise pissed at me?"

"Worried. She didn't want you to find out about us. Thought it might scare you off and she likes you."

"You can tell her I'm not going anywhere. This is my home." And it was, I realised. I wasn't giving it up, or going anywhere. Not anytime soon. I could, I would, have a life here.

"She'll be glad to hear that. I am." Gage caught my eye and held it until I broke away to gaze at my coffee. From under my eyelashes, I watched Gage raise his cup to his lips and take a swallow. I wanted to feel embarrassed that we'd nearly ripped each other's clothes off and almost had sex on my living room floor, but I really couldn't bring myself to be. But, my nagging conscience knew what we'd done wasn't right. When I thought that, I thought of Evan and I jumped, tipping a dribble of coffee over me. Gage snatched a cloth off the counter and passed it to me and I dabbed at my jeans before I could answer. Shit. Shit. Shit.

I hadn't even realised he'd spoken until he said my name softly and I looked up, guiltily. He was standing next to me, close enough that I could inhale his earthy scent. "I said, why don't you come out with me tonight? We could go to the movies again. Or out to dinner. A date."

"I can't," I sputtered.

"It's the daemon, right?"

I closed my eyes and nodded. When I didn't speak, Gage sighed and moved backwards and took his seat at the table across from me again. He rested his wrists on the table, big hands surrounding the mug.

"You knew what he was?"

"Of course. And he knows what I am too." Gage seemed surprised that I asked that.

"He never said." I felt bewildered. So that meant Étoile must have known too and neither of them had said anything to me. But I remembered Étoile telling me not to trust anyone; perhaps this is what she meant. It was all muddled in my head. They were so keen on me keeping me safe and free to practise my magic, but neither of them thought fit to mention that I was living next to wolves. Wolves who liked to roam in a pack throughout the woods behind my house.

"He should have. Or at least he should have taught you how to recognise others. You can recognise other witches, right?"

"Yes, I can feel their magic. And daemons, but they register differently."

"But not wolves?"

"I've never met one before. You're my first."

Gage grinned and I pulled a face at him. So not what I meant to imply.

"Do you love the daemon?" he asked after a quiet pause.

"I... think so," I said.

"That didn't sound very convincing."

So many thoughts and feelings were flittering through me. I thought I loved Evan, but he kept so much from me and his absence unnerved me. Now as much as it had when I didn't know whether he was alive or dead. He was secretive and mysterious and he only told me half-truths and wouldn't listen to me. There was passion all right, no question about that, but I wanted honesty and reliability too. Right now, I wasn't sure if I were getting that. "I don't want to talk about him with you," I said eventually.

Gage just nodded, then asked, "How much do you know about our world?"

"Not much," I confessed. "Evan and Étoile were teaching me."

"Then you should be wondering why your friends aren't teaching you everything." He got up and took his mug across to the sink. I heard the water whoosh out of the faucet as he rinsed the mug and placed it upside down on the drying rack while I was thinking about that. He was still behind me when he said. "You should be asking why your friends only tell you what they want you to know."

"It's not like that," I said, the chair skidding back as I turned round. "They've been really good to me. Both of them have saved my life." And I saved theirs, I thought, but I didn't say that.

"Then they should encourage you to live your life."

I didn't know quite what to make of that so I drank my coffee slowly until it was all gone and then I played with my mug, rolling it around in my hands until Gage took it from me and rinsed it out too.

"You're not their pet, Stella."

"I never said I was!" I exclaimed, looking up quickly. "You're making assumptions!"

Gage looked at me for a moment, his gaze coolly assessing. He set my mug on the rack next to his before leaning back against the counter and ran the tip of his tongue over his lower lip, like he was ready to say more but had just about decided against it.

"Listen, I'll go... unless you want me to stay." He waited for me to protest, but I didn't, not because I didn't enjoy his company – clearly I enjoyed it far too much – but because I wanted to mull over what he said. I didn't want to believe that Evan and Étoile were holding things back from me, but I knew they had and in a big way. When I thought about it, perhaps that was why I hadn't been so forthcoming about Chyler. What was that saying? Forewarned is forearmed. I was neither. "Come by later if you want to go to the movies. I'll let Annalise come too, so long as neither of you bullies me into a chick flick."

I smiled at the thought of that, Gage wedged between us as we giggled through a romcom, but having seen Annalise's stash of DVDs, I figured he'd seen his fair share already, even if he weren't ready to admit it.

"I'm not sure that's a good idea," I said. The right thing to do was put distance between us, to not cloud my already unstable thoughts.

With a shake of his head, Gage stepped towards the kitchen door and I followed behind him. At the front door, he turned back to me, his hand resting on the handle, not moving aside as I brushed past him to unlock it. "I'm glad this is all out in the open," he said.

I smiled tentatively. "Me too, though this magic business never seems to end. Witches, daemons, vampires, werewolves... What's next?"

"Well, you know what they say. I'll show you mine if you show me yours." And he was gone before

I even had a chance to gape at him. I rolled my eyes as I shut the door behind him. Trust Gage to get the last dirty word in.

CHAPTER TWELVE

Annalise was on my doorstep as soon as the hour was decent the next day. "Please don't be mad at me," she said as she hovered uncertainly on the threshold before I beckoned her in. She threw herself onto the sofa closest to the fire, folding her legs under her but careful to keep her shoes off the edge. I'd built the logs up and then thrown a shot of magic at it to kickstart the flames. "I didn't want to hide it from you; but it's not something you can really break out in conversation."

"Hi! I'm a werewolf!" I chirped. "Easy."

"Hi! I'm a witch!" Annalise chirped right back.

The corners of my mouth twitched upwards. "Touché. So why didn't you say anything? Gage said you knew what I was."

"I don't know. Maybe you'd think me running around the woods on all fours was creepy or something."

"I don't think you're creepy at all."

"When you moved here, Gage said we were to

respect your boundaries. We tried to stay off your property anyway; but you don't have to worry about us. I promise." Annalise's big eyes pleaded with me.

"Gage calling the shots, huh?"

"He is packmaster."

I looked at her sharply. "Say again."

She shrugged. "Gage *is* packmaster. What he says goes with the pack. If he gives an order, that's it. No one defies him."

"So, he's like head honcho?" I asked, wondering if I should check the documentaries on Animal Planet for the wolf lowdown.

Annalise nodded. "In Wilding anyway. We own most of the territory out this way so that's why we congregate out here."

"How much of the land?" I asked.

Annalise pointed towards the south. "Everything that way right down to the turn off." She pointed north. "And everything that way up to the interstate."

"And the whole lot in between?"

"Yep. The Loup, the woods, everything except your house and land, which was sold. I think my parents liked the idea of having witches around occasionally."

"Um, that's... nice," I said. Click click went the puzzle pieces in my brain. "So the Loup is... not just a members' bar?"

Annalise nodded. "It's for the wolves."

"Like a Cub Scout house but with fangs?"

She grinned. "Pretty much."

"So, what now?"

"I'm going for lunch with Beau." Her face was suddenly stricken and she flushed pink as she tripped over her words in a hurry to get them out. "I mean,

I'm not going to eat him! We're going to have lunch on Main. Do you want to come?"

"There's no way I'm crashing your date."

"Speaking of dates... has Evan come back yet?"

I shook my head. "No, he hasn't."

"Well, don't sit around moping," Annalise advised as she got to her feet. "Life's too short."

Life was indeed too short, but it seemed like I was just treading water, waiting for something to happen. Slowly it dawned on me, that throughout my whole life I'd been waiting and it had gotten me nowhere. Things had only truly changed for me when I started making real decisions of my own. That was what brought me to Wilding when I was scared and alone. That was what would drive me forward now.

I closed the door after Annalise and leant against it, wondering what the hell I should do. I could sit here and wait or start making plans of my own. I could wait for Evan to grow a pair and stop ignoring me, or go talk to him myself. It occurred to me that I didn't actually know where he was, but I guessed he was staying at the inn with Étoile, Seren and David, who all seemed to be giving me the silent treatment. I decided I would have to be the mature one.

I grabbed my jacket and bundled myself up, pausing for a moment to search for my bag, keys and the shiny new phone. I locked the door and tried the handle to make sure it was locked, because a little paranoia never hurt anyone and jogged to my car. It was freezing inside so I turned on the engine, switched the heater up to full blast, and tugged on gloves so the cold wheel didn't freeze me from the outside in and headed onto the road.

Wilding was fairly busy for midday with the

parking spaces on Main half full already. The sidewalk was bursting with people out and about doing their Christmas gift shopping. Our little town seemed to attract a number of tourists, the type of people who were day tripping or just travelling through, who liked the quirkiness of small town shops.

I drove down Main and turned onto Oak Lane, arriving outside the inn a few minutes later. I pulled onto the side of the road. The entrance to the Oak Inn was unlocked so I walked right in and asked for either of the Winterstorms but, before the receptionist could call up, I spotted Étoile and Seren in the adjoining sitting room. Étoile waved me over and I walked through, thanking the receptionist.

"Well, hello," said Étoile brightly, like they hadn't completely ignored me these past few days. "Take a seat. We were just talking about you."

"Oh?"

"All things nice, of course. How are you?"

"Fine." I wasn't fine, but no one ever truly cared to hear the real answer: my life sucks, I don't know where my boyfriend is, I nearly did something with my neighbour and I feel guilty as sin, oh, but my health is good, thanks very much.

"We kinda got that too," said Seren and I flinched. I would not get used to them doing that.

"You will," said Étoile with a smirk. "What was that about the neighbour?"

"Nothing." I flushed and stuffed residual memories in the back of my mind where they wouldn't leak.

A smile pulled at Étoile's lips. That made me think my feeble efforts to protect my thoughts were... approved. "Since you didn't ask but were thinking it anyway, Evan was here but he isn't right now," said Étoile, getting straight to the crux of my worries.

"Is he still mad at me?"

"He's having a little, jealous alpha male moment," answered Seren, in a way that would have been thoroughly condescending if Evan were listening, "but he's going to get over it."

I heaved out a sigh of relief. "Good to know."

"That doesn't mean he's exactly thrilled with you. Neither are we," chided Étoile with a pointed look. "But we do understand. It's okay to be suspicious of us. I would be too."

It sounded so unpleasant when she voiced it that I said, "I feel like I should apologise or something."

Étoile was surprisingly sympathetic. "Not at all. We swept into your life, took you away from everything you knew and when you needed us, we weren't there. Then we turned up again, out of the blue. We have not been good friends to you and we should have tried harder."

I tried not to look startled at Étoile's unexpected confession. "It's been a long year," I replied. "And I haven't even asked you how yours has been." Perhaps I had been a poor friend too. I'd been so eager to learn, to feel safe, that I'd forgotten a relationship had to work both ways for it to be a friendship. If they had failed, then, maybe, so had I.

"It's been tiring," Seren chipped in as she waved a hand to attract the waitress' attention so she could order drinks. "Our sister is very ill and she will be for a long time, but she's safe now, at least."

Étoile added. "And safe from everyone else. Astra's truly not a bad person, she's just not really ready for this world."

"I don't know what you mean."

"I mean, we'll keep her from the world because she can't handle it. She's... too much."

"Well, I'm glad she's all right," I said at last, even if I didn't throw any weight behind the nicety. We fell silent as the waitress laid a tray on the low table in front of us. When she left, I asked, "Do you know where Evan went?"

Étoile nodded. "He's been watching over the house where Chyler is staying."

"All this time?"

"No, just since yesterday. We've been coming up with a plan."

"And you didn't think to call and share?"

"You don't have a phone," pointed out Seren, "and we were too busy to drive over."

I slipped my new phone out of my pocket and held it up. Étoile whistled. "Well, look who made it into the twenty-first century!" She held out her hand and I passed it over as she said, "I'll program our numbers into it."

"And we'll take your number too," added Seren.

I looked around. "Where's David?"

"With Evan. Boys do like stakeouts." Seren winked.

"Are they coming back soon?" I wanted to know more about what they were doing, and what their plan was. I wanted to be a part of things, not an afterthought. Gage's chide taunted me. I wasn't their pet, even if I weren't entirely their equal.

"David will, but Evan won't. Don't look so glum, you'll see him later, and then you can kiss and make up." Étoile seemed very sure of that.

"If only life were that easy." I slumped in my chair

and stretched my legs for a moment before realising how unladylike I looked next to Étoile and Seren. I neatened myself up promptly.

"It's all down to Mrs Prentiss," said Étoile, plucking at my stray thought. "She was our cotillion teacher. If we slump, we still hear her shrieking."

"She was very mean," smiled Seren. "On our last day, we..."

"I don't think we should share *that* story," snipped Étoile and I wondered what awful thing they had apparently done for revenge. Strangely, it didn't exactly strike me as out of character and I felt instantly mean for thinking such a thing. I took my phone as Étoile passed it back and used my thumb to scroll through my phonebook. She had added Seren's and David's numbers, as well as her own, but not Evan's. I stuffed it back in my bag.

"You said you'd made a plan."

"Ye-e-es." Étoile picked up her cup and sipped. "But we haven't exactly put the finishing touches to it. Let's discuss at your house later."

"Today?" I asked and Étoile nodded, saying, "We'll all come."

"Do I need to get anything or do anything? If you need any..." I looked around. There was an older couple sitting in the corner and a middle aged man reading a book. It wasn't a big room, but there was enough space between all of us that we could talk with relative privacy. Even though, I hesitated to say things like *magic* and *spells* in the open. Instead, I said, "Uh, supplies, I don't have anything in the house that strikes me as useful."

"David will do that. All we need is you and us. David is the boss when it comes to the... other stuff."

Seren seemed rather proud of that. I wondered if his version of magic was as powerful as theirs, or more so. It didn't seem to me like many witches could outdo the sisters.

Étoile was introduced to me as something like a gofer for the Witches' Council. Then, later, she became a tutor. I never really understood what her job was with them. Evan explained that the Winterstorms were a very powerful family but I didn't have a frame of reference for that. The few witches I'd met hadn't exactly introduced themselves on a scale.

"It's just different. Either can be stronger. Many can do both, like you," said Seren.

"How do I keep you two out of my head?" I asked, changing the subject. I didn't see them plucking thoughts from David or Evan.

"You can stop us peeking if you want to; just like you did a few minutes ago," added Étoile, "though it's much more fun for us if you don't, obviously."

"You can see the future," I whispered back crossly, "isn't that enough?"

"I like living in the now." Étoile laughed.

Étoile and Seren both leaned forward and pressed a hand on each of my arms and I felt my spirits lift. "We'll come by this afternoon. Until then, we're stuck here waiting," said Seren.

"Fine. I'm going. Just turn up whenever you're ready." I stood up and shrugged my jacket back on and zipped it right to my chin. "Call me as soon as you've got some news?"

"We will," said Seren and they waved to me as I left. When I stepped outside, past the winter jasmines, I realised why I'd suddenly felt so calm and happy to go about my business. They had influenced me and I hadn't even seen it coming. I shrugged. Perhaps I needed it anyway; this feeling of serenity was much better than the familiar anxiety that had been tugging at me all morning. It had taken me some time to realise that they could do that, but today I didn't mind.

I stopped by the diner on the way home and sat at the counter while I ordered a grilled cheese sandwich and a Coke. I could see Annalise and Beau in the booth in the far corner but they were so absorbed in each other, they didn't see me. Darla, the ever present waitress, chatted to me between customers and filled me in on town gossip.

By the afternoon, I would probably be her new update. I provided her with an entire two weeks of juicy dirt when I first moved here. By the end of those two weeks, every time I opened my mouth and my English accent spilled out, just about everyone greeted me by name. Darla, wasn't just a small town gossip though, she was a one woman PR machine. She eased my route into the town like a well-oiled wheel so I made sure I tipped her well as I paid up and left. Although I tried not to think about how sharp and white her teeth were and not wonder if she were a member of the Wilding wolf pack, I failed.

I didn't go straight home. Instead, I picked up some books from the little bookstore across the street and the grocery store to collect more food. If I were going to keep on having visitors, I'd have to truly stock up, at some point. When I finally headed home, that calm, relaxed feeling was still with me and I was grateful for the Winterstorms' little intervention. It was about as close to feeling normal as I could get and I embraced it with open arms.

~

"I'm back," said Étoile brightly when I opened the door after flicking on the porch light. By now, it was early evening and the sun had just about set in the sky so I had all the lights turned on. I also set the fire crackling in the grate again, filling the room with warmth. I'd spent my day reading a mystery and playing CDs through my laptop. All in all, it had been a quite reassuringly – boringly, even – pleasant day thanks to my burst of good feeling. "And I brought reinforcements," Étoile added as two women stepped out from behind her. Neither of them smiled.

"Reinforcements for what?"

"For trapping that evil inside of sweet little Chyler." Étoile said like it was not only a completely natural thing to say, but also that it was completely absurd that I had to ask.

"You're going to do that? Where's Seren and David?"

"They're getting supplies. And Evan is still watching over Chyler. As soon as we're ready, he'll bring her here."

"Why here?" I hissed. It wasn't like it went well the last time.

"Where else? It's better that we do the incantation indoors. Besides, the inn is having some kind of weirdly provincial games this afternoon and several witches chanting is a sure way to ruin Charades."

"I suppose that would put anyone off," I agreed and held the door open so Étoile could step inside. She beckoned to her coterie to follow.

"This is Victoria, and this is Hayley. They are Chyler's aunts," Étoile said as she passed me, "and members of Andrea's coven."

"Hi," I mumbled to the two women who each nodded briefly to me as they stepped past without saying anything. Chyler seemed suspicious of them and I was instantly on my guard. That is, if it were Chyler who I'd been speaking to at that moment and not the malicious spirit. All the same, being wary of strange witches was one safeguard that I'd have to get very familiar with. Pun so not intended. I asked Étoile quietly, "Are you going to fill me in on what's going on?"

Étoile looked around the room, her hands deep in the pockets of her navy wool coat. It was spotless after their last efforts at summoning Chyler, no thanks to them on either count. "When Seren and David get here, they'll set up the circles again, but this time, they'll be spelled and they'll be stronger. Chyler and whatever that thing is won't be able to get out," she told me.

"And then what? You can't just keep them in a circle in my living room forever." I imagined myself inviting people in and *oh, just step around the witch shrieking in the middle and try to pretend she's not there.* Awkward!

"We're going to separate them." Étoile nodded at her companions who were hovering. "That's what they're here for. Extra muscle. We need to banish this thing and they can help us by looking after Chyler while we get rid of it."

"Banish it where?" I asked, addressing the hot topic first.

"It's probably dead," answered one of the witchy aunts. She was blonde and in her thirties and there was something about Chyler in her face, more so than in the other woman. "We'll send it back." She held out her hand and I shook it. Her grasp was cold. "Victoria," she said, her voice low and businesslike. "Thanks for looking out for Chyler. Étoile told us. We drove all day to get here."

"Uh, no problem." I was clearly not completely in trouble about that anymore which was a relief. Well, some, anyway. Evan still hadn't been in touch.

"It's clearly malevolent from what your friends here told us," added the smaller dark-haired woman, Hayley, who was ignoring the introductions and getting right to the point. "We think it killed Andrea and if it plans on staying in my niece, it's definitely up to something."

Victoria was willowy and blonde and dressed in a neat blue pantsuit with a white shell top. She would have looked more in place in a bank or a corporate office than around a cauldron, which was how I still thought of witches sometimes. Fairytales were hard to shake.

Hayley was more what I would have described as witchy in her long black skirt and polo neck top with a mass of mid-brown curls that edged their way down her back. She wore long silver earrings and had several large rings on her fingers. I wouldn't have had them pegged as sisters though, perhaps they weren't. Chyler said both her parents had sisters; that would explain the differences in them.

"Really?" I couldn't help keep the edge of sarcasm out of my voice.

"Hey, play nice with the other witches," chided Étoile, but softly.

"Bad witch, no cookie?" I shot at her.

"Bad witch gets evil witch," Étoile snipped.

"Tell us about Chyler," I said to the aunts, after our mini face off. I gestured for Hayley and Victoria to take seats and they sat on the sofa, at opposite ends. I got the impression they weren't close, despite the family connection. "All we know is what we've read on the internet about her, about your family, and what we've heard second hand. And I'm not entirely sure if I've always been talking to Chyler either, or if I've been talking to the spirit. Her behaviour was erratic every time."

"Chyler is a nice kid," said Victoria. "She's smart and popular and her parents were always very proud of her. She was just thinking about her college applications. She was the kind of daughter every parent would've been grateful to have."

"That's why we were so worried when she started dabbling," added Hayley. She had one of those commanding voices that made you automatically take note of what she was saying. "She just thought she could handle anything. She didn't want to be taught so much as to get on with what she thought she should be doing. Andrea was so worried. She came to the regional Council for help. She wanted to know how she could put Chyler off without coming down on her like an angry mom and making it all worse."

"What was Chyler dabbling in?" I asked.

Hayley shuddered, closing her eyes briefly like she could hardly bear to think of it. "Dark magic," she said after a long pause. "It all started when she believed one of her teachers had slighted her. She had been working really hard all semester on a project for her history teacher and she felt he gave her a lower mark than she deserved. She wanted revenge."

"Did she get it?" asked Étoile.

"Oh yes." Hayley paused. "She wasn't vicious but it was mean stuff. He'd lose things or trip inexplicably in the corridors. He'd talk gibberish instead of giving a talk. Stuff that made all the other kids laugh at him."

"It didn't stop there," added Victoria. "Her boyfriend dumped her a few months after that and she saw him with another girl. Chyler started a campaign designed to taunt the girl and that was mean. She made sure all her school projects failed, her homework disappeared or was marked down, and her grades hit rock bottom. The other kids started ostracizing the girl."

So far, Chyler was starting to sound like a mean girl. Everyone felt slighted in school, but Chyler had taken her revenge past whispering and pointed comments and used magic to make people feel as bad as she did.

"She realised just how much magic could do for her and, of course, there's the book that belongs to our family. It started showing her things that she shouldn't have been able to do, never mind encouraged to." Hayley slipped a sideways glance at me and asked, almost casually, "Do you know where the book is now?"

I shrugged. "I don't know." It wasn't exactly a lie; I had seen it, but I didn't know what Chyler had done with it or if she still had it.

"The book belongs with the family," said Victoria.

"Absolutely. I need to take it with me." Hayley added like it was an afterthought. "With my sister gone... Chyler's just not ready for it."

"It's very powerful?" murmured Étoile.

"Oh, it's just our family spell book," Hayley replied dismissively. She seemed to be taking pains to stay any interest in the book, speaking about it as if she were talking about a book of hand-me-down recipes rather than a book that not only absorbed power but also reinforced the magic of its bearer.

"We're almost certain Chyler has called something to her, another witch perhaps," said Étoile, switching direction. "What could have made her call something like that?"

"We've been talking about that ever since you mentioned it," said Victoria, pausing to glance at Hayley. "We don't think she did mean to call something. Chyler's got a mean streak and she's felt like she's had a hard time but we don't think she's evil or that she truly meant to do anything to hurt anyone, least of all her mom."

"Are you sure she hurt her mom?" I asked.

"Her fingerprints were on the knife," said Hayley sadly.

"Not that that means she did it," interjected Victoria, slightly defensively. "Her hand, yes, but she might already have had that thing inside her, controlling her. We don't think she killed her mom. Andrea just got there at the wrong moment."

"So how did this thing, this spirit, get into her?"

Victoria shrugged. "It takes something amazingly strong to come through and get inside someone else. It's not just possession; it's actually living, if what we've been told is true."

"We figured the more mean things she did, the more things she wanted to do and that made her more susceptible to anything malevolent. Perhaps the spirit was helping her; and the meaner Chyler got, the stronger the spirit got. The spirit would have just had to wait for the right moment," added Hayley.

"Wait. Spirit? Like a ghost?" I asked and they all nodded at me. I contemplated all the strange things I had to deal with that were living and breathing. I wasn't sure about dealing with the dead, too. "Don't dead things go to heaven?"

"Not always," said Étoile with a knowing look. "Some balance somewhere between the dead and living and some dead things... linger. They look for ways to come back."

"But why would it kill Chyler's mom?" I asked. "If it were about the book, it could have just snatched it, if it were already in her, right?" Too late, I realised I'd asked a question that I shouldn't necessarily have known to ask. Hayley was trying to brush the spell book off as just a family possession to be returned and I'd inadvertently exposed her attempts to gloss over what it really was.

"Chyler became the keeper as soon as her mom died. The spirit would have known that and it would have made her a very attractive target," said Hayley, echoing what I'd been told before but not volunteering any more information about the book.

"So this spirit, it has to be a witch, yes? Would anything else have been bothered about a spell book?" I had so many more questions, my mind was tripping over itself: do spirits think? How could spirits think? Were there lots of them?

Victoria surprised me by agreeing. "She's right. It could only have been a witch."

"So how do we narrow down which one?" I asked.

Étoile pulled a face. "I don't think we can. We can't even possibly begin to list all the dead witches. There's a lot." That did *not* sound promising.

"We have to entice it out," said Victoria. "It's the only way."

Étoile nodded. "We came to the same conclusion this morning." She turned to me. "Like I said before, Victoria and Hayley are the extra muscle. They're connected with Chyler in a way that we aren't – they're biological relatives and that counts – they can protect her as much as aid us. Seren and David are out searching for the things David will need to perform the right spells."

"David?" frowned Victoria. "Do you mean David Langstrom? The same one who..."

Étoile cut her off with a simple, "Yes."

Victoria and Hayley both looked impressed at the news and I wondered what I didn't know about David. The truth was I didn't know much. I knew he'd been attacked and it resulted in the long scar that cut through his face, but I didn't know what happened, or by whom. I also knew that Seren and Étoile trusted him and that Evan thought highly of him. Even if I didn't know much else about him, those were the important things. They had to count for something.

"When are they going to get here?" I asked.

"Soon." Étoile closed her eyes for a moment and her face was completely still. When she opened them again, she said, "They're on their way and they have everything they need."

When they arrived just ten minutes later, Seren and David didn't waste time chatting or on niceties. Instead, David busied himself in the kitchen preparing a foul smelling concoction of several herbs that he either boiled or crushed and mixed together into a curiously coloured paste, while Seren hovered around him.

I soon realised I was in the way and retreated to the living room where Étoile was questioning Hayley and Victoria further about their niece. I stood to one side, tucked out the way, listening and wondering where the hell Evan was. After a while, David and Seren returned with a plastic bowl and spatula and set them on the floor, in the widest part of the room, both kneeling beside the bowl.

There was symmetry in David and Seren's movements as they created two chalk circles side by side, each with an inner circle, leaving a small gap in the perimeter of each one. They chalked two lines between the two circles, creating a thin channel to connect the two. The thin strip between circles was daubed with the thick globs of the paste. Since my recent burst of homeowner's pride, I was not at all happy with what they were doing to the hardwood floors which, in my opinion, were the best feature of the house. The yucky paste mixture had better come up or the bitch in this witch was going to come back and bite them.

"Why are they doing that?" I asked Étoile as pleasantly as I could muster, trying not to wince at the mess Seren and David were making.

"When Evan brings Chyler, she'll need to be contained in one circle, and she'll need to stay contained when we separate the spirit from her. One circle will protect her; the other will keep that thing apart from her so it can't hurt her again. The chalk is stronger than the salt and the herb mixture is spelled so the thing can't get free. We won't lose it this time."

"You really think this will work?"

"It has to." Étoile did not look thrilled at any hint

of failure, but then she'd been sent to investigate. I wondered how much she had to lose.

"Enough," Étoile whispered and squeezed my hand.

"How can you even separate them? What if it won't come out of Chyler?"

Victoria said, "It's hard but it can be done."

"And if it doesn't work?" Chyler's aunts exchanged looks that made my heart sink. I asked, "She dies, right?"

"She's going to die anyway," Étoile said gently. "Two beings can't exist in one body, not long term. One eventually edges the other out. Chyler may be strong but it's doubtful that she will win. This is her only option. This is the only way she can survive."

It sounded to me like Chyler was stuck between a rock and a hard place. "What happens to her afterwards, if it works?" I asked.

"She'll be just fine, physically. We don't know what trauma has happened to her psychologically but she's a fighter. She's been fighting it. That's how she's lasted so long," replied Étoile.

"But it's only been a few days. Not more than a couple of weeks," I protested.

"And it's amazing that she's lasted that long. A lesser witch would have been destroyed by now." Étoile didn't sound overly optimistic and I wanted to ask more when David got to his feet and, after helping Seren up in a gentlemanly gesture, took the few steps towards us.

"We're ready," he said, looking over his shoulder at the almost conjoined circles. "Here's what we need to do."

We stood in a circle like hyperactive teens who

couldn't face sitting down while David explained what he wanted from us.

Bringing Chyler here was, apparently, the simple part. This time, we weren't going to practise a summoning spell. Instead, Étoile and Seren were to send Evan a message using their telepathy while the rest of us would wait in our assigned stations around the perimeter of the circles. While the potion David and Seren had daubed in the circles would ultimately act as a catalyst for his spells, we would link together, simply by holding hands. That way, he could draw on our collective power to fuel the spell that would separate the spirit from Chyler and then hold them both within the circles. It felt like we were a bit like the United Nations of Witches with our motley meld of spell casting and blood magic working in harmony. I hoped it would work.

When I moved to take my place, David motioned to me with a nod of his head to follow him. It was then that he explained the most dangerous part of his plan, the part meant just for me, the part no one else could know about, he murmured as I absorbed the enormity, the danger, of what he was asking me to do. I wanted to tell him he was crazy, out of his mind crazy.

"It's the only way," he said in his low voice and I could see how worried he was. "You don't know it yet, but you're going to be more powerful than any of us. We can all see it, Étoile, Seren and I, and that makes you important here. If I could ask any of the others, I would."

"I understand," I said, trying not to let my fear show. "I'll do it."

From my position, I could see outside that long

shadows were being cast from the house over the lawn and that the full moon hung low and heavy in the sky. I hoped fervently that Annalise and Gage had stayed away from home tonight. It was bad enough that my house was serving as the venue for all this, but I didn't want them stumbling across something they shouldn't. Certainly something I couldn't explain.

I didn't know if it were even okay to talk about what I was, never mind acknowledge that someone else knew what we were. Gage said that they each recognised each other for what they were but Étoile hadn't given me the wolves and the witches talk yet. There simply hadn't been time, and, as far as I knew, my friends still didn't know what I discovered literally on my own doorstep, all on my own.

I barely noticed the rustle of movement outside as I turned my back on the window and took my position. I concentrated on the circles. The six of us – Étoile, Seren, David, Chyler's two aunts, Victoria and Hayley, and me – formed an odd perimeter around the conjoined cages. Étoile and Seren were next to each other, to my left, and they linked hands first, their silence telling me that they were sending their message to Evan. With a nod from the two of them, we all quickly linked hands.

It was with a sudden rush of air that I realised Evan had shimmered into my home, seconds later, depositing Chyler in a heap in the circle closest to me. Then he hurtled forward at such a pace that he didn't stop until he crashed into the living room wall. I realised David must have left some kind of escape clause for Evan so he wouldn't be caught too, or maybe the magic was just aimed at witches. I couldn't be sure.

While I couldn't follow the chant that David was giving in his low baritone, each word said forcefully and clearly, I could complete the circuit so the magic could flow through me and channel into the spell casting. The wards were so strong that, to me, the air seemed to vibrate in columns the longer David spoke. It was like looking ahead on a hot day and seeing the heat wave in the air. Here, however, all I got was a cold chill.

"We can break the circle," said David at last and I blinked. Chyler had stumbled to her feet and was spinning around and around in her circle, bouncing off the invisible walls. Eventually, she ceased twirling and dawdled to a stop, staring at each of us in turn, her expression far from happy. She looked tired and drawn, like she had a severe case of anaemia, and her unfocused eyes had the glossy patina of someone not quite there.

"What the hell do you think you're doing?" she hissed, picking us each out in turn.

"To whom are we speaking?" asked Étoile.

Chyler smirked. "Chyler Anderson, of course."

"Oh, we know that's not the truth." Étoile's voice was soft but strong. She leaned in and whispered, taunting, "You're clearly not a very clever witch."

"Not a clever witch? I've been a witch for years. My family was revered." Chyler turned again, assessing her surroundings as if she were just joining us for afternoon tea and wasn't too pleased at the spread. "My family would have ruled the Council if it weren't for yours," she said, stopping suddenly so she could focus on Étoile.

"So you're a Lawley?" Étoile's eyebrow arched as recognition dawned on her. I watched Hayley and

Victoria exchange glances. They obviously recognised the name even if I didn't. I leaned in to Seren, "Fill me in?" I asked in a whisper.

"The Lawleys were an old and powerful family but they had a habit of dying out early. Spells gone wrong, illnesses, that sort of thing, not to mention that there was a long running feud with our family that didn't work out so well for anyone. Dina Lawley died twenty years ago when she performed a spell that backfired."

"It didn't backfire," snapped Chyler. "I was murdered. And now I'm back."

"So you *are* Dina Lawley." Étoile pursed her lips like she had just said something quite unpleasant. "How on earth did you get into Chyler's body?"

Chyler smirked. Or rather, Dina smirked with Chyler's face. "Like I'm going to tell you that."

Étoile put her forefinger to her lips. "Let me guess," she murmured. "Chyler's dabbling in dark magic somehow brought you back into the world and you're just hanging on by the barest of threads."

"Something like that." Dina shrugged. "But let's not dwell on it. Chyler let me in and I want to stay."

"You can't stay in Chyler's body," hissed Hayley, stepping forward.

"I remember your family." Dina looked at Hayley with scant regard. "Never liked you. You were always kinda whiny. Now Chyler, she's fun. She always wants to try out fun stuff."

"She would never have wanted this," Hayley protested. "She's only a kid. She didn't know what she was doing."

"Who cares?" came Dina's answer from Chyler's pouting lips.

"Regardless of all that, you won't be squatting in Chyler's body any more. Actually, you should probably say goodbye now," interrupted Étoile.

Dina's pupils widened in surprise before she rolled her eyes. "That is not going to happen. I need this body."

According to David's plan, it was time for me to step in. Our plan wasn't great, just a one shot wonder that stood a slim chance of working. If it failed, Dina would stay in Chyler's body, clinging on with all that she had, while Chyler continued to reject her. Eventually, that fight would drain Chyler and they would die. Even if Dina prevailed, she wouldn't be allowed to live as a parasite. Either way, Dina would return into the ether or the afterlife. And wherever she was destined to go, she would be right back to square one. No closer to life than she had been since her death. The only compromise was to offer her something that she wanted more.

"You can have my body," I said and took a moment to enjoy the surprise etched across her young, borrowed, face. "I'm stronger than Chyler and I won't fight," I added, tempting her further.

"I know you. You're Stella Mayweather. I knew your father. He was at school with me," said Dina. "I heard you were found."

"Oh, really?" How, I wondered, was she getting news updates when she technically didn't exist? I couldn't be distracted now. I held firm, saying, "The offer's there. Make your choice."

Dina shook Chyler's head. "It's a trap."

"There's no trap. It's an offer. A take it or leave it offer," I emphasised, with David nodding supportively. I hoped to hell his plan worked as Étoile and Seren regarded me with concern, Étoile just barely shaking her head.

Dina looked around at us, trying to fathom what the trap might be, but all she saw were hopeful expressions from Chyler's aunts who had no interest in me anyway. They only cared about their niece's safety, while my friends wore stone cold expressions. But the clincher for her was the fear that I could see, over her shoulder, in Evan's brown eyes.

"No, Stella." He shook his head desperately. "You can't sacrifice yourself."

"I can." I stiffened my jaw and refused to look at him.

"How're you going to do it?" Dina asked, peering at me.

"You know I can teleport?"

"Right, that thing you do. It's in Chyler's head."

Ick. I tried not to think about them sharing brain space. "Well, I can shimmer my consciousness out of my body. When I'm out, you're in. Simple." I tried to not look at Evan. I fixed on Chyler and kept my gaze even.

"Nothing's ever that simple."

"This is."

Étoile stepped in before I could start to shake with the effort of being brave. "You've got twenty seconds to agree or turn us down," she said.

"And what if I don't?"

"We'll kill Chyler."

Chyler's aunts started and Étoile had to shout above them to be heard. "Don't think that I won't." She checked her watch and looked at Dina expectantly, mouthing, "Tick tock."

I watched Dina weigh up her options. She had

twenty seconds to decide whether to stay in a body that was about to die. She couldn't risk disbelieving because if she were wrong, she would lose her one real shot at a second life. Or she could try and take my body, even though we could be lying about that too. Only one of those options offered her a slim chance of life.

She took the bait. "I'll do it."

"Stella, take your place in the other circle. When I give you the go ahead, shimmer out. Dina, that's when you leave Chyler's body. This is a one chance only offer. Understood?" said David, stepping forward.

"Fine," said Dina, her eyes fixed on me.

I stepped into the empty circle and faced the innocent exterior of my enemy. A thousand things were going through my mind and most of them were on the not okay end of the emotional spectrum. But most of all there was fear, and somewhere in the middle of that, hope.

"Stella, it's time to go," said David with a solemn nod, adding sadly, "Thanks for doing this."

I nodded and braced myself, summoning everything there was from inside me and the electric feeling crawled all over my skin. I visualised and, just as the room grew hazy, I blinked and the shouting started.

CHAPTER THIRTEEN

Seconds can feel like a lifetime when your life is hanging in the balance. In the moment that I left my living room, I felt my essence as it was caught and dragged in the slipstream of something amazing and terrifying. It lit everything around me in flames of gold and red. Just as quickly as it came, and I felt the heat lick at my skin, it was gone and I was blinking, trying to adjust my vision to the lowly lit room.

I was on my side, on the floor, the cool wood pressed against my cheek, but I was in my own damn body. Well, hallelujah! I shuffled awkwardly until I sat up, heat still prickling my skin. With a strange sense of déjà vu, I suddenly realised that this was exactly what I'd envisioned when we were in the restaurant and I had my first vision. Evan saved me, from Dina Lawley, and it was an experience as frightening as it was a relief.

I was surrounded by chaos. In front of me, I could see a newly drawn thick chalk line between the circles, splitting them. Seren sat panting on the floor, strands of hair flying out from her ponytail and settling around her face. Chyler's aunts knelt to her left, also on the floor and next to the circle in which Chyler had slumped into a heap again.

The thick prison of magic undulated around both circles now, but seemed stronger in the one that appeared empty. I shifted to my knees so I could lean in closer for a better look. Just as I started to topple forwards, a strong pair of hands landed on my shoulders and stopped me doing a face-plant on the floor.

The apparently empty circle was anything but. On closer inspection, the air seemed thicker. Something buzzed inside and it was angry. Very, very angry.

"That was a stupid thing to do," Evan whispered in my ear, his voice hard, as he held on to me. His strong arms felt like a vice around my torso.

"I knew you wouldn't let me die," I whispered back, dragging my eyes from the scene so I could look at him. My skin felt scorched from the heat that accompanied the way he teleported. A vague part of me hoped for a tan as compensation.

"You should have told me. I had a second to realise what you were doing. A second, Stella!"

"How could we say anything to you? For Dina to take the bait, your reaction had to look real. Besides, you've been gone for days." I couldn't resist slipping in angry words as I turned my head away, too close for comfort right now. I was both grateful and furious and I couldn't look at him. Saving me clearly outweighed any slight over the last few days, but that didn't mean I couldn't have a damn good sulk.

A part of me felt guilty that we, David and I, were relying on Evan's ability to teleport as extra protection for me. He had wrapped himself around me just as I shimmered, body and soul, and transported me through a plane Dina could never reach. We tricked Dina, but only just.

"I deserved that," Evan said after a moment and I could feel his warm breath on my neck. He didn't move his hands but he didn't try and hold me either. I could have wriggled away from him if I really wanted to, but I didn't.

"What happened to Chyler?" I asked, changing the conversation so I wouldn't have to think too hard about whether I was mad at him, or angry, or relieved, or... anything.

"I don't know. I've only been here a minute or two longer than you. You were unconscious. I think you got knocked out."

"What was that anyway?" I asked. I cooled rapidly but I could still feel the heat against my skin. In those seconds, it had been intense and relentless. I snuck a glance at Evan; he didn't seem even remotely affected by it.

"I caught you at the moment you shimmered," Evan confirmed what I already knew, "but I had to move you through a different plane so that Dina couldn't attack you. But I thought you knew that?"

"I knew you'd be able to get me, but I didn't think it would be like that." What Evan had done was amazing and terrifying, but I wasn't sure I wanted to experience it again.

He added, "It's different for you."

I dipped my head, nodding briefly, even though I wasn't sure if it were a question or a statement.

Étoile stepped over to us, navigating her way around the circles, her heels clicking on the floor.

"That went well, don't you think?" she asked brightly, stooping to kneel on one knee so she was level with me. She inclined her head towards Evan. Almost reverently.

"Is Chyler all right?" I asked.

"I think so." Étoile held her hands out to me and when I took them, she tugged me up, as Evan's arms slipped from where they had encircled me. She pointed to the twin circle that was now occupied. "We've contained that thing."

"So all we have to do is get rid of it... her?" Evan asked, stepping forward so he was abreast with me, so close that if I moved a muscle, I'd brush against him.

"Hmm, well there is one small problem."

"What's that?" I asked, wondering what else could possibly go wrong now.

Étoile looked embarrassed. "Apparently we've drawn some attention to ourselves. We can feel other witches arriving. Your wards are strong so they can't enter the house and Seren will strengthen them in a moment, but they're outside. Waiting."

"So, basically everything is fine, we just can't go outdoors because of the witches? And we don't know whose side they are on?"

Étoile nodded. "That seems to sum up it up."

"Oh, crap," I muttered.

"We want to take Chyler and go," said Hayley, her voice forceful as she interrupted us. "Whatever is going on out there has nothing to do with us."

"Whatever is going on out there has everything to do with Chyler," hissed Seren.

"I agree. Besides, I don't think it's a good idea to go, not when we're surrounded and not while Chyler is unconscious," Étoile added.

"But Chyler isn't a threat to anyone, not anymore," protested Victoria.

"We don't know that. More importantly, they don't know that and we don't know what they want." Étoile jabbed a finger to the door.

I used the distraction caused by their bickering to move away from Étoile and Evan and edged around the periphery of the room to the big window that looked over the front of my house. I could already feel the vibrations that I got when another witch was present; but this was stronger and more forceful. Several small clusters of people were dotted around, no more than three or four to a group, and they all took care to keep a good distance between themselves. I could see a small line of cars on the street so it was obvious that some had come the regular way. They were all facing the house, waiting.

I stepped back. "If we tell them Chyler's fine, will they go?" I mused to no one in particular.

"They might be here for that." Seren nodded at the buzzing inside the circle. It was getting slower and more solid and seemed to be taking shape; legs, a body, arms, a head, all translucent but nevertheless, there. I could make out a face of a woman. When she spoke, her voice was surprisingly strong. "We had a deal." Dina was apparently back in the building.

I grinned at her. "There's no honour among thieves."

"I want out. Now." Semi-visible hands felt their way around the circle, testing its strength, until she came to a stop and looked at Chyler, slumped on the floor. Dina gave a wisp of a sigh and folded her semi-corporeal arms.

"What would they want with her?" I asked,

nodding at Dina. She turned to me, flicking her ghostly hair, and narrowed her eyes.

"Who wants me?" she asked. Dina had taken a couple of minutes longer than I coming around to make herself almost completely visible, so she was behind the rest of us in noticing the supernatural cannonball race pitching up on my lawn.

"Witches," I replied.

Dina seemed to shrivel for a moment, then her form came back slightly stronger. I could still see through her. "I don't want to go to them. Help me, Stella. They'll imprison me for years and years. I'll never move on."

"Is that why you came to me? So I could help you?" I frowned at her suddenly wheedling tone.

"You dumb bitch! Chyler came looking for you. But when I realised who you were, it suited me to stay. I needed you because you killed Eleanor Bartholomew. Because you're a murderer. A witch killer," Dina spat.

I shuddered and it was all I could do not to take a step back. I said, "I didn't murder her, it was self defence." It didn't matter how I said it though, the end result was still the same. I was responsible for another being's death.

"You ripped her heart out." Dina smiled at me. Actually smiled.

"Not because I wanted to," I protested. "I was just trying to stop her."

"Like I care. You killed her and you can kill them, you can kill them all. Do it or..."

"Or what?" I hissed. "You're nothing. You barely even exist."

"I'll kill Chyler," she said smugly. "She's given me

the strength to get me this far. All I need is to suck a bit more of her life-force. I probably don't even need a body now. I can become me again and you can help me do that."

I mulled the idea over in my mind. She'd been co-habiting with Chyler long enough to become incredibly connected to her and Chyler had tried desperately to warn me about the malevolent spirit that occupied her. It may have been Chyler who came to me for help, but it was Dina who tried to manipulate me into doing what she wanted. There was no way I could let Dina go; I couldn't be sure what she might be capable of. If she were strong enough to linger here, where she didn't belong, and still able to leach life from another, who knew what she would do when she got what she wanted: her life.

"I can't do that," I said finally, with a guilty glance at Chyler.

Dina pulsed a little more strongly, becoming a little more solid. She smiled when Chyler whimpered on the floor, her face contorted in pain, hands balled into fists as she drew her knees to her chest, curling up like a baby. Despite everything we had done to separate them, to force Dina from Chyler's body, somehow there was still a connection and Dina was drawing on it.

"It's the circle," gasped David. "The circles are joined and that's keeping them connected. We have to break it." He rushed out of the room and, a moment later, reappeared with a wet cloth. He wrung it as he jogged back, leave a trail of drops on the floor behind him. "If I break Chyler's circle, only Dina's will stand. Chyler will be safe."

"It's that simple?" I asked.

David nodded. "I should have realised earlier." He knelt on the floor next to the junction of the circles. Hayley and Victoria sat back to let him wipe out the chalk lines that kept Chyler captive. Dina vibrated around her prison like a tornado, shrieking and hurling abuse at David until the last trace of the circle was gone. The room was eerily quiet while we all waited for Chyler's face to relax. She drew in a sharp intake of breath, gasping and coughing like she had never tasted oxygen before. Next to her, Dina screamed.

"Keep an eye on her," David said to Chyler's aunts but I saw his eye flicker to Evan, and his head dip in a brief nod at the two women cradling Chyler. His message was clear. They were to be watched too. For whatever reasons David had, he didn't trust them. Chyler didn't either.

"We need to find out what's going on out there," I said, turning away from the scene so I could check outside again. More people had turned up in the minutes we were breaking Dina's connection to Chyler and I could feel the faint trace of power bouncing off the barriers of my wards.

"Can you feel that?" I asked Étoile.

"Yes, they want to know who is in here and what we're doing." She motioned to Seren who came by her side and they linked hands. "We'll send out our own mental feelers and find out what they want."

"Okay." I watched them stand there, blank expressions across their faces for a short while until Seren said, "They want to punish Chyler for dabbling in the dark arts and some are holding her accountable for her mother's death."

"I did that!" piped up Dina. We ignored her.

"Some of them know Dina is here. That group," Étoile pointed to a crowd of five on the driveway, "want Dina to be punished. And that group over there want to take Dina with them."

Seren added, "There's another group thinking about Hayley and Victoria a lot. They want Chyler and I think they are fairly safe, given that everyone else is thinking quite malicious thoughts."

I clarified, "So, they're all different groups and they all want different things? That's good, right? Better than having a whole bunch of them against us."

"Oh, most of them are against us." Étoile seemed strangely cheerful about it. "But they're not exactly ready to help any other group out either. Seren, do you feel that?"

Seren cocked her head and was quiet for a moment. "That blank spot?" she asked.

Étoile nodded. "Someone is blocking their thoughts."

"Someone is prepared for us," said Seren thoughtfully.

Some of that, I decided, could count as good news to me. There were just seven of us inside the house – Evan, Étoile, Seren and David, Victoria and Hayley and me. Chyler too, though she was unconscious. Plus, there was Dina though not quite visible at the moment as she flitted around. Not that it mattered, she was the reason my house was surrounded by witches. And not just one band; there were several who wanted Chyler tonight, or at least Dina's spirit. I was adamant that we were not going to surrender Chyler.

As far as I was concerned, she was an innocent in

all this. She may have been mean, but she hadn't asked to be possessed and she did try to get help. I had no guarantee any of the witches out there wouldn't just kill her and be done with it. After all, what was Chyler to them? Just another teen witch who had stupidly dabbled in something she didn't understand and paid the price. She was the perfect scapegoat.

Of course, there was the small matter that maybe one of these groups was rather intent on keeping Dina, and not banishing her at all. That would mean death in all but body, seeing as she didn't have one. Dina was a powerful witch; just moving into someone else's body was proof of that. There would be others seeking her skills, especially now that the Witches' Council had fractured so severely. Perhaps they wanted to give Dina the very thing she'd been drawn back to this world for. I didn't have to take a moment to think how bad it could be… Speaking of which...

"How come some of them are thinking about Dina?" I asked. That puzzled me. How could any of them know Dina was here?

"That's a very good question." Evan drifted closer to me but if he were worried, he didn't show it. "Did you get anything from any of the witches? Any thoughts about how they knew about Dina?"

Both sisters shook their heads and Seren said, "They weren't thinking about that when we listened in."

David bent down to Chyler, two fingers pressed against the pulse point on her neck. Her breath was shallow and every so often, she'd gasp a long breath before falling still again. "If we're going to get a plan together, we need to do it now," he said urgently.

"Now we're not protecting her, I cannot guarantee her safety."

"Shh!" Étoile flapped a hand at him from where she had positioned herself by the window. I was the other side of her, trying to see if there were any signs of movement from my neighbours' house. For the first time, I cursed the house being built at a right angle to the road. I still hoped Gage and Annalise were out and wouldn't be back any time soon. It wouldn't be fair for them to get caught up in this. Our small crowd would easily draw them out if they were at home and who knew what would happen then? "I think I see something," Étoile continued. "Way back, at the edges of the woods."

I peered through the dusk to see. There were more than forty people on my lawn now and they kept carefully to their smaller groups. My enemy's enemy was supposed to be my friend, but I didn't think I could count on that any time soon, seeing as my enemy and my enemy's enemy were both apparently very keen to get what they wanted. I followed Étoile's gaze and, sure enough, I could see the scrub rustling. A cold chill passed down my spine.

"What the hell is that?" Evan asked from behind me. "More witches? Did they program their WitchNavs wrong?"

I stifled a giggle.

Étoile shook her head as the scrub parted and something stepped out. "Something much better. Wolves."

I felt my heart thump. When I hoped Gage and Annalise would be out for the night, I hadn't meant quite like this. A drink in one of the nearby towns, maybe, or the movies, or over at a friend's house...

anywhere but here.

"Damn wolves," said Evan, his voice cold.

"Depends whose side they are on. We're already outnumbered. If they're here to help, we need them," Seren pointed out. She looked at me, asking, "Are they here to help?"

"I don't know." I was puzzled. What were they doing here anyway? My brain searched for a plausible response to this implausible situation. Maybe they had just been out running and stumbled across the gathering. Maybe they just felt the magic in the air. Even from this far away, I could hear the low rumble of their growling. It was an ominous sound, the kind a dog makes when it hears a prowler and it gives a first warning.

Several more wolves stepped out of the scrub and I saw the witches turning to see what was going on. I saw the big frame of Gage at the head of the middle group. Several witches shrieked and stumbled backwards at the sight of the wolf pack. I caught sight of one witch stepping forward from his group and raising his hand. He was pounced on and tackled to the ground before he could do any damage.

I was riveted to the scene as two large wolves stood over him, their teeth bared as the male witch froze, not daring to move. Clearly, no one else was foolish enough to approach the pack, but chaos was beginning to disrupt the groups, distracting them from us.

While this was going on, a larger group fanned out, positioning themselves squarely in front of the house. A woman stepped forward and she walked steadily towards the house, a long coat swishing around her ankles giving the appearance that she was gliding. Maybe she was. She stopped at the foot of the porch steps, and I saw her tentatively push a foot forward then draw back again. I felt the breath in my lungs catch. The wards I had woven were there to protect me from harm and no one could enter my house if they intended any ill will towards me. This woman was positively seeping with it.

"I want to talk," she said simply and loudly enough that we could all hear. Her eyes flitted over to the window and we locked eyes for a moment before I turned away.

"Georgia Thomas," breathed Seren and beckoned me away from the window.

"You've mentioned her," I said. When they first told me about the Council having problems, her name came up as one who saw herself as a potential leader, whether they wanted her or not.

"The blank spot. She was also one of the biggest critics of the Witches' Council under Robert Bartholomew's leadership. This is bad news." Seren looked over to Étoile and pulled a face. "Georgia wants control of the eastern seaboard at a very minimum. We've heard she's been canvassing all over the country for support."

"And she's on my lawn?" I asked.

"Seems that way," replied Étoile. She looked over to the spirit. Dina was taking on a corporeal form again, and she was substantially more solid than before, despite the severed connection. "From what I've heard, she was an old cohort of Dina's. She's very dangerous and very devious."

"Could she have anything to do with Dina being here?" I pondered.

Seren pursed her lips in concentration. "Maybe.

It's certainly no coincidence that both are here now."

"Stella Mayweather," called Georgia Thomas, a little more forcefully. "Seeing as you are not inviting me in, will you step outside to talk?"

"I suppose we should have known that she would have worked out who owned the house. Still, at least she's not tried to blast her way in," said Étoile.

"Yet," added Seren, unhelpfully.

"Do I have to talk to her?" I asked, panic rising. Devious and dangerous were two "d" words that I wasn't overly fond of. Now if they said "donut" that would have been an entirely different matter.

Étoile nodded. "We have to find out what she wants, and she asked for you. I wouldn't be surprised if she's behind all this, if she's behind Dina's return."

"I'm not going to talk to a mad person." And *fyi*, I won't go in the basement or the attic, I wanted to add.

"Oh, she's not mad, she's just horrible," said Étoile. "One doesn't have to be insane to be a bad person, just ruthless."

"I'll deal with her," said Evan, muscling up to the challenge. He was by the door, raring to go, seemingly ready to protect me, my honour and anything else of mine he thought the witches might threaten. I wasn't too sure about anyone else's chances though. He'd already made it clear I was his priority and I didn't want that tested.

I shook my head. I didn't know much about witches but I knew a lot about bullies. If I didn't stand up for myself, I might as well paint a target on my head myself. "You can't do that. I'll face her," I said.

"Seren and I will be with you. We wouldn't let you

go out there alone," said Étoile emphatically.

"Um, thanks," I replied, realising that it came out much more sarcastically than I'd intended. Even so, Étoile flashed me a smile and said, "You're welcome!" like she was doing me a favour.

"I'm coming with you," said Evan, flashing me a dark look as if to say *I dare you to say no*. There was no chance of that though, I was happy to take all the back-up muscle I could get.

"David, Hayley and Victoria," said Étoile, her voice all authoritative, "you watch Chyler and that... Dina, while we find out what Georgia Thomas wants."

I didn't like the idea of splitting our group up, any more than I liked the idea of standing on a porch with two witches and a daemon to face a growing crowd of witches and wolves. There wasn't even a punch line to fall back on. I felt like a frightened novice who was putting on her capable game face while quaking inside... which was exactly what I was doing.

"Let's do it," I said, opening the door, stepping out onto the porch, Evan just a step behind.

Georgia Thomas was waiting for me at the base of the steps. She was a tall woman and appeared to have been strikingly beautiful once, though she was aging well. I put her at around her late forties with fine cheekbones and raven hair that swung in a glossy bob, cut severely at her chin. Her long coat was thick velvet, dark as night, and pooled at her feet. It was finished with a thick collar made of something fluffy and tactile that buried her neck right up to her chin. She held herself with the absolute assurance that she would get, and could get, whatever she wanted. She was a woman who clearly did not take "no" lightly.

"So you're Stella," she said, running her eyes over me, starting from my toes and working upwards. "A little older than I expected."

"Right back at you," I said tartly.

"Oh, a wit too," she smirked. "Étoile and Seren Winterstorm, I see. And Evan Hunter too. How interesting." She gave them a polite, if rather cursory, incline of her head, then paused. I followed her gaze and watched four wolves prowl to the front of the house. They climbed the steps, my wards accepting them willingly, and sat in front of me, absolutely tense. I recognised Gage, the big wolf at my feet, and Annalise's smaller frame but not the other two.

"I don't like wolves," Georgia said, looking across at them as she fingered the thick fur of her collar, a cruel smile playing on her lips.

Gage growled. The chills they sent through me made me glad I was behind him.

"Let's cut to the chase, Georgia," said Étoile. "What do you want?"

"Always so blunt," murmured Georgia, not taking her eyes off me. "You're harbouring a fugitive."

"If you mean Chyler Anderson, she's not a fugitive. She's a frightened kid," Seren protested from behind my right shoulder.

"I do mean Chyler Anderson. And this 'frightened kid' has committed crimes of magic that have required a certain level of cleaning up, that we prefer not to do. Has anyone taken responsibility for her?"

"We have. And her family will look after her now," said Evan. I could feel his presence brooding behind me and he gave me the strength not to quake in front of the formidable woman. Ahead of me, Gage's ears flicked backwards, angry.

"She's a murderer. She needs to answer for her crimes."

"She's not a murderer. She didn't kill her mother, and you know it," Étoile spat.

"Oh? Is there something else I should know about? Like, for example, what is going on in there?" Georgia asked with a smile and I wondered what her real game was. Behind her, the other witches had drawn closer, their obvious dislike for one another overthrown by their desire to hear what was being said. The wolf pack prowled behind them skittishly, fanning out as though they were herding, which perhaps they were.

Georgia tried to look past me into my house but the door was closed behind us. I didn't know if she had any kind of powers that would enable her to read minds, or see the future like Seren and Étoile could, but we were still in the boundary of my wards and I hoped the occupants of my house were protected enough that she had to rely on good old curiosity and guess work.

"What right do you think you have over Chyler? You can't take her into custody," said Seren. "Only the Council can do that, and that most certainly is not you."

A murmur rippled through the small crowd and Georgia flashed a look at them that quieted them in moments. It struck me that there was some play for supremacy here, and some of the witches were here to watch what Georgia did, as much as others were here for Chyler. This wasn't a simple inquiry about a crime, there was a subtle challenge playing out that I didn't quite understand.

"That's right," piped up a female voice

somewhere behind Georgia. "Chyler will be taken care of by her own family. We all know she wasn't herself when her mother died."

Georgia smiled up at us. "Was she really not herself? Who was she?" she asked, a small gleam of interest sparking in her eyes. With a faint feeling of unease, I wondered if Georgia knew exactly what the answer would be and if Dina Lawley's return were entirely down to Dina or if she had help. It struck me that if Georgia were building her camp ready for a coup, she would want loyal followers, not to mention someone who was vicious and powerful. Dina fit the bill on all counts, the only problem being that she was technically dead. However, if she could raise her...

"We won't let you take Chyler," said another voice, a man this time, but he didn't step out where he could be seen under the porch lights now that the sky had faded to night. If Georgia was the vengeful type, I could understand that he didn't want to mark himself fully as an enemy. I wasn't overly happy about the position I was in either; by virtue of my friends I was already clearly marked as not on her side. I felt like a target was being painted on me with a big fat marker pen.

"Chyler was possessed," said Evan after a long silence in which I could hear nothing but the undercurrent of anxiety from the crowd. "She was attacked by Dina Lawley."

Dina's name rippled through the people, all of them having something to say except Georgia. I caught rumour, accusation and more than a few undercurrents of fear. Behind them all, the wolves whined in chorus, their throats thrust upwards to the sky. Georgia, however, didn't even look surprised.

"Dina's dead,' Georgia said simply, then, after a moment, "Are you saying Dina is inside Chyler?"

"No, we're saying she was, but we've separated them. Chyler isn't a danger to anyone anymore," I answered.

Georgia pressed on. "So Dina has gone? You've destroyed her?"

It was Evan who answered. "We've still got Dina."

Georgia's eyebrows perked at that and her eyes flashed. So she could be taken by surprise... "I'd like to see for myself. Stella, relax your wards and let me in. I pose no threat to you."

And I was a monkey's uncle! I glanced either side of me. Seren and Étoile weren't making any moves, but Evan shook his head in such a slight movement that I barely caught it.

"You'll have to take my word for it," I said. "Dina possessed Chyler, but we've separated them. Dina's still with us, but she doesn't have a body to move anymore."

"Stella, you seem like a clever girl. Put your wards to one side and let me in. I can assure you, no harm will come to your house. I'll take Dina with me."

If Georgia thought that was supposed to be reassuring, she was wrong. It wasn't my house I was worried about: it was everyone in it. Everyone except Dina Lawley that is. As far as I was concerned, the sooner we were rid of Dina, the better. Georgia just wasn't the right person for the job.

"No," I replied firmly, and started to turn away. Evan was by my side in a flash.

"I encourage you to reconsider," said Georgia, her tone dripping with acid. "I wouldn't want anyone to get hurt."

In front of me, Gage rose to all fours, and the wolves flanking him reciprocated. They looked poised to spring.

"Don't start anything you'll regret, Georgia. Remember who you're dealing with," said Étoile, stepping to flank my other side.

"The Winterstorm family? I hardly think I need worry about you two! Without your third wheel, you're no threat," Georgia scoffed.

"Don't count on it, bitch," snapped Seren, in an uncharacteristic burst of anger.

Adjusting her collar, Georgia called, "I'll be waiting, Stella, but the clock is ticking." As we retreated inside the house, she added, "I'll play with your... puppies while I wait, shall I?"

I waited until the door was firmly shut before speaking. "So that went... um..." I struggled to think of how it went. We weren't attacked, so, good. But Georgia wanted Dina. Bad.

"Georgia Thomas wanted Chyler," Étoile told David and Chyler's aunts, quickly recapping our conversation. They pulled Chyler onto my sofa and she was lying with her head in Victoria's lap, her breath shallow. "But as soon as she heard Dina was still here, she just focused on her."

"You think Georgia knew Dina was possessing Chyler?" David asked.

"Yes," said Étoile. "I think she knew the whole time."

"Then let me go," said Dina. She was much more real now than before and not quite as translucent. She seemed almost solid. She was an attractive woman, um, ghost, with a long swathe of dark hair. Her eyes were absent of colour but just milky orbs with pinprick black pupils. "You don't have any reason to keep me."

"Other than you being a murderer and a nut job?" I asked.

"Hey, it was just one time, so it hardly counts."

"Just once?" Étoile looked sceptical. "And how exactly do you plan on leaving here?"

"Georgia will have a way. She always does." Dina plastered a self-satisfied expression over her face, sealing our suspicions that Georgia had been behind her summoning all along. "Georgia said she had a plan."

"You're not seriously going to let her go?" I asked the others who were eyeing each other speculatively.

Evan shook his head. "Of course not. She's got to be sent on. The dead are the dead. There's no place for them here, no matter what the likes of Georgia Thomas think."

"Like, sent on to the afterlife?" I asked.

He shrugged. "Who cares? So long as she's not here."

"No! No!" Dina shouted and she fuzzed out of focus before rippling back into view. "I was murdered and I want my revenge. You can't send me back! Georgia promised. She promised I would live again!"

I empathised with her briefly at that moment. I could understand wanting revenge, but then I snapped out of it. Possessing Chyler, killing Andrea, and nearly killing Chyler in the process too, that just wasn't cool in my book. Plus, the thought of unleashing her to Georgia's custody gave me gooseflesh. I may not know either woman, but my sixth sense was screaming *no way*.

"So how do we get rid of her?" I asked, just as Dina let out an ear-splitting scream: "Georgia!"

The blast that rocked my house was huge. I felt like an earthquake was happening right under my feet and might have lost my balance if Evan hadn't wrapped an arm around my waist, letting me lean on him for support. "What the hell was that?" I whispered into his chest.

"Georgia Thomas," he muttered, tightening his hold on me as another blast hit the wards. Through the windows, I could see sparks scattering from the barrier. My wards were holding for now, but I'd never tested my own before, so I couldn't guarantee how long they would last. Terror edged through me as Evan said, "She's holding back. That was just a warning."

"She must want Dina really badly," I said still confused. There had to be more than friendship in it for Georgia to be so intent on getting Dina.

Evan said, "I've got a theory 'bout that. She's got some support, but not enough to stage a coup. I think she's trying to bring back all the witches who'd support her and are dangerous enough that no one would dare fight back. That would give Georgia absolute control. She could take the Council."

"And you think Dina's the first? Or do you think there are others?" I looked over at David. He was whispering something and I watched him walk around Dina's circle three times as she screeched at him. I was just thinking about putting my hands over my ears when her abuse came to an abrupt halt. When I looked, her mouth was still moving but nothing came out. David had spelled her into silence. Not only did we get a break from her screaming but she couldn't call out to Georgia anymore.

"If Georgia were successful, Dina wouldn't be the last. We were only lucky that Chyler fought back and came looking for you. Otherwise, she would probably have gotten away with it. There's no telling if she's done it before, but I would take a guess and say Dina was the first, an experiment that went wrong."

I slipped my arms around Evan's waist and buried my head in his chest for a moment so I could kill the panic bubbling in me. He stroked my back gently and I had a brief moment of wondering if everything were okay between us. I gulped. Now was not the time to be wondering about my romantic life. Not when there was a homicidal witch outside and her maniac sidekick inside.

"What's Georgia doing?" I asked, when I realised the blasts had stopped at two.

Seren pulled the curtains closed with a sweep of her hand from across the room so I couldn't see outside anymore. "She just pissed the wolves off," she answered, hurrying over to look through a chink in the material. "They're keeping her occupied for the moment."

"We have to get rid of her now," said David with urgency in his words as he nodded at Dina. "We can't risk Georgia breaking through."

"I can distract Georgia. She won't be expecting it," offered Evan. "If there's one think I know for certain about her, it's that she's got an overblown sense of her own importance."

"How are you going to do that?" I asked but he just winked at me. Then a rush of hot air that made me blink told me he'd gone. I was hugging air. I let my arms drop to my sides.

"Everyone gather round. We're going to form another circle around Dina. Hayley, Victoria, we're going to need you too." David seemed to think it was safe to leave Chyler unwatched and no one challenged the wisdom of that. Her breath was still shallow, but even. Plus Dina was the more pressing issue.

Hayley scrambled to her feet and Victoria slid out from under Chyler, replacing her lap with a pillow. They joined us in a circle while Dina threw herself against the invisible walls keeping her in place. Her silent screaming and shaking was disturbing. I linked hands with Étoile and Victoria to complete the circle and the strange feeling of our magic mingling and multiplying tickled over my skin.

"Everyone concentrate. When I give the signal, channel your power at Dina and use it to send her back when I perform the spell," David instructed us, flinching as Dina hurled herself towards him.

"Send her back where?" I asked.

"The afterlife," said David, his jaw set firmly. His voice lowered, he focused on the vibrating essence, commanding, "Dina Lawley, we send you back. Dina Lawley, we send you back. Dina Lawley, we send you BACK!"

Magic surged through me and I felt the electricity erupt from within. The flash that ripped through Dina blinded me momentarily and I felt the back draft of the enormous volume of magic burn like fire as it tore past me, sucking out the oxygen with it. I could hear ringing in my ears and I choked for breath.

For a moment, I felt like I was in the midst of nothing – my house was gone, the world was gone, then I snapped away like the moment never happened. The air felt still again and the silence deafening. Slowly, like a newborn child, I opened my eyes. I sank to my knees and reached forward with shaking fingers. The circle was now nothing more than chalk and paste on the ground. Dina, and her terrifying brand of unruly magic, were gone.

"We sent her back?" I asked, looking up at faces gaping at me. "What?"

"She's gone all right," said David. "But I didn't perform the spell."

"But I heard you. You sent her back," I mumbled.

"You sent her back yourself. The spell was much more complicated than that and I hadn't finished it." David's voice spoke of approval and reverence. "It should have taken all of us to send Dina back to the afterlife, but it was just you. *You* did it."

"I did it?" I stammered

Étoile sniggered. "You had a premature magiculation."

"Pardon?" I asked, arching an eyebrow, but the sound of worried voices outside distracted me. I got to my feet and quickly crossed to the window. I inched back the curtains and peeked outside. The assembled witches were staggering around, looking confused and shell-shocked. I couldn't see Georgia Thomas anywhere. I turned back to look at our group. "What did Evan do?" I frowned.

"I took Georgia Thomas on a little trip," said Evan, surprising me into jumping and letting the curtain slip back into place. I wasn't sure I would get used to him being able to sneak up on me like that. When no one else reacted, I surmised that there must be some kind of early warning system that I was missing. Just something else to learn.

"Where did you take her?" I asked.

"Arizona."

"Oh." I thought for a moment, then narrowed my eyes, "Where exactly in Arizona?"

Evan grinned. "The Grand Canyon."

"Oh, Evan. How will she get out?" chided Étoile, in a not exactly displeased way as she chided him. "You know Georgia can't teleport herself."

"Who cares?" he laughed. "She's going to be very, very cross when someone comes to get her."

"So basically, you just made her a bigger threat to me?" I snapped, leaning against the wall to keep myself upright, my legs like jelly. At once, I regretted snapping. "Evan, I'm sorry, I didn't mean it quite like that. I just meant, now she's going to be *really* mad at me."

"She was already mad at you and she would have been madder when she found out Dina was gone. I've just bought us some time."

"Georgia would have held a grudge anyway, especially as you're with us," explained Étoile. "If you're not with her, you're against her, in her eyes."

"It's the way of witches," added Seren. "We're often a clannish bunch. Speaking of which, how do we get rid of the ones outside?"

"I can't take them all to the Grand Canyon," said Evan. He dropped in the armchair, crossing one leg over the other. This was his third shimmer in less than a few hours and I didn't know how much energy it took out of him, but he looked weary.

"I've got a much easier way than that," I said, stomping past him to the door, feeling stubborn. I threw it open and strode outside until I stood on the edge of the porch. In front of me, the assembled witches argued, fought and shouted at each other, turning my lawn into a sea of chaos. I put my fingers in my mouth and blew an ear-splitting whistle that stopped the crowd pushing and shoving at each other. They turned to me, intrigued, confused and angry. The wolves circling them stopped growling a moment later, ears flicking.

"Get lost!" I yelled, my hands on my hips. "Dina Lawley is gone and if anyone even thinks about taking anything out on Chyler Anderson, you'll have me to deal with. Now, get the hell off my lawn and I don't want to see any of you here again." I stomped back inside and slammed the door, leaning against it as my heart pounded. Inside, I was being gawped at again. Evan jumped to his feet.

"You go, girl," grinned Seren, surprise etched all over her face.

I put my head in my hands and then forced myself to stand up straight, pushing my hair back from my face. I felt like throwing up. Outside I heard an engine start up. "I just pissed off a whole bunch of people, didn't I?" I said to the room.

"Yeah, but you just impressed a whole bunch too. They'll take your warning seriously especially with the demonstration of power you displayed when you banished Dina. Whatever happened in here, they felt it. Hell, I felt your magic and I wasn't even in the state," said Evan.

And if he thought that was reassuring, he was very, very wrong.

CHAPTER FOURTEEN

After my outburst, I couldn't help glancing out the window every few minutes to see if my lawn were emptying out. When the last stragglers eventually left, a pair of wolves snapping at their heels, I opened my door wide, ready for a few more guests.

Four wolves strode over the threshold like they belonged there while the rest stopped by the porch steps, sniffed and circled away in a pack towards the woods. I easily recognised the fine black and grey fur of Gage and Annalise's smaller frame with her pink-flecked coat. Two big wolves flanked them both. Inside, they sniffed suspiciously at the circles and then Chyler, whose aunts shrank back and tried to shoo them away like dogs. Gage nudged at my hand with his cold nose but it seemed rude to pet him. Instead, I placed a hand on his and Annalise's heads in what I hoped was a friendly gesture while resisting the urge to run my fingers through their soft, thick fur. I was also trying to shake the unpleasant image of Georgia's fur-trimmed coat, and the way she stroked it.

I collapsed onto the empty sofa and Annalise curled up on the floor at my feet, her nose resting on her paws as she watched us. Gage stood next to her, his feet firmly planted on the floor. He growled when Evan took a step towards me and I heard Evan swear lightly under his breath but he stepped backwards all the same.

One of the other pair of wolves keeled over and, for a moment, I thought it was hurt until his legs began to stretch and his bones cracked as they reshaped themselves. Fur receded and, moments later, there was a very naked man stretched out in front of the fireplace. I grabbed the coverlet that was still folded over the back of the sofa and tossed it to him. "Thanks," he said with a grin at me as he wrapped it around his waist.

I leant forward so my head was level with Annalise's ear. I wasn't entirely sure if she could understand me in her current form. "If you want to change, you can use my room. The door's open. Help yourself to clothes."

She nudged my hand and gave my fingers a quick lick before rising and trotting down the hallway. Gage looked up at me with his big, black eyes.

"My clothes aren't going to fit you," I said.

I wasn't sure if wolves could smile, or even laugh, but his tongue lolled out from his mouth and his chest heaved in a strange imitation of laughter. He waited until Annalise came back wearing my running pants and top, still barefoot, before he padded into my room. A few minutes later, he came back, one of my towels wrapped around his waist. His chest was bare and muscular, only a light dusting of hair remaining. I held out my hand and called for clothing from his house, and my hands depressed with the sudden weight of jeans, tee, socks and boots.

"Neat trick," he said reaching out to take them from me. He turned his back on me and trotted off and I heard the bathroom door shut a moment later. I thought I saw Étoile crane her head for a longer look.

"What about you?" I asked the naked man by my hearth, my coverlet loose about his waist.

"My clothes are in the Dodge across the street."

I put one hand on his warm shoulder to get a read on him and called his clothing. "Do you do pizza too?" he asked hopefully. Then he took the untidy bundle from my outstretched hands and hoisted it under his arm.

"You can change in the spare room," I replied, pointing the way and averting my eyes as the last wolf began to change in front of us. It seemed like an oddly personal thing to do in front of people. I guessed they were largely used to changing around each other and after a while, nakedness probably didn't bother them so much. Me? I wasn't so used to it. I called for his clothes too and he tugged them on immodestly.

"Jay," he said, shaking my hand as he fastened his shirt, before settling his eyes on Étoile. She arched an eyebrow at him and he grinned back. I rolled my eyes.

"You get used to changing," said Annalise, turning to me. "Though I prefer not to let it all hang out in public."

"No objections there," I replied. There were some things that were most definitely not best shared between friends. I waited for Gage and the other man to return and, once introductions were out the way, I gave the condensed version of events quickly.

"So what happens now?" Annalise asked. She looked from the broken circles chalked on the floor to Chyler huddled against her aunts. We were a shell-shocked weary bunch, but we were alive. She pressed her hands to her ears when everyone started talking at once.

A spectacularly loud whistle stopped the cacophony and we turned en masse to look at Gage. "The pack will be around tonight to keep an eye out. They'll stay outside so you won't have to worry about them."

"Thanks, I appreciate it," I said, meeting his eyes and seeing the uneasiness that flashed in them. He was worried, yes, but I didn't feel like I had any right to claim his concern.

"We'll put extra wards around the house," added Seren, before looking at me with admiration. "Though Stella's were pretty good." Which was apparently all the praise I was going to get for keeping our asses safe.

"I need a drink," I muttered, lurching off the sofa and walking quickly out of the room

"I'll help," said Gage and I heard him follow me into the kitchen.

I ducked my head inside the fridge and pulled out a six-pack of soft drinks and set them on the table, wishing I had something stronger. A lot stronger. Most of all, I just wanted to occupy myself with something normal. When I shut the door, Gage was pouring coffee grounds into the pot.

"It's getting cold out," he said conversationally, as if nothing particularly exciting had just happened. Me? My nerves, were like jumping frogs, I felt so wired.

"Seriously? That's all you have to say?" I said, my voice bubbling into what could be reasonably construed as hysteria. "It's cold out?! How about it's terrifying outside... oh! And maybe, how did you get rid of the evil witch inside Chyler? Or how about, is she going to live?"

"I kinda figured she was okay," said Gage, looking at me oddly. "She looked all right to me."

"Well she is now," I moaned. I stomped from the fridge and started pulling open the cabinet doors, searching for the biggest box of cookies I could find. I guessed we could all do with a sugar high right now. "It only took spells I've never even witnessed before to separate the spirit possessing her, a big threat from the wicked witch, not to mention, me risking my body and magic I don't even understand. So, yeah, Chyler's doing fine now."

Gage crossed the kitchen in a few quick steps and wrapped his arms around me. I just sank into him, my legs sagging with the weight of holding myself upright. My whole body succumbed to trembling. "Tell me," he said and I let the story tumble out.

After I finished, he held me still, one hand stroking the small of my back, the other resting on my hair, holding me to him. "It's okay now," he murmured from the top of my head where he rested his chin. "I'll protect you."

"You already did," I mumbled into his warm, strong chest. The wolves proved an extra boon to the cause when they corralled the witches and added extra weight to my threat. Some of the witches may have been prepared to attack, but not when the odds of them being bitten were high. I shuddered when I thought of the damage Georgia Thomas could have done.

"I'll always..." Gage started to say, but he was cut off as I felt him pull away from me. Not quite ready to support myself I almost sank to the floor but, unfortunately for Gage, he stumbled and knocked me over. I landed on my butt with a thump.

"What the hell?" I gasped. Gage managed to catch himself on the table and was rising back to his full height. Evan loomed over him, his face thunderous as he threw a punch that knocked Gage back. Gage rubbed his cheek where Evan landed his punch, his face reddening and body taut. For a moment, I was afraid he would change in my kitchen. Instead, they stared at each other with venom in their eyes. I scrambled to my feet and positioned myself between them, a hand on each chest pushing them apart as they pressed in.

"Don't take advantage of her," Evan said, his voice laced with anger.

"I was looking after her," Gage growled. "You should try it some time."

Evan's voice was a low, warning rumble. "Keep your hands off her. Stella's with me, not you."

"You sure about that? Doesn't seem like you're around much," taunted Gage.

"I'm here now." Evan moved closer.

I pulled my hand from Gage's chest to push both hands firmly at Evan, pleading, "Stop this! This is my house and I won't have either of you fighting in it. This is not okay." I hoped the finality in my voice was getting through to both of them.

"I'm sorry, Stella," said Gage after a moment and, even though we weren't touching, I could feel him step away, leaving an empty space behind me. He walked around the table and out of the room, picking the soft drinks up as he went, without a backwards glance.

"What were you thinking?" I whispered furiously at Evan. "You hit him!"

"I've seen the way he looks at you."

"So?" I replied, because that's all I could think of saying. "You can't hit every guy who looks at me in a way you don't like, or who gives me a hug. That's just not okay."

Evan relaxed and rotated his shoulders to shift the tension in his muscles. He rested against the counter, his face still guarded as he asked the one question I didn't want to answer. "Did anything happen between you two?"

I paused for a moment, not sure how I wanted to play this. Sure, we kissed on our poker date and we kissed a few days ago when I didn't know if Evan were coming back, but I put a stop to anything more. It was wrong, and I didn't want to be the kind of woman who cheated. Not that I was even sure if it were cheating. Evan left me in such a hurry and without a word, that we hadn't had a chance to talk properly yet. I kept it simple. "We've kissed."

Evan opened his mouth like he had something else to ask, but then he seemed to think better of it and closed it, shaking his head. "I love you, Stella," he said, after gaining some control of the connection between his brain and mouth. "I shouldn't have walked out on you. I should have stayed and listened. I'm not going anywhere, if you'll still have me."

"I love you too," I said quietly, "and I don't want you going anywhere. But you've got to be straight with me. Tell me if you're leaving and never coming back. Don't just leave me waiting and wondering. Don't hide things from me. And don't hit my friends."

Evan was quiet for a moment, then he answered, "Done." He wrapped his arms around me and I found myself standing in the same spot, hugging a second man in less than five minutes. He tipped my chin up to kiss me gently. "I can make the coffee faster, you know?" he murmured and nodded to the table. A moment ago, it was empty. Now, a fully laden tray with a steaming coffee pot and all my mugs were laid out on it, along with sugar and creamer.

"Very cool," I smiled, not letting it be lost on me that there was some one-upmanship going on. I didn't want a cute trick to cover up my being cross. I looked up when I heard a light click of heels and Étoile entered.

"Need any help?" she asked, her face fully knowing. She looked from the tray to Evan. "Apparently not. Perhaps Evan could carry?"

Evan released me and picked up the tray before it occurred to me that it might not be such a good idea to shepherd Evan into the same room as Gage. It was a good job I was short on furniture; any fighting would demolish it.

"Gage seems to have a bruise developing right here." Étoile pointed with her forefinger to her cheekbone, then upwards to her eye. "He didn't appear to have it until he came here."

"Evan hit him."

"What an asshole," she said, looking at the door as if looks could sting. I hadn't realised she had taken to Gage so much. Apparently, I was wrong. Unless something else was going on that I'd been missing.

"He may be an asshole, but he's my asshole."

She turned to me, arching one perfect eyebrow. "Bet you meant that to come out much more romantically."

I stifled a giggle. "Yes."

"Are you okay?" Étoile asked, putting on her concerned face.

"It's all a huge mind fuck," I said, breathing out heavily. "A year ago, if someone had told me this was my life, I'd have laughed. The Brotherhood tried to kill me, the Bartholomews, possession, dead witches trying to come back, Georgia freaking Thomas! What happened to my nice normal life?"

"It gets better," Étoile smiled, reaching out for me. I placed my hands in hers and she held them for a moment, then nodded. "Yes, it does get better for you."

"What did you see?" I asked.

She hooked an arm through mine and gave me that secretive smile of hers. "Now that would be telling!"

~

Chyler woke up an hour later, looking around in disbelief. She shuffled on the sofa until she sat upright, blinking in surprise at everything she saw before bursting into tears and pushing her aunts away. I knew how she felt. Before anyone could fuss over her, admonish her, or say anything downright stupid, I caught her in my arms and bundled her into my bedroom. If there were protests, I didn't hear them.

I let her curl up on my bed, sobbing. When she was ready, I filled in the gaps of her memory while she gaped at me as if I were telling her a particularly awful bedtime story.

"Stella, I don't want to be a witch." Chyler shifted uncomfortably until she was sitting on the edge of my bed, her shoulders hunched like she was trying to make herself invisible. "I didn't ask for this. I just want to be normal, like everyone else."

"But you were raised with this." I sat beside her, so close that I could feel her body shake with frustration.

"I know and I have this amazing lineage. Everyone tells me that. Everyone thinks I should be so proud and that magic is part of who I am, but I just don't want it." Chyler wiped her eyes with the back of her hands. "The tricks are cool, and they're fun, but this... This is all messed up! I'm seventeen. I shouldn't have to deal with... spirits and daemons... and werewolves. What the fuck is all that about? I want to finish high school and go to the prom. I want to have a boyfriend and I want to get drunk without worrying that I'm going to blow out all the lights with some stupid spell that I never meant to say!"

"Can't argue with that."

"I don't want to live like this." Chyler looked so small and alone. A long time ago, when magic had seemed more like a curse than a gift, I knew just how she felt. Yet Chyler had lots of people waiting to help and guide her, if she wanted. She grew up accepting and being part of the supernatural. "I want to have a choice. I don't want this forced on me," she finished.

I thought about all the decisions that were snatched from me. Even when Étoile showed up to rescue me and insisted I come back to the States with her, I never questioned why. Now I wondered how much of that was her influence. And how much was just my naivete that magic couldn't be part of my life.

It never occurred to me that I could make it all go away. It had never even been an option. But that didn't mean it had to be the same for Chyler.

"I once knew a couple of guys who were spellbound," I said slowly, trying to think through what I was saying, what I might be offering. "One just had his magic bound so he couldn't use it at all. The other one was a nice kid, but he struggled to control it, so he asked to be bound. He could use some magic but not so much that it made problems for him."

"I want that," said Chyler. "Not just a little bit of magic. I want all of it gone. I don't want magic, even if it wants me. Can you do that for me, Stella? Can you make it go away?"

"I think so, but I think you should talk to someone else first. Maybe your aunts, or your dad?"

Chyler shook her head. "They would convince me not to. Magic is too much a part of them and their lives. They can't imagine life without it. I think they even look down on regular people."

I could hear Étoile and Seren laughing as they passed the bedroom door. Well, didn't that sound familiar. "It's your choice," I said simply.

"Can you do it? Can you take it all away? Please. I just want to be normal."

I nodded. "I haven't done it before but, yes, I think I can."

"The book can stay with you."

"Huh?"

Chyler pointed to my dresser. The top was empty a moment earlier but now the book, which was mysteriously absent over the last few days, was sitting there. "I don't think it likes my aunts much and no one knows it's here. Plus, if it's here, it chose to be here. It made sure I found you."

"It tried to warn me too. Are you sure, Chyler?" The book was old and powerful and represented a tremendous gift.

"I'm sure. It will stay as long as it wants and you'll be able to use it. I'm sure of that." She looked at me with her big eyes. "Please try. If it weren't for magic, and the temptation, none of this would have happened and my mom would still be alive."

"Okay." I was going to have to wing this one. I placed my hands on Chyler's temples and felt the connection between us. I eased my will into her and felt the familiar tingle of magic flow through me. I held my hands at her head until I felt her magic ebb away.

"Is it gone?" she asked when I let go of her.

"Yes," I said, "but not completely. I willed your magic to be hidden but you can call it back anytime you want. You're in control."

"How do I call it back, if I ever want to? I don't, but, you know, if I did?"

"It's like a safety switch. You just have to will it, as powerfully as you can, and it'll be there." I couldn't, in good conscience just take Chyler's magic away, but I was glad to give her the option to restore it, if she wanted or needed to. "Like I said, it will always be your choice."

"But otherwise, it's gone?" Chyler's face filled with hope.

I smiled and nodded. "You don't have to worry about it anymore."

"The Council won't try to hurt me?"

I shook my head. "They never did. Dina must

have made you think that. They actually tried to help." It pained me to think it, but if the Council hadn't tried to intervene, we probably wouldn't be having this conversation.

"My head was really messed up." Chyler sucked in a breath. "Will you tell my aunts about the binding?"

"You're on your own with that one."

"Will you at least come out with me?"

"Sure."

Chyler stood up and smoothed her clothing with the flats of her hands. She took a deep breath and walked to the door, then, with her hand on the handle, she paused for a moment. "I'm nervous," she said.

"You don't have to be. They should respect what you want."

"Do you respect me?" Chyler seemed desperate for some kind of approval.

"Yes."

"Well, okay, then. Thanks, Stella. Thanks for everything."

I followed Chyler out of my room but I let her approach her aunts on her own. I watched her for a moment, just long enough to see Hayley cry and Victoria hugging Chyler before I turned away. This wasn't a scene meant for anyone but them.

Gage was in the kitchen holding an ice pack against his eye and cheek, nursing the purplish-blue bruise that stained the surrounding skin. I was angry that Evan hit him, but relieved that he was so restrained. It could have been so much worse if a fight had sprung out. It didn't escape my notice either that only Gage had apologised to me.

"Are you okay?" I asked. I wanted to reach up and

peel away the ice pack and check his progress, but I thought I'd be over-stepping the boundary if I did, so I kept my hands to myself.

Gage nodded. "I'll be fine in a few days. Wolves are good healers. How's Chyler?"

"She asked me to bind her magic."

"Did you?"

"Yes, but she can break it if she wants to."

"You've been a good friend to her." Gage peeled off the ice pack and tossed it on the drying rack. Annalise, coming through the doorway, rushed to his side but he brushed her off and she hung back anxiously. "Now that everything has calmed down, we're going home. But, like I said before, some of the pack will hang around. Not that we're expecting anything," he reassured me.

"Okay." I didn't know what else to say. I couldn't ask Gage to stay without giving him the wrong impression. And, if I offered to help, I didn't want to insinuate that he wasn't masculine enough to deal with this problem himself. So, I said nothing but followed him and Annalise through the house to the front door, where their two men were waiting.

I caught Gage and Evan glaring at each other, but other than that, Evan gave him a wide berth, sticking to leaning against the mantle-piece. I hoped my warning had sunk in. I couldn't change what happened between Gage and me now, but I could ensure he wasn't punished for it. He hadn't done anything wrong.

"Bye, Stella." Annalise kissed me on the cheek and stepped outside. She obviously had a lot on her mind but we both knew now was not the time to say it. The men followed her out, flanking her sides like they were her personal bodyguards. Maybe they were, for all I knew. I think one of them, Jay, winked at Étoile.

Gage followed them, then turned to me. He surprised me by dropping a kiss on my other cheek and held my hand for the briefest of moments, just enough for his extra heat to radiate warmth through me. He pressed a little object into my hand and curled my fingers over it. "See you soon, Stella."

"Bye, Gage," I murmured as he stepped out. It was fully dark now, only the silvery glow of the moon, hanging low and heavy in the sky, for light. In the black of the countryside, I heard a wolf howl and shivered. How had I not realised Wilding was so... wild?

Across the room, Evan smiled at me. I dipped my head and uncurled my palm to see what Gage had pressed into it. There was a small round blue button. It had fallen from my shirt when he ripped it open as we kissed. I balled my hand again. Oh yes, I got the message all right. He wasn't going to give up without a fight and he just made sure that I knew that, right under Evan's watchful eyes.

CHAPTER FIFTEEN

Despite their enaction of the most powerful displays of magic I ever saw, with me in a front row seat, my visitors left by car. After the teleportations and ghostly banishments, it was pretty disappointing to see them depart so normally.

Hayley, Victoria and Chyler left first. After Hayley's third bout of tears and a lot of hugging and reassurance from Victoria, to the point where Chyler needed rescuing, they seemed strangely calm and tolerant of Chyler's rejection for their way of life. I hope that meant she wouldn't be punished for wanting a normal life, if she even really knew what that was. I hoped that losing her mom was all the punishment she suffered.

"Thank you," said Victoria, holding my hands between hers. We were standing on the porch watching Chyler buckle herself into the back seat. "Not just for saving her life, but for making sure she can call her magic back when she's ready."

"If she's ready. She might never want it back," I pointed out.

"But you gave her the option and we'll look after her until then."

"She's going to really need supportive people around her. It's not easy going through all that when you're so young." Get me. I was only seven years older than Chyler. I could practically still taste my teen years.

"And yet you've turned out rather well," Victoria replied with a smile. "We'll get her in therapy and back to school. She can go to college, have a career and, when she's ready, we'll all be waiting. She won't be punished for any of this. We know Chyler didn't kill her mother."

It seemed to me like Victoria thought Chyler's resolve would not last. I didn't have any hopes either way. I just wanted Chyler to be happy and I hoped her aunts wanted that above anything else, especially their personal gain. Magic was so ingrained in their way of life that I couldn't be sure.

"I hope she finds happiness," I said and Victoria nodded to me. I waved to them as their car pulled away and, within minutes, they disappeared behind the tree line.

Seren and David were the next to go. They stayed through the night and now that it was early morning, they were eager to depart. Sharing the car that they arrived in, they squabbled shortly over who was going to drive. I rather thought they just wanted to be together, in the same way that I wanted to sink down next to Evan and pretend this had all been just a bad dream.

"Are you sure you won't come?" Seren asked her sister for the umpteenth time.

"I'm sure," replied Étoile, hugging first her sister, then David.

None of us slept that night and I was busy stifling a series of increasingly longer yawns. Étoile asked me, over breakfast, when it was just the two of us, if she could stay. After a moment of silence, in which her impeccably unreadable voice started to approach something close to pleading, I laughed. "Of course, you can."

"I won't get under your feet," she promised, slugging back a coffee that was so strong, it should have blown her socks off.

"I'd rather you did," I replied. "I'm done with being lonely and I'm glad you're staying."

"Will lover boy mind?" Étoile asked. Evan was stretched out on the sofa, asleep, having crashed out the hour before. After throwing a cover over him, I left him there.

"It's my house," I reminded her, "and he's a guest too."

"I'll pay rent."

"You can help me get some furniture," I suggested, ignoring her offer for now. "Not that I'm expecting you to pay for it. I just need help choosing it."

"Sure," said Étoile, but I wasn't sure if she were disagreeing, or agreeing with me.

I showed Étoile the empty spare room and she looked around it, opening the closet door. She looked out the window to see the view, and finally, gave me a pleased smile. "I really need a break. I've looked after Astra for so long and she is getting better, but it's so

291

exhausting. Even when she was missing, she was exhausting."

"Seren won't mind?"

"It's Seren's turn," Étoile answered simply. "It's not forever. She'll be okay."

"It's a done deal, then," I said, and settled it. Étoile was here to stay for as long as she needed and I had gotten myself my first roommate.

The four of us were standing on the porch now, going through the motions. Seren hugged me and David did too, with just as much affection as they had shown Étoile. "We'll be back as soon as we can. And maybe you'll come out to us. There might be a wedding," Seren added coyly with a wave as she backed away. "You'll have to come home for that."

"Of course," Étoile agreed and then said so softly that only I could hear. "You'll love our family. Most of them are nuts."

"Couldn't miss that."

Étoile linked her arm in mine. "You might even find you need me if those two alpha males are going to keep on butting heads," she murmured. We both looked at Gage's house and then over to the window, through which we could see Evan rolling onto his side, still deep in sleep.

Evan and Gage's horn-locking was still fresh on my mind. "They'll just have to get along. I'm not a prize to be fought over. I've made my choice," I said, even though a little part of me felt sorry for not choosing Gage. Something inside me deeply adored him and that part would have to stay dormant if we were to reach anything like a platonic friendship.

"Did you?" Étoile asked pointedly, but I just pulled a face at her and she went inside, muttering something about searching online for some decent furniture.

Despite the amount of coffee replacing red blood cells in my veins, I crashed, fully clothed, in my bed. Six hours later, I woke up feeling guilty for being such a dreadful host. I provided my first housemate with an empty room, with no furniture of any kind, and promptly flaked out on her. As I dragged myself out of bed, I couldn't really bring myself to feel any shame. After all, we spent the evening fighting and conquering evil. My stomach grumbled. Apparently, battling necromancy stimulated my appetite.

Étoile and Evan were waiting for me in the kitchen when I stumbled through.

"I didn't think you were ever going to wake up," said Étoile, with a shake of her head. She had a stack of magazines spread out in front of her: *Martha Stewart Living*, *Elle Decor*, *Living etc.* I hoped she didn't plan to redecorate. I was only just getting the hang of having my own space, plus, I didn't think my budget ran along the same lines as hers, not that I was complaining.

"Hey," Evan smiled at me. "Feeling better?"

I stretched my arms to the ceiling, feeling my aching muscles pop and settle. "Much."

"No one came back through the night or today," said Evan, like he was reading my mind. I was wondering if there would be any sneak reprisals, but sleep insisted on taking me before I could even consider staying awake any longer.

"That's good, right?" I said, searching through the fridge for something immediately edible. I gave up and sighed. If there were going to be three of us in my house, someone else would have to do the shopping besides me. When I turned back to the table, there was a full plate waiting for me.

"Did you do that?" I asked Evan, who was looking smug.

"It was the least I could do."

"Meals out of thin air. That could come in handy."

"Out of your fridge, actually. I just sped up the cooking process."

"To light speed?" I sat down and ate like I hadn't seen food in weeks while Étoile ignored me and Evan thumbed through the messages on his phone.

"Étoile's staying," I said to Evan between mouthfuls and he just nodded, saying, "She mentioned that. Said you were going to have to get furniture."

"I can stay at the inn until then," Étoile chimed in, looking up from her magazine. "I'm paid up until the end of the week."

"We can go get a bed, at least, tomorrow?" I suggested. "Hey, didn't Seren and David take your car?"

"Yes, but don't worry about giving me rides, I'll just shimmer if I need to."

"I guess I'm driving to the furniture store then."

"Hmm. Guess you are." Étoile gave me a warm smile and looked between the two of us. It was all very scrupulously polite. "I don't suppose you'll mind if I disappear? I need to sleep and I imagine you have some talking to do." She didn't give me a chance to protest, she just blinked out of my kitchen.

"Hah," I said looking at the space she left behind. "Will it ever get to the point when I think people walking out of doors is unusual?" I took my plate to the sink and rinsed it before sitting down again. Étoile might have forced my hand, but Evan and I did have some talking to do. The least I could do was make sure it was over a tidy table, Étoile's magazines excepted.

"Why didn't you contact me while you were gone?" I asked, throwing all my eggs into one basket. He might have given me his love, but he hadn't offered up an explanation as to where he had been yet.

"I didn't know what to say. I was angry, and worried, and pissed off that you lied to me."

"I didn't exactly lie. I just didn't tell you what I knew about Chyler."

"All the same, you should have said something." Evan rocked back in his chair. "You have a lot of power, Stella, but you're still new to this. You're still untrained. You can't fully control what you do yet. David told me what you did with Dina... but that was by chance, not by design. You can't rely on luck like that to keep you safe. You'll get hurt, others could get hurt."

I breathed in. Everything he said was true. "I know."

"But I should have kept in touch. I should have realised you would be worried," Evan conceded.

"I thought you left me," I said, my voice so thin it was just a whisper.

"Sweetheart, I would not leave you. But I can see why you thought that."

"The last time I didn't hear from you, I thought you were dead. I... panicked."

Evan leant forward. "I want to be part of your life. I don't want to be the guy you see occasionally. I want what we had at the safe house when we first met. I want you every day."

"How can we have that when you want to be in Texas, and I want to be here for now?" I asked, feeling tears prick at the corners of my eyes. I blinked them back.

"I've been thinking about that. We could stay here. I can still run my business, though I'll be away occasionally. You can start going to State if you want to go to school. We're more out of the way here and it's quieter, so strangers will be recognised easier. It might even be safer than the city."

"You would do that? For me?"

Evan nodded, sincerity and hope etched across the fine planes of his face. "Yes. I'm not saying forever. I'd want you to come with me sometimes and see my home too, see how I live. You could transfer credits if, eventually, you decided to move away from here. Maybe even work for me, if you wanted?"

"I could do that," I said carefully, trying to think things through before I launched into any major decisions. All the things Evan offered ran through my head: living with him, an education, a job... it was a lot to take in. It was everything I wanted, and more. "I'd like to see where you live. Wait, did you just offer me a job?"

"You need one, right? And I can use someone with skills like yours."

"What would I do?"

"We'll deal with that when it comes up."

"I'm not calling you boss." I grinned.

"And I'm not going to sexually harass you in the photocopy room."

"It's not harassment if I'm enjoying it," I pointed

out.

"You'll have to keep your mind on the job," Evan quipped without missing a beat.

We were quiet for a moment, then I said, "You have to know that Annalise and Gage are my friends. If you're staying here, you'll see them. I'm sorry that I kissed Gage, and that it upset you, but I'm not going to avoid him."

"I can deal with the wolves. Annalise is a nice person. Gage ... I'm not too fond of him. I can't help it that I don't like that you've kissed each other, and maybe there was an attraction there and that makes me jealous; but I won't do anything that would make you uncomfortable." Evan seemed sincere but a part of me wondered if it would be that easy. He seemed to think so. He didn't know that Gage had already implied that he wasn't giving up and I wasn't going to fan the flames by telling him that. I was a one-man woman and I aimed to stay that way, werewolf attraction or not.

"So what now?" I asked, trying to temper the butterflies in my stomach. Evan was staying. My mind and body were both struggling to accept it as fact.

"We could celebrate?" The smile Evan gave me then was anything but friendly. Instead, it bordered firmly on being devastatingly carnal. Feelings that I had, up to now, tempered bubbled to the surface.

"Oh?" I raised my eyebrows and barely had time to squeal before he scooped me up, his mouth on mine. A wave of worry rushed through me at the thought of him teleporting, and I mumbled against his lips. "Don't shimmer, or whatever it is that you did before."

"I'm familiar with using my legs to get about."

Evan carried me into my room and settled me on the bed, falling next to me, kissing me all the while. Struggling out of my clothes was a welcome chore and I pulled him to me, eager to finally have him in my arms again, to feel him as part of me. When he finally was, the pleasure was sweet and intense and I never wanted it to end.

~

I was engrossed in Étoile's magazines when she came back, pinging into the living room quietly, making me jump. I really needed to find out how they always knew when someone else was coming. At least, they never seemed to be surprised the way I was. Only Chyler's entrance had given me any warning, indicating there was some difference between spell craft and innate magic.

Étoile changed into skinny indigo jeans, a bright yellow silk blouse that billowed around her arms and long tan boots. Her hair was freshly washed and she'd applied a fresh layer of make-up. In short, she didn't look like she had been up all night banishing dead witches. I, however, still did. I refused to feel bad about that.

"How're things?" she asked, sitting next to me on the floor and curling her legs under her.

"Evan's staying," I told her with a smile.

"Thought he would."

"As if I wouldn't," interjected Evan. He stretched out on the sofa, a book in his hand, a scene so familiar to me, like when we first met. Back then, I'd barely ever seen him without a book.

He lit the grate too, kickstarting the fire with a flame flung from his palm, so the living room was filled with warmth and the sounds of the logs crackling. I didn't know what happened to the floor, but the chalk and paste were gone, and the hardwood looked buffed and shiny. I was never letting that happen in my house again. Any spells could be performed on the driveway in future. Or in the next state. Or another country.

I looked up at Evan and smiled when he ran a hand over my hair. With him here, I had what I wanted. I had the chance of a home with him. He gave me love and I loved him back. He would protect me. Most of all, I was just happy at the thought of waking up every day, knowing that he was sharing my life.

"I've had quite enough of the gooey stuff with Seren and David," sniffed Étoile, but she wasn't upset when she added, "You people disgust me."

I traded glances with Evan before he put his nose back in his book. Neither of us bothered apologising. If Étoile were going to live with us, and dip into my head, she would just have to deal with it.

"What about your job and your apartment?" I asked Étoile as I flipped through a magazine. I wondered how she could leave her life behind on a whim, and then I remembered that I, very easily, walked out of my life and stepped into a new one.

Étoile sighed and sat down, her back warming against the fire. "Everything went on a hiatus when I was working for the Council, but now they're gone, I can do as I please."

"Are they really gone, or are they just regrouping?" I asked. I wanted to know more about the Council and what was happening. It seemed strange to think that such an apparently powerful structure could disintegrate without something rising from the ashes, especially when people like Georgia Thomas wanted to pick up the pieces.

"Not quite." Étoile paused and I could see her thinking about what I should know.

"Out with it," I urged.

Étoile picked at a piece of thread from the hem of her top. "You know already that the Council governed everything, but without a leadership, it's a shambles. A long time ago, before we were anything like organised, it was just lots of covens dotted about. Then we unionised, as it were, so witches could converse better, share knowledge, help each other... It used to be a good thing, but like all good things, there's always someone who wants more power. Controlling the Council is a powerful job and it takes a powerful witch to keep everyone in line."

"There's a European Council too," added Evan. "And in Russia, Asia, Africa, the Middle East. Australia. I hear their conventions are a blast."

"You don't go?" I asked, not sure if he was being a touch sarcastic.

Evan shrugged. "Daemon."

"Oh, right."

Étoile picked up where she left off. "Anyway, the remains of the Council board are still there and they were the ones that asked us to investigate Chyler. The problem is, they don't have anyone to lead them and no one on the board is individually strong enough. It used to be that the Council was elected fairly. The smartest, the wisest, the most benevolent. Then, of course, politics got involved and it was the strongest, the richest and the best promises lobbied to get a backing for election. That's where the Bartholomews excelled. They had it all, including power."

"So if there were an election, there would be a new leader?" I asked.

"Theoretically, yes, but the Council is supposed to elect a new leader before the old one goes. Obviously, that hasn't happened this time so we've been without with a leader for six months. That leaves the Council wide open for lobbying, and I don't just meaning shaking hands and kissing babies' heads. Some witches will do anything to get the spot."

"Like Georgia Thomas?"

Étoile nodded and I wondered if it were my imagination that she paled a shade. "Georgia isn't the only one who wants to collect an arsenal of witches so strong that no one would dare defy her. There could be a takeover. A new Council could be declared."

"And she's having to resort to bringing back the dead?" I asked. "Doesn't sound like much of a recipe for success."

"She's determined and she'll try anything. Thankfully, it didn't work this time, but there's no telling what Georgia would do if she forced her way onto the Council, never mind the leadership."

I thought about that. "It would be that bad?"

"Georgia *is* that bad," Evan said, turning the corner of his page and closing the book.

Étoile added, "She knows our house wouldn't support her, but you're not allied as such, except through our friendship."

"What do you mean by 'house'?"

"A lot of magical families have houses. Even when names change and there's distant cousins, marriages and so on, they're all part of a house. It keeps us aligned and ensures some degree of protection. The house of Winterstorm is an old house and we've extended our backing to you, but that doesn't mean it's absolute."

"Well, thanks," I said. "Were my parents part of houses? Would their house still exist?" I'd finally laid my parents' memories to rest but it did cross my mind that I might have distant relatives that were unknown to me.

"I'll have to ask my mother," Étoile answered. "She's got an excellent memory when it comes to all the houses and their histories."

"This is a lot to take in," I confessed, leaning back against the sofa. I wondered how my thought processes would ever straighten out enough to think all of this through in a vaguely coherent manner. I asked, "So what happens if I'm not a part of a house?"

Étoile shrugged, "Nothing much, usually. Like I said, it's a way to organise, more than anything. But things are changing and I can't say being aligned to a house would be good for protection in the future, not when Georgia Thomas and the likes of her are canvassing for power. A threat is much weaker if you've got the backing of a house. Lone witches will be targeted, I can guarantee that."

"And there's the Brotherhood," I said, the group forever on the periphery of my mind.

"There's nothing to suggest they go after houses, just individual witches," Étoile replied.

I turned to Evan. "What about daemons?"

He raised his eyebrows. "What about us?"

"Do you have hierarchies, or councils, or houses?"

"We're not nearly as organised and there aren't as

many of us as there are witches," Evan said. "Many daemons aren't even that close to their own families. It's not like being a human, where you're ruled by emotions and connections. Daemons are very self-serving."

That seemed a little harsh to me. "You're not like that," I protested.

"I'm not one hundred percent daemon, thanks to my mother."

"Hallelujah for that," muttered Étoile.

"What happens to witches on their own?" I asked, curious as to exactly what Étoile's family backing really meant. I appreciated them offering it, but I still wanted to understand what I was receiving.

"There's a good chance they'd be bullied into picking a side," said Étoile. "They'll be forced to pick a side if they want to live, and the side they pick will all depend on who threatens the worst, and/or who provides the best protection."

"And what happens if a side loses?"

Étoile sighed. "I really don't know. I would imagine they would be forced to surrender to the winning party, or face the consequences."

That didn't sound promising. I could only imagine what Georgia Thomas would do if she won. But, would it be as bad as her retaliation if she lost? Finally, I wondered if the Brotherhood were as dangerous to witches, as the witches were to themselves. That was not a happy thought at all.

"What about wolves?" I asked, thinking this seemed the opportune moment for me to finally learn more about the strange world I lived in.

It was Evan who answered. "They are split into packs regionally. As far as being organised, they pretty much have it down. Often they congregate in one place, like Wilding."

"And vampires?"

"Who knows? Shifty, devious creatures. Let's hope they keep to themselves." Étoile's mouth was set in a firm line, like she wanted to spill the gruesome details, but couldn't quite bear to bring it all out in to the open.

I stifled a snort. That coming from a witch! None of the witches I'd met struck me as being solidly honest.

"Don't look so worried, Stella." Evan picked up his book again, and was thumbing through to his dog-eared page.

"It's hard not to," I replied, trying to wipe the frown from my forehead as my mind filled with thoughts.

"Étoile and I won't let anything happen to you."

"I know you won't, but it's not like things are looking great. Georgia Thomas, and who knows who else, want to rule the Council and you've already said we stand a chance of getting caught up in that; even if only because we're forced to choose. The Brotherhood will always be a threat..." I trailed off, slightly despondent.

Evan pulled me up onto the sofa next to him and held me close. "You're not alone anymore, Stella. You'll never be alone again."

CHAPTER SIXTEEN

It took me a moment to realise that the strange ringing noise wasn't just in my ears. I scrabbled around the sofa for my phone, plucking it from under a pillow to answer on the fifth ring. "Hello?"

"Hello. Stella?"

"Yes," I said hesitantly, thinking the voice on the other end sounded familiar, like I should immediately know who was calling.

"Stella Mayweather?" the woman asked again.

"Who's this?"

"Stella! I can't believe you asked me that! It's Kitty."

Didn't I feel like a moron? "Kitty! Oh, I'm so happy to hear from you. How's your leg?" I asked while mouthing at Evan, who glanced up from his laptop: *it's Kitty!*

"Out of a cast, at last. You would not believe how long it took to shave my legs. It was beyond gross. Anyway, I just got out of hospital. Literally! I'm still in the parking lot. I was thinking of coming to visit you, in time for Christmas, if you like?"

I beamed. "I do like. Actually, I love the idea. Come when you like for as long as you like." I couldn't wipe the grin off my face. Seeing Kitty again was a huge boon. She had been my first proper friend and I missed her enormously in the months since we last saw each other. "Is Marc with you?" I asked.

"No, Marc left a few days ago. He had to go back to New York. Witchy business, you know, but he said to say hi and he's looking forward to seeing you soon." Marc had even less time than I to come to terms with his magic. He would have had years of training, however, were it not for a powerful spell that bound his powers. He had a lot to come to terms with.

"That's nice of him. It seems like forever..."

Kitty cut in, "Well, it doesn't seem like nearly long enough ago for me. Oh, don't get me wrong, not seeing you has been far too long, and I think we have a lot of catching up to do, but the less I think about what happened that day, the better."

I nodded in agreement, and then, remembering she couldn't see me, said, "When can you get here?"

"Sometime in the next couple of days I think. I have everything packed and all I need to do is turn on the engine. My leg aches a little so I'll be taking it easy."

"Great. Étoile is here, but there's more than enough space for the four of us. Evan is staying too."

"I can hardly wait to catch up. I want a blow-by-blow account of everything and, as a special bonus, for you, I'm going to bring some good weather with me. See you soon, honey." Kitty was a weather witch. She had been learning how to control the elements when I first met her and I was certain she was responsible for the perfect weather wherever she went, not to mention the orchard that she once forced to grow despite the salty climes of ocean-side living.

"See you soon." I hung up. Kitty's imminent visit was the cherry on the icing on the cake. I felt the need to be surrounded by friends. I had Étoile, I had Annalise across the street. Kitty would be here within days. Seren and David may have gone, but I knew I would see them again. There was Evan, who was here solely for me. And Gage; he would be my friend even though what I felt for him was tempered. I was surrounded by people I adored and people who wanted to be with me. Happy was a good feeling.

Even better, the happy vibes were waylaying the angst that sat heavily on my shoulders since Georgia Thomas' inauspicious visit. True to his word, Gage kept up his offer of keeping watch and his wolves were patrolling the area for the last few days. Now, however, they were less reticent about being seen by me. Much as I wanted to sit by the window and observe their wild behaviour, it felt strange doing so, knowing they were my neighbours and townsfolk. Evan and Étoile barely gave them a second glance, as if such beings were completely natural in their world. Thinking about it, they probably were.

Now the wolves were out in the open, they had taken to howling in the woods all night and, for a while they, kept me awake with them. I thought about stomping onto the porch as dawn broke, yelling "Shut up!" But it seemed arrogant to try and break them out of their natural state, especially when they were not only my protectors but were generally on the lookout for anything unusual in the area, anything that could be a threat to us. So I resigned myself to live with the howling.

When I finally went outdoors, there were still a few wolves, in their animal forms, milling around the porch of Gage and Annalise's house. I was watching them when Gage came across, and they parted to allow him a path. They trotted on his heels to my porch before wheeling away again to the woods that bordered my land. I lost sight of them as they leaped through the scrub before bursting playfully back through in another spot, nipping at each other's tails.

"How come they're still like that?" I asked him. "You're not."

"We don't just change during full moons. Many of us can change whenever we want."

"Ahh."

Gage leant against the railings and watched them with me. "Besides, it's the weekend and they can just be themselves out here, especially now they don't have to worry about you seeing them."

"I'm sorry for disrupting the pack."

"Don't be. We have to hide from everyone, so they understand. With your house standing empty for so long, they had free run of the land around here. When you came, we took a motion and agreed to stay off your property. It's no problem at all that you're here. If anything, a witch is more welcome than not." Gage took a deep breath. "Though it should be said they're all anxious at the moment. All those witches created a huge surge of energy in the area. We hear rumours."

"What kind of rumours?"

"That energy like that brings trouble, one way or

another. You should be on your guard."

I felt a chill travel through me. "On my guard against what?"

"Georgia Thomas, for one. Other witches, too. I've put feelers out to other packs to see what they report and what I hear isn't good. Her coming here was bad news. You attracting her attention was bad news, and there's no telling if or when she'll come back. She's a powerful witch and she was humiliated last night. I doubt she'll take that well, at all. And, of course, there could be any number of other supernatural creatures... as well as those that want to harm us for just being us."

"Like the Brotherhood?" I asked.

Gage nodded. "They'll be attracted to the power, just as much as anything else; and just because they target witches, doesn't mean they won't come after the rest of us. You need to be prepared for that. You need to understand what it is to be part of this world, not just someone who got sucked into it. You need to learn to defend yourself."

"I have been learning," I protested.

"Not enough. You need to demand to learn. You need to know how to protect yourself against werewolves – yes, even us – vampires, daemons and witches. You need to know what will work and what won't. You need to know how to run, if you can't fight."

"I need to learn a lot, huh?" My shoulders fell a little. Everything he said was true, of course. So far, I'd been flying by the seat of my pants, performing magic – like Dina's banishing – that I didn't understand, rubbing shoulders with creatures I couldn't even recognise. He was right. It had to stop.

I had to accept the protection extended to me could only go so far, and it wasn't fair to take theirs – Gage's, Evan's, Étoile's – without offering anything in return. "I don't know how to do all that," I said.

Gage's jaw locked and I stabled myself for a furious answer at my apparent ineptitude but instead, he said, "You've got teachers. Make them teach you properly, and faster, and more intensively. You can train with the wolves here, but you'll need to meet other supes to learn about them."

"Won't that just expose me?" It didn't escape me that I had been hidden my whole life and that all that was now for nothing.

"The way I hear it, and I've been asking around, is that business with the Witches Council already exposed you. People know who you are, even if they don't know where you are. But soon enough, they'll know that too. Georgia Thomas is pissed at you; other witches will see you as her enemy and they will want your power. Rumours will start about Chyler and Dina and there will be nothing you can do to stop them. Other supes will want to know what you can do for them, and you won't know if they're friend or foe." I didn't need to look at him to know how serious he was.

I let it sink in, before saying more to myself than to Gage, "Basically I'm in a world of shit."

"Something like that."

"Will we be safe here?" I liked Wilding. I liked the town and I liked my home. I'd done my absolute best to keep any magic I used to a minimum here, and my control was now in great condition. But I seriously doubted that I was up to protecting myself against a legion! Not that Georgia Thomas had turned up with a legion, but my imagination was allowed a minor freak out. That she, or the Brotherhood, could force me into leaving, into running again, was something that didn't sit well with me. That was before I even factored in the danger that the town and its inhabitants could be in.

I felt a brief moment of shame when I wondered if I should have helped Chyler at all. She seemed to have brought a lot of problems with her, and now, it was likely we would be left with the fallout. A daemon, a witch, two novice witches and a town of werewolves might not be enough to defeat a very angry, very powerful witch, or the sinister Brotherhood. I sincerely doubted we could deal with both, or more.

Gage shrugged. "We're all on the lookout. If anything comes this way, we'll know about it," Gage said, which didn't exactly answer my question. I wondered: if I pressed the point, would I like what I heard? He added, "You're safer here than anywhere else."

He turned back to me, ignoring the wolves sniffing around his house and chasing each other, nipping at tails. He nodded towards my house. "Is the daemon staying?"

"Yes," I replied simply. We had some stuff to work through, but Evan was staying. We'd see what happened later. "Étoile is staying too, and my friend Kitty is coming."

Gage frowned at her name. "Is she a werecat?" he asked.

"A Katherine," I clarified, in case he was thinking of eating her. "She's a witch."

Gage drew a lungful of air and rested his hands on

my shoulders. "It'll help that they're here." He moved closer to stand by me, so close my shoulders rubbed just above his elbows, so close I could feel his heat and draw in a lungful of that earthy scent of his. He looked down at me, and for a moment, I thought I saw a flicker of sadness in his eyes. "I'm still your friend... even if I don't want to be."

"Thanks, I guess."

"You know what I mean. You know I don't want to be just your friend." He bent down and kissed my cheek and his head lingered there for a moment, his stubble brushing my cheek, while part of me wanted to turn my jaw that extra inch to kiss him properly, firmly. But I didn't, and he drew back hesitantly.

I couldn't say anything else. I'd hurt him enough already by rejecting him and I couldn't justify why I'd picked one fine man over another equally fine man. More to the point, it wouldn't be fair, and Gage wouldn't want to hear it. I rested my head against his chest for the briefest of moments and he wrapped his arms around me, sighing as he hugged me to him.

"See you around, Stella." Gage untangled himself and loped off the porch. I couldn't stand there and watch him go while my heart ached, so I turned my back and went inside. Just as I closed the door, I heard the sound of his motorbike's engine roar into life and he thundered away.

For a moment, my house seemed empty. Then I saw Evan had set up his laptop on the table in the small dining area off the living room. I uncovered it under a pile of dust covers in the unused sun room and he carried it into the dining room and made it his makeshift desk.

It was scrubbed pine and old and there had been a

stack of matching chairs underneath it, like my parents once planned on getting rid of them but never gotten around to it. Evan offered to help me sand it down and oil it so it would achieve a rustic sort of perfection. Until then, it was serving as a sort of office for him.

He still hadn't told me much about his business, but it seemed he was able to coordinate things remotely. He also mentioned having a loyal assistant who was at his beck and call, for want of a better phrase. I was just grateful that he was able to be with me for now, especially with threats hanging over our heads like pointed swords.

"You okay?" he asked, taking in my thoughtful expression.

"I'm fine."

"What did he want?" Evan nodded at the front door. I didn't know if he and Gage would ever get to the point where they could have any kind of friendly relationship, or even a vaguely polite one, and I had to take some responsibility for that. But I wasn't going to get into that now, not when there were more important things at stake.

"He thinks all the witches coming here has started something."

Evan hesitated before he said, "I hate agreeing with him but he's probably right."

"So we should be worried?"

"No point worrying until something happens."

I thought about what Gage told me. "You know the easiest way for me to protect myself is for you to teach me how to control what I can do. No more flukes. I need to be able to protect myself and, if it comes down to it, I need to be able to stand up and fight, not be a hindrance to you or anyone else. Plus, I can't make decisions when I don't understand this world properly. If Gage is right, and something is coming here, I don't want to run into something that I can't recognise, and can't fight." I took a deep breath before I added, "I know you all want to protect me and I know I'm lucky, and I'm so grateful, but I need to be the best I can be. I need to be prepared for whatever is coming."

Evan leant back in his chair, legs crossed. A moment later, I could feel the air behind me bristle as it was suddenly parted. I could feel the sudden heat of his body close to mine as the chair in front of me still wobbled from his abrupt departure. He brushed a lock of hair back from my face with his hand as he whispered in my ear, "I'll teach you everything I can."

I let a broad, happy smile blossom on my face as I twisted to look at him. I still had to pinch myself that he was really staying. As I gazed into his delicious eyes, a familiar trickle of magic lit my skin, playful, at my command.

"You'll have to catch me first," I teased, and then I disappeared, and the sound of Evan's laughter swept along in my wake.

Continue the Stella Mayweather series with Devious Magic, out now in ebook and paperback!

Witch hunters who will stop at nothing.

A deadly foe who wants to harness witches' power.

A secret supernatural world that is on the verge of revealing itself.

When the recent surge of supernatural activity in the secretive town of Wilding apparently draws the fearsome Brotherhood, Stella knows she could be risking her life to give in to their demand to return to England.

But defying them sees her world fall apart as her best friend is kidnapped. Lured home to her birthplace, Stella's powers are tested to the limit as she battles magic and trickery at the heart of the Brotherhood's operations. But flight across the world brings as many questions as it does answers, and Stella can never be sure who is on her side and who will betray her.

www.ingramcontent.com/pod-product-compliance
Lightning Source LLC
Chambersburg PA
CBHW020249200626
46816CB00001BA/212

* 9 7 8 0 9 5 6 9 0 8 6 5 0 *